"You need any h
his voice a differe

"No." She certainly didn't need any help with the prescriptions. She might, however, need a prescription to get rid of a very real headache named Jimmy Murphy.

"How is Ray?"

Ever the calculating journalist out for information any way he could get it. She'd dealt with people like this before. They had agendas; she had animals to take care of. They had deadlines; she had animals to feed.

Still, it felt different when the one asking the questions happened to be the one who got away.

Dear Reader,

I've long been an animal lover. Growing up, I had cats, dogs, rabbits, hamsters, birds, guinea pigs, turtles and fish. Every Christmas from age six to about twelve, I asked for a horse. We lived in the city, and boarding a horse would have cost about the same as what we paid to rent our house. The closest I came to getting a horse was the Christmas I got a bike. My dad said the bike could take me to "almost" all the same places as a horse could. In my twenties, I was a kindergarten teacher. My classroom had birds, fish, hamsters, lizards and, for a short while, ferrets. One night the hamster escaped and attended a school board meeting. Apparently, Goober wasn't recognized right away for the hamster that he was. We had new rules about pets in the classroom after that. Right now, I'm typing with a cat pressed against my arm. What a great life.

The heroine in *Holiday Homecoming* is Meredith Stone. She introduced herself to me in *Katie's Rescue*, the first Scorpion Ridge book. We've all met that person at work, school, church, who is the powerhouse that gets things done. Well, that's Meredith. She gets things done, mostly when it comes to the animals under her charge. But now, she has to slow down to help care for her grandfather. It's a time for reflection. Of course, nothing's that easy.

Jimmy Murphy's whole world changed when his wife died, and he realized that a vagabond life didn't work well for his daughter. Now he's caught between the old and the new. His career still means a lot to him, but his latest story is in direct opposition to what Meredith believes in. Jimmy's first love was Meredith, and sometimes first loves are meant to be forever loves.

I hope you enjoy *Holiday Homecoming*. If you'd like to meet some of the Harlequin Heartwarming authors, please visit www.heartwarmingauthors.blogspot.com. If you'd like to learn more about me, please visit www.pamelatracy.com. I love to hear from readers!

Pamela

HEARTWARMING

Holiday Homecoming

—

Pamela Tracy

Recycling programs
for this product may
not exist in your area.

ISBN-13: 978-0-373-36699-6

Holiday Homecoming

Copyright © 2014 by Pamela Tracy Osback

All rights reserved. Except for use in any review, the reproduction or utilization of this work in whole or in part in any form by any electronic, mechanical or other means, now known or hereinafter invented, including xerography, photocopying and recording, or in any information storage or retrieval system, is forbidden without the written permission of the publisher, Harlequin Enterprises Limited, 225 Duncan Mill Road, Don Mills, Ontario, Canada M3B 3K9.

This is a work of fiction. Names, characters, places and incidents are either the product of the author's imagination or are used fictitiously, and any resemblance to actual persons, living or dead, business establishments, events or locales is entirely coincidental.

This edition published by arrangement with Harlequin Books S.A.

For questions and comments about the quality of this book, please contact us at CustomerService@Harlequin.com.

® and TM are trademarks of Harlequin Enterprises Limited or its corporate affiliates. Trademarks indicated with ® are registered in the United States Patent and Trademark Office, the Canadian Intellectual Property Office and in other countries.

Printed in U.S.A.

PAMELA TRACY

is an award-winning author who lives with her husband (who claims to be the inspiration for most of her heroes) and son (who claims to be the interference for most of her writing time). She started writing at a very young age (a series of romances, all with David Cassidy as the hero, though sometimes Bobby Sherman would elbow in). Then, while earning a BA in journalism at Texas Tech University in Lubbock, Texas, she picked up writing again—this time it was a very bad science-fiction novel.

She went back to her love and was first published in 1999. Since then, Pamela has had more than twenty romance novels in print. She's a winner of the American Christian Fiction Writers Carol Award and has been a RITA® Award finalist. Readers can find her at www.heartwarmingauthors.blogspot.com or www.pamelatracy.com.

Books by Pamela Tracy

HARLEQUIN HEARTWARMING

KATIE'S RESCUE
WHAT JANIE SAW

Visit the Author Profile page at Harlequin.com for more titles.

To Aimée Thurlo,
a gifted author who opened her heart to both
people and animals.

We miss you, Aimée.

CHAPTER ONE

"I CAN'T GET a hold of Grandpa. He's not answering the phone—again." Meredith's brother's tone was more annoyed than frantic. For the last three months, Grandpa Stone had been acting more like a teenager—disappearing for hours, not answering questions directly, grumpy.

"You are still coming, right?" Zack asked.

"I'm just ten minutes from his house." Meredith pressed on the gas pedal while assessing the dirt road that was more *dirt* than *road*. A few miles back some idiot in an old black truck—its windows so darkly tinted she couldn't see the driver—had almost run her off the road. That was the last thing she needed if Grandpa truly was in trouble.

If...

Raymond Stone was eighty-two, born a little more than two decades after Arizona had become a state. He was hard of hearing, so the phone was more miss than hit lately. Thus her brother's exasperation.

It was Grandpa's forgetfulness and wandering, however, that had led to a recent powwow between the two oldest Stone siblings. They had agreed that someone had to stay with him for a while. Family emergencies weren't Meredith Stone's forte anymore. But this time it was her grandfather who needed her, and she was the best choice.

The only choice her grandfather might tolerate.

She put her cell phone on speaker so she could talk more easily. "I really hope we're just over-reacting and this isn't necessary."

Her brother, Zack, didn't hesitate. "It's necessary."

Ah, the theme of her youth. *Necessary* was an important word in a household that had a father and mother who were gone too much. Both had been high-end real estate agents working a three city area. When Meredith was young, they'd worked seven days a week because it was necessary. By the time the real estate bubble burst, Meredith was a junior in high school and it was too late to suddenly have mother/daughter chats or attend father/daughter dances on a Friday night.

Zack and Susan, being the middle and youngest children, had those memories, but not Meredith, the eldest.

Meredith had been raised in an atmosphere where chaos reigned. She, of all the siblings, craved order and control. The drive to excel, make goals and persevere had been necessary for her, as way too often, she'd been the parent. It had gotten her to where she was today: head animal keeper at a small but well-known habitat and at only twenty-eight years of age.

Only once had "necessary" been too high a price. The repercussions from that disaster still kept her awake at night, and it was the biggest reason she'd left her hometown of Gesippi.

She hadn't gone far.

Zack obviously wasn't going to say anything else, so Meredith tried once more. "You really think Grandpa needs someone with him all the time? He seemed fine at his birthday party. And he's made it clear he really doesn't want me living with him."

"That party was five months ago." Zack's tone changed from worried to resigned. "Plus, he had the whole family doting on him. Even Dad showed up. With the Fourth of July celebration going on, nobody else noticed anything amiss, just me. You didn't come home two weeks ago for Thanksgiving…"

No, she'd worked instead so that the other employees, the ones with spouses and children, could take the day off.

"All night, Grandpa kept looking over his shoulder as if he was expecting someone. I'm worried he was looking for Grandma. And in the last week, it's gotten worse."

Yikes, it was the beginning of December already. Time to decorate for Christmas. Had it really been five months since she'd visited? Bad granddaughter. Bad.

But it was Zack's nature to fret. As middle child, Zack knew his job description. When they were kids, Meredith had made the rules: bed at nine, lights out at nine-fifteen. Zack had been the nurturer. He'd read Susan her bedtime stories; he checked under beds for monsters. His whole life, he'd expected to find one. He'd have battled it; Meredith would have fed it. Susan would have handed it her doll and ordered, "Play."

Her parents would have sold it a haunted high-end mansion. The house, of course, would be in foreclosure now.

Zack continued, "Yesterday morning, I stopped by to see how he was doing, and he was clear out past the field. Claimed he was searching for Rowdy. I'm not sure how far he'd have gone if I'd not have showed up."

Okay, now Meredith understood his worry. Rowdy had been her grandpa's beloved border collie. *Had been* being the operative words. Rowdy had died when Meredith was eighteen: a decade ago. He'd died the week after her almost wedding.

"What did you do?" she asked.

"I reminded him that Rowdy had gone on to greener pastures and led him back to the house." Zack was in his second year of community college and determined to be a doctor no matter how long it took. He'd know how to gently break the news of Rowdy's passing to Grandpa again.

Raymond Stone had never been without animals, both wild and tame. Under his tutelage, she'd learned how to work with the wild ones: how to mend broken wings, sew stitches in a rabbit's side and bottle-feed a baby white-tailed deer. She had always been drawn to animals that had no one looking out for them. Maybe because back then, at home, no one had been looking out for her, and she very much wanted someone to.

On Grandpa's farm, she'd also learned to milk cows, groom horses and feed chickens.

This past week, Meredith, as head keeper at a zoo, had been stepped on by an ostrich, kissed by an orangutan and sneezed on by a bear. She loved it, and she had Grandpa to thank for pushing her toward doing what she loved.

"The dog is another thing we have to worry about. Twice now Grandpa's gotten up in the middle of the night and tripped over Pepper."

Pepper was a big, old black-and-white dog. He was hard of hearing, like Grandpa, and no longer had the oomph to do much more than follow Grandpa around and sit and wait. Meredith figured the mutt was part golden retriever, part shepherd and possibly a bit standard poodle. Big dog; big heart.

"Grandpa would be miserable without a dog." Meredith had no idea how she'd manage it, but she'd make sure Grandpa kept this one. Grandpa needed Pepper just as Meredith needed all of her animals. At last count, she'd cared for one hundred and eleven different species. All of which needed her, many of which loved her. But canines were what she did best.

Right now, she didn't own a dog. Not really. Yoda, her favorite at the zoo, wasn't really a pet she should keep in the backyard or take to dog parks. Yoda was a high-content wolf dog: half wolf, half German shepherd. He came when he was called and walked on a leash, but he was a little too wild to keep in her tiny apartment. He required space to run and dig and howl.

Plus, Yoda was the property of Bridget's Animal Adventure, BAA for short. Except that he, like Meredith, didn't really belong anywhere. At the moment, he was being sequestered in a barn off the property, away from the other two wolves BAA had because of a territorial battle between them that had resulted in a torn ear, twenty-nine stitches and new digs for Yoda.

But she shouldn't be worrying about Yoda

right now. She had her grandpa to think about. Still chatting with her brother, Meredith turned off the main road and drove past a dozen barbed-wire gates that guarded farms full of grease-wood, paloverde trees and dirt. It took a good three miles before the tiny town of Gesippi came into view. A minute later, she drove by her parents' house—the biggest in town—and tried to listen while Zack filled her in on the rest of the family.

By the looks of things at her parents' house, only her mother was home. No surprise, since Mom rarely left. Her job now was cutting coupons and cleaning the house. Dad's car wasn't in the driveway. Instead of real estate, he now sold medical products at trade shows, traveling four out of every five weeks, often to different states. Today, she knew, he'd driven into Phoenix for a meeting and Zack said he wasn't answering his cell phone.

Zack had just given her the update on Susan, who apparently was in the throes of young love, when Meredith pulled into the driveway of her grandfather's house.

"I'm glad Susan's happy," Meredith said. "But I'm here now, and you know how Grandpa gets if you talk to a phone instead of him. I'll call you in a bit."

While his grandchildren were busy grabbing at

life with both hands, Grandpa was hard pressed to find things for his hands to do. The end of his story was nearing, and no one in the family—especially him—was prepared for the conclusion.

Meredith turned off her phone and pocketed it, then took a deep breath and tried to figure out what to do first. Should she act as if this was just another visit? No, that wouldn't work. She'd never stayed overnight...not in a decade, anyway.

At eighteen, thanks to Grandpa's insistence and money, she'd traveled an hour away to Tucson and the university there. After earning her degree in zoology—in three years instead of four—she'd secured a job at a major zoo in California. As the new kid on the block, her responsibilities hadn't been as hands-on as she desired. Plus, she hadn't liked being so far away from Gesippi and her family. What if she were needed?

So, after just one year, she returned to Arizona and found work at BAA in Scorpion Ridge, only seventy-five miles from her home. Far enough away so she didn't keep bumping into her past; close enough to be available to help her family if they needed her.

But since returning to Arizona, she'd never spent the night in Gesippi.

Grandpa knew the reason why, and he'd be suspicious when he saw her bag, so it would be better to just jump right in and tell him the family's concerns, and that she was staying indefinitely. Yes, that's what she'd do. Hopefully, Zack would show up in time to help.

She studied the place where her early childhood had flourished thanks to horses, tree houses, creeks and Grandma's cookies. All the Stone children had basically lived here while their parents worked evenings and weekends. But once Meredith hit fifteen, she'd been more interested in the boy next door and spending time in the tree house and creek with him. She'd also learned to make Grandma's cookies because he liked them.

The way to a man's heart and all…

Too bad the young man in question had been so intent on leaving Gesippi, getting an education and making a name for himself as a journalist that he'd managed to break her heart.

Ten years later, her grandfather's horses were now gone and the tree house was in as much disrepair as her heart. The boy next door had moved away, married, had a daughter and indeed was making a name for himself by writing and filming documentaries.

He was now a widower. Not that Meredith cared.

His shy younger brother was moving on, too, and getting married.

Good, she wished him the best after their misguided relationship.

Switching off the ignition, she shook away those memories and opened the door, pausing before stepping from the car. The house had always been painted white. Grandpa saw no need for any other color. But now, it was weathered and looked a bit like a white-and-gray-speckled egg. Not a pretty one, either. The gutters circling the house were loose and in one place a section was missing.

Luckily, it was a small house, so, if necessary, she could probably do the painting herself these next few months. The Rittenhouses, Luke and Katie, her bosses at the animal habitat, had kindly changed her schedule so that she was only working weekends. They'd told her to take all the time she needed to settle things here in Gesippi. If Zack was right, she might have to take a full leave of absence. She'd heal the house even if she couldn't heal her grandfather.

"I've got the time," she whispered to herself. "I might even enjoy it."

She gazed beyond the house to the barns and stables, now empty. Beyond, Grandpa's land, currently farmed by someone else, spread as far as the eye could see. When she was young, she'd thought it spread to the ocean. When she hit fifteen, she knew it bumped against paradise.

A boy named Jimmy Murphy.

Slamming the door to her SUV, she stepped down not onto the walkway that led to the front door but onto grass that grew across the pathway that led to the front door.

One more thing to do: mow.

"Grandpa! Where are you?"

Used to be, he was at the front porch door before a visitor could even exit the car. It had driven the family crazy. He'd invite strangers in and offer them something to drink, talk their ear off about his family, his animals and his God. But as his hearing worsened, he couldn't hear cars approaching. Today, if the volume of the television was any indication, he hadn't heard her arrive, either. She'd wanted to surprise him, but maybe she should have called.

"Grandpa, it's me. Meredith!"

The screen door was unlocked, so she stepped onto the porch. Grandpa's jacket hung on a hook by the door. A pair of old brown boots waited underneath. Two chairs faced the windows. Newspapers were spread over one—Grandma's. The other chair was empty, although Grandpa's reading glasses and a half-empty coffee cup were on a nearby table.

The door to the house was unlocked also. Meredith pushed it open until she could see into the living room with its olive green couch, antique coffee table and large-screen television, which had a morning-news show blaring. Meredith turned off the TV before hollering Grandpa's name again.

When Grandma was alive, something half crocheted always waited in a basket on the floor and partly read books lay open over the couch's armrests. After five years, very little remained of Grandma's presence, and if loneliness had a smell, this was it. Meredith knew it well.

Somewhere in the distance she heard Pepper bark. Maybe Grandpa was in the backyard where he liked to feed the squirrels; Pepper liked to chase them.

Veering off the front walk, she headed through the grass—which was past her ankles and full of weeds—and to the backyard.

As she made her way to the backyard, she saw more signs of neglect but no signs of her grandfather. Meredith fought the out-of-control feeling threatening to make her turn around, tuck her tail between her legs and flee.

In Gesippi, she was a Stone and had been what the kids called an overachiever, voted Girl Most Likely To Get Whatever She Wanted. No one knew that in high school she'd filled her calendar—along with her siblings' calendars—with so many things just so they wouldn't have to go home.

And, even more funny, the yearbook with that predication had arrived the day after she'd lost what she wanted most.

Jimmy Murphy.

Twelve months after that, one rash act had made her rethink who she was, where she was going and why. Thanks to her grandfather, she'd sidestepped a huge mistake with Jimmy's younger brother, Danny, and she'd left Gesippi. In the years since, she'd rarely returned because while many were forgiving, none had forgotten.

It was only on television that leaving a groom standing at the altar made for good entertainment.

CHAPTER TWO

JIMMY MURPHY LEANED against his shovel and watched as the brown SUV sped across the dirt road, skidding slightly while taking the bumps too quickly. Clearly an outsider who cared little about the vehicle's alignment.

"Ray expecting anyone?" he called to his brother. Danny was on the other side of the truck, messing with a roll of plastic ditch.

Jimmy had been stuck with the digging and was glad for a break.

"Not that I know of." Danny didn't even sound winded.

"Any of the Stones get a new car?"

"Not that I know of."

Jimmy could have asked a few more questions, but obviously Danny wasn't in the mood to speculate. He was getting married in less than two weeks, the Saturday before Christmas. Although their mother and Holly, his bride-to-be, were doing all the work, Danny was stressed. Thus, all the Murphys were stressed.

They deserved to be. The last time Danny had

tried to get married, his bride hadn't shown up for the wedding.

Meredith Stone, the girl next door. Both Murphy boys had loved her. But it had been Jimmy who had owned her heart, only to walk away from her. Danny had tried to fill the empty space, but failed. In the end, everyone had gotten hurt.

For years, he and his brother had maintained a polite friendship. It wasn't until Danny had gotten engaged that the laughter returned. Looking in the direction the car had traveled, Jimmy wiped sweat from his brow. It wasn't easy pulling a shallow ditch, and what he and his brother were about to do was even more strenuous. Jimmy wished for the millionth time that he was back in California, sitting across from his boss, hashing out his next assignment. But his boss had asked him to take some time after Jimmy had gone over budget and still hadn't delivered a good story on his last two assignments—a story on pandas in China and bears in Alaska

It was probably overdue. After the death of his wife a year ago, he'd been dragging his daughter to faraway places, gathering stories and losing himself.

But really losing six-year-old Briana.

The grief swelled, threatening to take him to his knees. Instead of letting it consume him, Jimmy stomped his steel-toed boot on the shovel's edge, driving it into hard dirt by a good inch. Then he did it again, and again, and again.

Still he was mad, mad at a world that didn't include Regina. Asthma wasn't supposed to kill a twenty-six-year-old mother who took care of herself and carefully monitored her disease. And it certainly wasn't supposed to kill her as she went into the bathroom to get her inhaler because she was having a little trouble breathing.

In all, her death had taken twenty minutes. It had begun as a persistent cough when she was in bed one night. When it turned into a short, strangled intake of breath, he'd still not been concerned. This had happened before. She'd finally rolled out of bed, her face taking on the blue, pinched look he knew so well. She hated her asthma, hated that it attacked her without provocation. She'd stoically and quietly walked the length of the room—not wanting to wake Briana asleep on the other side of the wall—and gone inside the bathroom. He'd heard the sounds of the medicine cabinet door opening followed by water running and something else…her hand slapping against the counter maybe.

Then, he'd heard her hit the ground.

He'd been by her side in seconds, doing CPR with his cell phone on the floor beside him so he could scream for help.

Help that had arrived too late.

Briana had slept through the whole ordeal. He'd woken their next-door neighbor to watch his little girl while he followed the ambulance to the hospital. The next morning, he'd had to tell Briana that Mommy was gone, not coming back.

She hadn't believed him at first and continued to look for Regina, watching the door and the phone.

Meanwhile, he'd numbly called the dentist office where Regina had had an appointment the next week. Then, he'd found the number of the woman in charge of Regina's book club. Finally, he personally visited the gym where she'd taught aerobics part-time and cleaned out her locker. There he'd accidentally encountered the grieving dark-haired personal trainer who'd known Regina was married but didn't care.

His wife had been having an affair.

Jimmy blamed himself. He'd been passionate about the wrong things, had been gone too much and loved too little. He wouldn't make the same mistake with Briana.

He wouldn't mess up love a third time.

Still, he didn't want his family to know how broken he was, so instead of screaming his frustration at life, he asked his brother, "Think this irrigation technique will work?"

Danny said something under his breath.

"Wasted effort?" Jimmy queried.

"No, it will work."

Jimmy and Danny's parents lived five miles away, just down Pioneer Road. While their dad, Mitch Murphy, ran a cattle and sheep operation, his brother Matthew—where they were working today—farmed beans, squash, corn and whatever else struck his fancy. Against his wife's wishes, right now Matthew also rented a few acres from Ray Stone.

The women in Jimmy's family held long grudges.

"Not Ray's fault the girl ran off" was Matthew's feeling.

Jimmy agreed. Not Ray's fault. It had been Jimmy's for not being mature enough to listen to Meredith, to think things through, give her time. She'd been all of seventeen when he'd asked her to leave with him."

He'd thought she'd said "No, I can't" because she didn't want to be with him. Only later, after he'd been in school awhile, lived a little, grown up, had he realized it had been a "No, I can't right *now*."

But it had been too late to change things by then. She'd stood up his brother at the altar and had left Gesippi. Seemed both he and Meredith had run away.

"If you're sure it will work," Jimmy said after

a moment, referring to the irrigation technique. Danny had been quiet for too long.

"I'm sure the concept will work." Danny came around the truck, a bright yellow roll of plastic ditch now on the back of his quad. "I'm just not sure if I have enough plastic."

Something about bright yellow stripes running down the center of cornstalks didn't work for Jimmy. Gesippi, Arizona, was once home to the Tohono O'odham and Akimel O'odham Indians, expert crop growers who would laugh at Danny's efforts. From the nearby Santa Catalina Mountains, to the Saguaro National Park, to every lake in between, Jimmy preferred natural beauty. Yellow plastic–striped rows of corn just didn't do it.

"I'm thinking," Danny said, "that I'll stop the quad at the end of a row and walk the plastic down."

"Walk?"

"Well, more like unroll," Danny admitted. "Maybe just the first few to get a feel of how I want it placed and how it's going to settle."

"What do you need me to do?"

"Nothing right now. I'll anchor it on the quad. Shouldn't be too hard to unroll."

"Okay, see you back at the house."

Jimmy could tell him that this was a two-man job. The roll would get stuck and one brother would need to run back to untangle it while the other pulled and straightened. But if Jimmy volunteered to stick around, he'd not be able to ride down the road and satisfy his curiosity about the SUV. Clearly the mysterious SUV was connected to Raymond Stone, and that both worried and relieved him. Strange how quickly Gesippi had settled around Jimmy, tapping him on the shoulder and reminding him that he could leave the small town but the small town wouldn't leave him. He and Briana, his daughter, had only been back a week, which had been plenty long enough for Jimmy to notice that Ray's body was weakening, his mind was somewhat confused and he was uncharacteristically grumpy.

As they were Ray's nearest neighbor, Jimmy's aunt and uncle had plenty to say about Ray being alone. Mostly how lately they sometimes saw the beam of his flashlight in the middle of the night and heard him shouting in the distance. "As if he's calling for someone or something," Aunt Shari had said.

He wondered if he should go over there. Jimmy didn't care what the Stone family thought of him; he'd more than paid for his decade-old lapse in judgment. Looking over at Danny, Jimmy felt a moment's guilt. Actually, Danny had paid more dearly. But maybe now with Danny getting married to the right girl this time, the relationship between the Stones and the Murphys would start to heal.

Besides, Jimmy loved Ray Stone as if he was his own grandpa. The man had taught Jimmy to sit a sheep, wrestle a steer and ride a bull.

His mind made up, Jimmy headed for his white Dodge 250 truck, brushing his hands on his shirt. He thought briefly about going inside and washing up, but if he did, Aunt Shari would either want to feed him or want to know what he was doing.

As he approached, he noticed the brown SUV was parked in front of the house. That told Jimmy the driver was a return visitor. A stranger would have stopped just past the road.

He parked behind the SUV as the porch door opened and a slender girl came out. No, not a girl, a woman. One he knew well. Meredith Stone, all long golden-brown hair, pink sweaters, and endless energy and smiles.

At least that's how he remembered her.

Today her hair was pulled back in a loose ponytail, and her hoodie was black. Judging by the way she hurried down the front walkway toward him, the energy was still there, but the smile was gone.

This wasn't good.

He almost opened his mouth to tell her how not good her sudden appearance was. Now was the worst time for her to return, just weeks before Danny got married.

Danny still avoided mentioning her name.

Heck, sometimes Jimmy couldn't choke it out, either.

But before he could say anything, Meredith skidded to a stop right in front of him, panic in her eyes, and said, "I can't find Grandpa."

CHAPTER THREE

WHILE JIMMY CALLED his aunt Shari and quickly gave her the rundown, Meredith paced. She hadn't changed, not one bit, in the years since he'd seen her last. Today, she was like a two-year-old colt, not quite broke and wanting to move. She wanted to search some more, with or without him.

Hanging up, Jimmy said, "Aunt Shari will get a hold of the neighbors. We'll spread out and cover more territory. Don't worry, we'll find him."

"My brother's on his way," Meredith said. "He's trying to get a hold of my parents. I—I didn't know who else to call. I was about to call your uncle, when you drove up."

Considering that the Stones and Murphys had been neighbors for more than thirty years, she shouldn't have hesitated. "You can always call my dad, me, my uncle—" he looked her right in the eye "—my brother."

"I'm so flustered," Meredith muttered, "that I

couldn't remember a phone number for anyone in your family."

Any other day, any other moment, Jimmy might have smiled. There'd been a time when Meredith had talked to both him and his brother on the phone daily, either talking or texting. Usually she'd been trying to organize their day to her liking. He'd always reorganized. Danny had actually followed her directions.

But now she looked ready to cry, something she didn't do easily. He knew that firsthand.

"I'm usually spot on in an emergency," she muttered.

He knew that, too. "You're sure Ray's not in the house?"

"I'm sure. The house wasn't that hard to search."

No, Jimmy had to agree with that. There were three bedrooms, which made up half the house. A kitchen, bathroom and living room made up the other half.

"You went downstairs?"

"I did."

She'd never much liked the basement, Jimmy remembered. It was half finished, which bothered her to no end, and most of it was dirt walls. Sometimes snakes managed to get in.

Though that had never bothered Meredith. She'd just caught them, taken them outside and let them go. He'd helped her—and fallen in love. Who wouldn't fall in love with a girl who thought snakes deserved a second chance?

"Pepper keeps barking," Meredith said impatiently. "I can hear him in the distance. I've shouted his name until I'm hoarse. I tried to follow the sound, but I can't figure out where he is. Once I thought he yelped, like he was hurt, so I decided to come back and get help. On top of everything else, I had to keep searching for a location to get cell-phone reception."

Jimmy checked his own phone again. All the bars showed and the signal was strong. "You want to stay here at the house and wait, or come with me?"

She didn't hesitate. "I'm coming with you."

As they stepped out the back door, in the distance Jimmy, too, could hear Pepper's barks.

"Sounds like Pepper's well past the end of the field."

Meredith agreed. "At least to the foothill."

Surely Ray hadn't walked all that way. Jimmy had stopped by to check on him just two days ago. Ray'd had trouble just getting up from the easy chair and heading to the kitchen for a snack.

But Meredith was already moving through the backyard and toward the sound. "I don't get why Grandpa would come out here."

Jimmy thought for a moment. "Maybe he did

what we're doing. He heard Pepper barking and wondered if something was wrong."

Meredith had never acted like a rich girl when her parents had had money. She'd preferred being out here with her grandparents and with him and his brother. And right now, she followed Jimmy and didn't mind that her shoes were getting dirty or that her hoodie was getting snagged.

It had been almost a decade since he'd seen her this close. His family, though, had kept him informed a bit. He'd been in Australia doing a crocodile story when the Stones had thrown Ray a big eightieth birthday two years ago. Jimmy hadn't received an invitation, but his mother had told him about the event. She'd said Meredith looked good and was doing what she loved.

Mom was wrong. Meredith didn't look good; she looked great.

Meredith spoke up. "Maybe I should have kept looking for him."

"You did the right thing, coming back for help," Jimmy reassured her as she stepped around a paloverde tree and almost lost his balance as the terrain started to slope.

"The right thing is finding him."

"If you'd found him injured, you wouldn't have been able to get him home on your own and even more time would have been wasted."

"He might not even be with Pepper," she muttered. She muttered a lot more than she used to, that's for sure. "He might be out looking for Rowdy, and Pepper's just out here playing with us."

"Rowdy? He's been dead for—"

"Almost ten years," Meredith finished. "Zack says he had to remind Grandpa of that fact just the other day. Grandpa's getting forgetful."

"Or maybe Pepper's out here on his own and your grandpa went into town."

"Leaving the television on? His breakfast plate still on the kitchen table? Plus, Zack organizes all Grandpa's trips into town. No, Grandpa's next doctor's appointment isn't for a month, and that's a specialist in Phoenix, and Zack is taking him."

"And he wasn't expecting you?"

She shook her head. "We were afraid if he knew I was coming, it would upset him. I'm…" She hesitated. "I'm moving in for a while."

"Good. He needs someone." Jimmy upped his pace, refusing to take the time to consider how having Meredith next door again might affect the balance of his family: Danny getting married; Jimmy home again but intending to leave as soon as the next story, next locale, called.

He followed the barking as it grew louder, more frantic, and Meredith had been right, it seemed to come from different directions: right, left, straight ahead. It echoed, too, and he overheard Meredith say, "Almost sounds like two dogs."

No wonder she'd turned around when she'd been searching by herself.

"Ray!" he hollered. He followed that by whistling for Pepper.

Only the dog responded, with a strange echo.

Jimmy's cell phone sounded. Instead of a hello, he answered with, "Tell me what's happening?"

"There's a bunch of us in Ray's living room," Danny said. "Where are you and what do you want us to do? We've called the sheriff, and Dad's all for organizing a search."

Meredith stepped next to him, closer than she'd been in years. Tears shimmered in her eyes, just below the surface. Jimmy wanted to reach out, touch her, but he knew she'd step away, so he didn't. Instead, he said, "We're about five minutes north of Bandit Hideaway. We can hear the dog but can't seem to get to him. I've got the first-aid kit with me."

Danny said something Jimmy couldn't hear, and then Zack Stone took the phone. "Doc Thomas is on his way and bringing his dog. Zeus loves Pepper and will lead us right to him."

"Hope Doc gets here soon," Jimmy said, ending the call and then sharing the information with Meredith.

They spent the next fifteen minutes investigating different paths and trudging through under-brush. Jimmy felt the first inklings of real fear. No way should Ray have come this far alone. The man was a veteran of not one but two wars, had been part of the volunteer fire department and lived alone at age eighty-two. Two days ago he'd showed no signs of poor judgment. He'd been distracted, yes. Almost as if he was expecting someone.

But Ray wasn't careless and didn't take chances.

"If we don't find the dog or Ray in five minutes, we're heading back to the house to re-group—"

Two things happened then.

First, they rounded a corner and found Raymond Stone. He lay on the ground, conscious, but obviously in pain.

Second, Ray wasn't alone.

"THAT'S A WOLF!" Jimmy stopped so quickly he almost stumbled.

Meredith stepped in front of him. She didn't need him to go all heroic, not right now. "It's a wolf dog. Just stay still. Grandpa, are you all right?"

"I will be if I can get up without that fool animal attacking me." Ray held a stick in one hand.

Even though he now had two rescuers, he still shook it at the animal.

"Did he bite you?"

The wolf dog barked, thinking Grandpa wanted to play.

"He nipped me on the leg. It was enough to knock me down, but he didn't break the skin. Pepper lit into him after that."

Pretty impressive for an old dog. Glancing around, Meredith found the mutt hovering a few steps behind Grandpa, shivering, limping, but still ready to fight if his owner was threatened.

"Stop waving the stick," Meredith said. "He thinks it's an invitation to play."

Grandpa dropped the stick to the ground.

To Jimmy, Meredith said, "I'm going to deal with the wolf dog, lead him away from Grandpa. You help Grandpa, make sure he's all right, no broken bones."

Jimmy stared at the animal. "Wolf dog? You're kidding. How did one get way out here?"

"Since she's got a collar, I'm thinking she must have escaped from her owner. Let's hope she's trained."

"How do you know it's a she?" Jimmy asked.

"I'm guessing."

Walking sideways, Meredith slowly moved closer to the wolf dog. Behind her, Jimmy knelt at Grandpa's side and helped the elderly man to a sitting position. The wolf dog kept looking at Grandpa, clearing wishing that he would start playing with her again. Meredith wasn't sure what the wolf dog thought about her.

A bird chirped in the otherwise silent world. The wind picked up, blowing Meredith's hair into her eyes. She resisted the urge to pat it back into place. Instead, crouching down, she moved even closer to the animal. Now the wolf dog was on alert. Her eyes stayed on Meredith, and her tail stopped wagging. The wolf dog didn't know whether to meet Meredith's eyes and try to establish dominance or whether to be submissive. When Meredith got within a foot of the wolf dog, she halted, waiting to see what the animal would do.

"I'm not sure this is wise," Jimmy said.

Meredith agreed with him, but… "Look at the collar. It's tight, hurting her. We can't let her run off without trying to help her."

"We need to help your grandfather first," Jimmy pointed out.

"I'm fine," Ray said.

That the wolf dog hadn't run off indicated that she had been a pet. But the tightness of the frayed collar suggested that she'd been in the wild for quite a while, probably abandoned or maybe an escape artist that the owner hadn't found.

Or looked for.

It made Meredith furious.

Her favorite animal in the world was a wolf dog named Yoda. But if Meredith had her choice, Yoda would be a dog, nothing else. Breeding wolves with dogs was a risky endeavor. Most people who chose a wolf dog as a pet got rid of the animal within a year. They were hard to train, expensive and destructive.

By the time the owners realized the commitment involved, the wolf dog was no longer a cute puppy but a demanding teenager quite willing to eat a couch.

Forget about shoes. A wolf dog could actually chew his way out of a wire cage.

Shelters didn't want them.

Neither did zoos. They didn't quite fit anywhere.

Slowly, the wolf dog's tail went between her legs, and she turned her head away. Meredith didn't wait for another sign. She reached for the collar, praying she'd not lose any fingers. The collar was too tight for her to get a grip, but she managed to force the wolf dog to look her in the eyes. After a moment, the wolf dog sat, lay down, then finally put her head down to rest.

Meredith let go of the collar.

"You're either a miracle worker or stupid," Jimmy said.

Meredith wasn't a miracle worker, but she

wasn't about to admit that what she'd done *was* a little stupid. "How's Grandpa?"

"I can answer for myself. Help me up."

"Right, Grandpa." Meredith left the wolf dog and headed for Grandpa, going down to her knees to stroke his forehead. "Where do you hurt?"

"Everywhere but the bottom of my left ear. Help me up."

They'd just got him to his feet, though he was clearly favoring one leg, when Pepper starting barking. A group of people, dogs and horses appeared from behind a small hill. Afraid the loud noises and sudden movements would spook the wolf dog, Meredith turned to her.

She was gone.

But it only took a groan from Grandpa to convince Meredith not to pursue the wolf dog. Jimmy got Grandpa to his feet and slowly the trio started toward the noise.

Meredith's brother met them halfway and the two men hoisted Grandpa between them.

"Don't ask me to get on a horse," Grandpa said.

When they finally made it to Grandpa's house, it echoed with people. Meredith's brother went right to the phone, trying to get a hold of Doc Thomas, who'd not made it to the house yet.

"He's got a sprained ankle at least," Zack predicted. He was more than annoyed that Grandpa refused to go to the hospital in Adobe Hills.

"You've already iced it," Grandpa called from the bedroom.

Zack ignored Grandpa's protest. "Doc says he wants you in his office at two o'clock tomorrow."

Grandpa muttered something Meredith couldn't quite hear. He'd gotten crustier in his old age.

"We're having a family meeting on Friday. Today changes everything," Meredith said.

Zack took Grandpa back to his bedroom, propping Grandpa's foot up, taking his temperature, giving him an aspirin and making him comfortable. When they were little, Meredith had rescued animals, but Zack had fixed them. Their little sister, Susan, had stuck bows in the animals' fur. Jimmy, of course, had made up stories about them.

Leaving Grandpa with Zach, Meredith headed for the kitchen. Sitting at the table was Danny Murphy, bigger than she remembered and missing the smile that had driven the girls wild in high school. Of course, it had been a long time. Maybe the smile was a thing of the past.

Jimmy sat next to him, tapping the table with his fingers, looking as if he wanted to be anywhere but where he was.

"You say this dog was part wolf?" Danny's

brown eyes met Meredith's green ones. She couldn't ignore the stoic expression on his face or how straight he sat. Because of her, he clearly felt like a stranger in her grandpa's house.

But then, so did she.

"Probably more than half," Meredith said.

Danny leaned forward. "Could it kill a cow?"

"Did you lose one?" Meredith countered.

"You didn't tell me you'd lost any cattle," Jimmy said.

"I've lost three head."

"Were they old or young?" Meredith asked.

"Both," Danny said. "Two were just calves and one was old, losing her teeth and all. I expected her to die, though, not disappear. Why?"

Meredith thought for a moment. She was mostly familiar with the behavior of wolf dogs in captivity, but she could generalize. "Wolves do go after calves, but they generally leave cows alone. Cows don't act like prey."

"She's right," Jimmy said. "A cow tends to look danger in the eye and ignore it. Confuses the heck out of predators. Plus, for a wolf, given the size of its mouth, it's hard to find a place on a cow to grab on to. Cows are big. Kinda like trying to bite into a whole watermelon using your teeth. Wolves prefer something a little smaller."

Meredith stared at Jimmy in disbelief. "And you know this how?"

"I specialize in doing documentaries on wild animals and writing for *Nature Times* magazine. I know just as much about animals as you do."

"I know you write for *Nature Times*, but wolf dogs aren't endangered. There's no reason for you to have researched them."

"Wolves are endangered, so I've done plenty of research. When we went multimedia and started doing documentaries, we started small. The gray wolf was one of my first stories."

She didn't remember that, or remember that at one time *Nature Times* had only been a magazine. Usually she agreed with what his pieces, at least when it came to disappearing habitats and hunting for sport or seizure. But then he'd climb on his animals-belong-in-the-wild soapbox, and criticize zoos for making tigers lose their natural inclination to hunt, or making chimpanzees depressed, or forcing bears to wear silly hats and tutus.

Okay, she didn't *have* to read or watch him. She'd just been drawn to. She'd loved him, after all.

And still missed him.

She'd been engaged to Danny, but it was Jimmy who had been the love of her life. And if she was being honest, he, James Henry Murphy, was the reason she was still single. No one made her feel the way he had.

Even though he'd more than once written about the cruelty and injustice that wild animals suffered in captivity, never once acknowledging that there were sanctuaries like Bridget's Animal Adventure, which actually saved animals' lives.

But then, he'd always been a bit tunnel-visioned, seeing what he wanted to see. Isn't that why he'd refused to wait for her?

CHAPTER FOUR

IN THE END, sitting at the table in Ray's tiny kitchen, Meredith convinced Danny that the wolf dog had probably not been responsible for the disappearance of the calves or the adult cow. A pack of full-blooded wolves maybe, Meredith had allowed, but a lone wolf dog, no.

And not one wearing a collar and leaving no carcass.

Jimmy'd seen wolves in the wild. They were cunning, creative and callous when hungry. He did, however, agree with Meredith that calves were a more likely target. He also was somewhat sure a lone wolf could do the job, too, especially on an old or already wounded bovine.

But this hadn't been a wolf, not really. It had been a wolf dog, the first one Jimmy'd ever seen.

He'd have to Google them when he got home tonight. Maybe little Gesippi, Arizona, would have a wild-animal story to offer, an assignment that would appease his boss—who was already acting as if Jimmy was on his way out instead of merely taking a break—and give Jimmy something to document, both in words and film.

It worried him that his last two shoots had been less than stellar. It worried him even more that his boss wasn't phoning and asking him for new ideas.

On the other hand, Briana was actually smiling again. Something she'd not done much of during the year he'd dragged her to exotic locales. No, during their travels she'd been well-behaved but almost eerily silent. Nothing like the happy child she'd been before…

She missed her mother; she missed having a permanent home and friends; she missed having a routine. So, for her sake, Jimmy tried to be glad about being home. And in those moments when she smiled and talked a million miles a minute about her new friends, it was all worth it.

Jimmy thought of his own friends that he rarely talked to, the people that he'd allowed to slip out of his life. He was glad he'd been able to visit Ray twice since he'd been home. The first visit had been for old times' sake. The second had been because Jimmy had realized that visiting Ray Stone was a now-or-never venture.

But both visits had been slightly off-kilter. Ray had been twitchy, insisting they sit on the porch and rarely taking his eyes from the road, though he claimed not to be expecting company. Jimmy had chalked it up to a by-product of old age.

On his first visit, neither brought up Meredith's name, as if instinctively knowing she was off-limits. On the second visit, Ray had been a bit more forthcoming, talking about Meredith and how she was faring, and expressing some concern that she still felt she had to stay away from her home.

Gazing at her now across the table, Jimmy had to admit that Meredith was even more beautiful than he remembered.

She'd always filled a room with her personality and passion. That hadn't changed. Back when they'd been dating during most of his junior and all of his senior year, there were moments when he couldn't imagine his life without her. But there'd also been times when she'd almost consumed him, made him lose who he was, made him question if he could compete with her.

Which he shouldn't have cared about because he'd loved her...but he had. His brother had never felt that type of angst. Danny would have followed Meredith anywhere, happily, without question. And he hadn't questioned her when she'd agreed to marry him. He'd been unable, or maybe unwilling, to believe that Meredith didn't love him.

"I'm heading home." Danny pushed himself up

from the chair, his face still stoic, his demeanor tired. Younger than Jimmy by just one year, he looked five years older.

"I really appreciate all you guys did," Meredith said. "Grandpa, well, he's special."

Danny nodded even as he exited the kitchen. Jimmy wasn't sure why he stayed; there was nothing else to say. And sitting in this kitchen with Meredith wasn't something he should do. For her to move back to town a mere eleven days before Danny's second attempt at marriage and just as Jimmy's life was falling apart was a cruel fate.

At some point Meredith would challenge Jimmy about his job. He was highlighting the changing and vanishing habitats of wild animals. He was saving the world for the next generation, as Ray had taught him to do, albeit on a smaller scale. She managed a man-made habitat that put wild animals behind bars and robbed them of freedom.

If there was to be a debate, he wanted to start the round. "So, you work in a zoo?"

"You've been keeping track of me," she accused.

"Someone told me last week." Though Jimmy *had* already known.

"It's a habitat, not a zoo, and a dream job," she stated, looking him full in the face. She'd always been sure of herself. "I work with all the animals, but the wolves and the birds are my main charges. I have a wolf dog."

"You own one?"

"No," she corrected herself. "We have one at the habitat. I named him Yoda, so yes, I'm perfectly capable of handling one."

"I saw that today."

She shook her head and gazed out the window. He knew she was wondering where the wolf dog was and that she was bothered by the fact it still wore a too-tight collar.

"You're going to search for her?"

"Not tonight, but if Grandpa's better tomorrow, then yes."

"Do you remember how to get around?"

"It hasn't been *that* long," she said indignantly.

"Ray says you haven't stayed here for any length of time in ten years."

She gave him a dirty look. Ten years ago, she'd been putting together a wedding. The I do's would have been at the Gesippi Church; the reception would have been here at Grandpa's. They'd not planned on a honeymoon. Neither'd had the money. Meredith must have found some money, though. She'd managed to take off right before the wedding, find an apartment in Tucson and start taking classes at the university.

He'd always been afraid to ask why she'd made

the decision to accept Danny's proposal but then to leave him right before the wedding, but maybe it was time to put the wrongs of the past behind them. Tonight, maybe he'd find that he hadn't been to blame.

"In all these years," Jimmy said, "I don't think anyone, at least in our family, knows why you stood Danny up."

She gazed at him, eyes hooded, chin jutted out in defiance. Oh, she'd apologized, said she was sorry. Had written Danny a letter explaining that she was too young and scared to get married.

She'd never acted young and scared. She'd always seemed years more mature than her age. As for scared, she'd pick up a snake before he would.

For a moment, she waffled, wanting to change the subject. But she was still the stand-up girl he remembered from his youth. She'd never played games like the other girls. She'd always known exactly what she wanted and how to get it.

"I didn't love him, not the way you're supposed to love the man you marry."

"But you said yes when he proposed, you set the date, people were actually in the church waiting for the wedding to begin."

She looked tired suddenly. Part of him wanted to reach out, move the stray strand of hair away from her eyes, see if it still felt like lightning when he touched her.

Her cheeks flushed. "When I agreed to marry Danny, I thought maybe love, the happily-ever-after kind, would grow between us, in time. But I had a conversation with someone very wise who made me realize that I was cheating myself and Danny," she admitted. "It wasn't fair to him. He deserved more."

He'd always wondered if she'd gone from loving him to loving his brother. Now, hearing her say that she'd never loved Danny, he should feel a sense of freedom. Instead, he felt loss.

She looked at him expectantly, clearly waiting for a reply.

"I used to believe in happily-ever-after, too," he admitted.

"Used to?"

Before he could answer, someone in the living room called her name. She almost knocked over the kitchen chair in her haste to exit the room.

He walked to the door and watched as she stood amidst her family, somehow apart from them, as if she believed she didn't quite belong.

But then, he didn't belong here, either. Jimmy made his way out the front door and to his truck. No one tried to stop him.

SUNLIGHT SPLASHED THROUGH the window. Meredith groaned. Really? Christmas was in two weeks. Surely the weather could pretend a chill.

She'd slept until almost nine. Unheard of. Back at BAA, she always rolled out of bed at four, knowing she needed to get the animals ready to face the day.

Today it didn't matter, though. Grandpa was still asleep. Last night had been a lot of excitement for him. Her, too, but some of the excitement she could have lived without.

She let him sleep a while longer, busying herself with returning phone messages; walking the property looking for the yesterday's wolf dog, and finally by making breakfast. It was ten before she finally woke him up.

"I usually just eat cookies for breakfast," he confessed.

She always had a big breakfast. She'd learned her first week at BAA that sometimes there was a chance for lunch but sometimes instead there was a grumpy camel to soothe, a depressed black panther to cheer up, a peacock with a injured wing to repair, or enclosure malfunctions to fix.

"A decent breakfast will do you good," she scolded. "How do you feel?"

"Like I fell off a wagon and then it ran over me."

"Perfect, then you're not numb," Meredith said, loading a plate for him. "How's your ankle?"

"Doesn't hurt. And where that fool dog nipped me isn't sore at all. It's my back that's sore."

"Zack made a two o'clock appointment for you. I figure we can go into town about noon, grab some lunch at the diner, and then head to the doctor to make sure you're all right."

Grandpa winced. "I don't need to go into town. I'm sore. When you're eighty-two, you get to be sore. It's called old age."

"If you're spry enough to chase after a wolf dog and then fight it off with a stick, you don't get to use old age as an excuse." She put two plates on the table and then sat down across from him.

"I didn't chase after that wolf dog. I heard some noises and…" His voice trailed off and for a moment Meredith wondered if he would continue. Then he added, "I thought…it was Rowdy."

"Rowdy's been dead for—"

"For more than a decade. I know." He slowly folded the paper and put it next to his plate, his face looking pinched and stressed.

"You feel all right, Grandpa?"

He made a face instead of answering. Before he picked up his fork, he put his gnarled hands together and bowed his head. Meredith did the same, trying to remember the last time she'd prayed before a meal. It had been a while. She usually was too busy filling up the hours and days on her calendar to think about taking a moment to thank God for all she had.

After the amen, Grandpa took a bite, forced a smile and swallowed before saying, "I still miss that fool dog. I just knew that I'd heard something. By the time I realized how far I'd gone, there the animal was. You'd have gone looking, too, had you been here. And don't think I don't know that you were out there early this morning searching."

"I got that determination from you."

Instead of being pleased, Grandpa scolded, "I don't want you out there wandering alone. It's not the same kind of place it was when you were a kid."

"I'm fine."

"No," he said. "You need to listen to me— take care."

She nodded, not understanding or agreeing but knowing she had to appease him. He'd rarely looked so stern when talking with her.

Satisfied, he said, "There were too many people here last night, so I didn't get the chance to ask. That thing I went after really was a wolf dog, huh, like Yoda?"

"Yes, I'm certain of it. She had the long legs of a wolf and I recognize the snout. I must have walked back and forth across two miles this morning, but I couldn't find her. She's skittish. I'll try again tomorrow."

"Skittish?" Grandpa asked.

"Yes," Meredith answered. "Plus leery. You've heard me talk about Yoda."

"The wolf dog you use for public relations back at BAA. Your favorite."

Meredith always felt a little guilty when people remarked that Yoda was her favorite. She loved all the animals, even BAA's grumpiest camel who liked to spit on her. But she and Yoda did have a special bond.

"Obviously, you managed to get him to trust you." Grandpa finished his orange juice, but he'd only eaten a tiny corner of of the hash browns she'd prepared, maybe two bites of one sausage, and he'd scrambled the eggs a bit more so she'd not notice he'd not even tried to eat them.

Hmm…

"He was my first assignment. Somewhere, under all Yoda's fear, was a dog who wanted to be loved."

Grandpa pushed his plate away. "You always had a way with animals. Remember Blackie the cow?"

"I remember her following me around."

"She trailed behind you whenever you were on horseback. Your grandma and I always considered Blackie somewhat of a guardian. We thought if you fell off, she'd drag you home with her teeth. Now, finish telling me about Yoda and wolf dogs."

"Well, your visitor looks a lot like Yoda, maybe a bit bigger. I figure she's at least half wolf. If I had to guess, I'd say that she was here searching for her owner."

That seemed to worry Grandpa. He'd been starting to relax, just a little, but now he went back to the pinched look. Meredith hurriedly added, "She was most likely a pet, one that got a little too hard to handle and so her owners tried to release her into the wild."

"I don't think so." Grandpa sounded sure.

"It happens more than you'd believe."

"So," Grandpa said, "ignorant people drop an animal like Yoda off in the forest thinking maybe he'll find a wolf pack in Arizona? I don't think I've seen wolves in the wild in the last fifty years."

"And whoever released our wolf dog didn't take the time to remove her collar. That's just wrong."

"Maybe they just didn't care."

"I hate to think that," Meredith said. "I'd rather believe that the wolf dog got loose and couldn't find her way back. Maybe somebody's looking for her."

Grandpa gazed out the window. "I doubt it. That wolf dog's owner might be sending a message, a warning."

"What? Grandpa, why would you say that?"

His lips pursed together. "I just know."

Meredith wasn't sure about this sudden change in Grandpa's mood, but pressing would probably just make him more irritable. "Whoever lost the wolf dog had good intentions," she said. "They just get overwhelmed."

Meredith could manage a whole animal habitat without getting overwhelmed. And yet she'd not been back in Gesippi but twenty-four hours and she already felt the crush of responsibility. This elderly man sitting across from her was the only one who'd truly understand.

"It was strange having both Jimmy and Danny in the kitchen talking with me."

"Danny's moved on," Grandpa said. "His fiancée's nice. I've talked to her a time or two. Her name's Holly. She rides her bike up and down Pioneer Road on occasion. She likes my chickens."

"He deserves happiness."

"Always," Grandpa agreed. "You talk to Jimmy about anything special?"

"He asked why I didn't marry Danny."

"What did you tell him?"

"The truth. That I didn't love Danny that way."

"Did you tell him who you still loved?"

Standing, she gathered up their breakfast dishes and asked, "Do you need help getting to your bedroom and getting dressed?"

"No. And don't try to change the subject."

"I'm not *trying* to change the subject. I *am* changing the subject."

No way was she going to talk about Jimmy Murphy. Ten years put a lot of dirt over the casket of unreturned love.

Grandpa waited a moment, then nodded. In the time it took Grandpa to stand, walk to his bedroom and shut the door, she finished clearing the table, washing the dishes and putting everything away.

The phone rang just as she set the towel on the edge of the sink. Her first impulse was to answer it, but this was Grandpa's place, and she needed to remember that. After a moment, she heard him answer.

"This is Ray Stone... What? I can't hear you. Speak a little louder." She was about to knock on his bedroom door and offer to help, when apparently whoever was on the other end must have made himself heard.

"No," said Grandpa, "I've not lost a wallet or any money. Really? That's interesting, but my wallet's on top of my dresser. I've no idea why my phone number would be in a wallet containing that much money."

The conversation ended, and when Grandpa didn't call for her, she decided it wasn't her place to pry. She headed for the small hallway bathroom and brushed her teeth, redid her ponytail and then went outside to sit in Grandma's rocking chair and call Luke Rittenhouse. Next to her, he understood Yoda the wolf dog most and would be able to help her with this new animal.

"We can't take another wolf dog," he said, surprising her. Used to be, he'd open BAA's doors to any animal. "Yoda's struggling to find his place, and he's been at BAA for years. Technically, wolf dogs are not wild animals. They're pets."

"So's your beloved iguana."

"My iguana is a not-so-wild wild animal that someone attempted to turn into a pet. Your new wolf dog is a hybrid, so it clearly falls under the pet category. I know there are rescue—"

Meredith protested, "You know as well as I do that there are more wolf dogs than there are people and places that will take them. We've already done the legwork with Yoda. And this new one will be harder. She's been in the wild. Yoda never was."

"First you have to find her," Luke said calmly. "Then we'll worry about what to do with her."

"Easy for you to say," Meredith muttered, frustrated.

Luke laughed before asking her a few questions about the birds and giving her an update on Ollie the orangutan who, like Meredith's grandfather, was losing the battle of aging.

The moment she hung up she realized that

Luke hadn't told her how Yoda was faring. Which meant there was something Luke didn't want her to know.

She started to redial, but Grandpa shuffled out from his bedroom. He'd lost weight. She could do something about that, like make him eat a second helping of her hash browns and three bites of sausage. He had less hair. She didn't care; he was still handsome. His hands shook. After a moment, *The Price is Right* blared on the television. Grandpa's favorite show.

"I don't need to go see Doc Thomas," he stated. "He's just going to tell me to take a pill if my back hurts and to baby the foot and try to stay off of it. Use my walker more."

"You should use your walker more," she scolded. She'd said she wouldn't pry, but her curiosity got the better of her. "Who was that on the phone?"

For a moment, she thought Grandpa wasn't going to answer, but then he said, "The sheriff. Someone turned in a wallet. My number was written on a piece of paper inside."

"Who'd you give your number to?"

"Nobody I remember."

She let him watch television while she cared for the chickens. It wasn't all that different from taking care of Crisco the bear or Ollie the orangutan. She fed, watered and cleaned their bedding. The only thing she did that she couldn't do with Ollie or Crisco was gather eggs. The five chickens ignored her, not even appreciating the fact that she was making sure they had plenty of shavings.

After doing a few more odds and ends, she took an hour, put on clean clothes and woke Grandpa up.

"I wasn't sleeping," he insisted.

"Maybe not," Meredith appeased, "but you do need to get up and out, eat something besides cookies and make the family happy."

"I always make the family happy."

"Not true."

"You're one to talk," he grumped.

"I'm the one most like you."

That earned a smile and got him out the door, into her car and agreeable.

About halfway to town, he asked, "So, why were you in Gesippi last night? And why are you the one driving me around today?"

It took Meredith a good three blocks to answer. She didn't want to give him room to argue. "I'm here to stay with you during the week. Zack will stay with you on weekends."

"Because I fell! That's silly. I fall all the time."

"Yes, Grandpa. You fall all the time. And we want to be there to make sure you always stand up. What if I hadn't shown up last night and realized you were missing? Would you have eventually gotten up? Or would you have spent the night out in the cold? And maybe still be there now?"

"It's December in Arizona. Doesn't get really cold."

"You didn't use to lie," she accused.

"And you used to listen."

"I'm staying."

"No, you—" he started to protest.

"I'm staying because I love you."

"And because I love you, I want you to go on with your life."

"You are my life."

He didn't respond; he stared out the window as tears pooled in his eyes. She didn't know if he were happy because he was loved or miserable because he needed to rely on other. What she wished was that he'd reach over and pat her knee, give her some sign that he appreciated what she was doing and recognized the need.

Gesippi hadn't changed much in the ten years since Meredith had stopped calling it home. Sure, she'd been back a time or two. But she'd mastered sneaking into town for a few hours and then hightailing it back to Scorpion Ridge. Today her trip into town would take much longer.

Downtown Gesippi was three long blocks. Tyler's Antique store was the biggest. Old-time Christmas decorations graced its window. A combination drugstore and restaurant was next to it. Someone was out front ringing a bell hoping for donations. A Native American trading post, the Crooked Feather, had opened when Meredith entered high school. It had a wooden plaque in the front window advertising Victor Lucas as proprietor. He'd obviously not found a moment to decorate for the season. His daughter, Kristi Lucas, had been in Meredith's grade but had dropped out of high school. A tiny movie theater, which played movies months after their release, offered a film Meredith had meant to see. Already a giant Christmas tree was in the tiny park by the school. A big sign notified the public that Santa would be visiting on Christmas Eve.

"You want anything from the drugstore?" Meredith asked.

"Cookies."

She laughed. "Anything besides cookies."

She parked in front of the drugstore and hurried around to help Grandpa out. The wind added a bit of red to his cheeks. Impulsively she reached up to pat one. He caught her hand with his and smiled.

"I'm glad you're here, Merry."

She'd not been called that in years.

Unfortunately, he added, "But you needn't put your life on hold to take care of me."

She didn't bother to respond as she followed him into the Drug and Dine.

"Hey, Ray."

"Keith, good to see you. Thought we'd stop and get something to eat." Grandpa didn't mention that Meredith had had to nudge him out the door to get here. "Not that I'm hungry. The granddaughter, here, thinks I should eat more."

Keith, wearing a Santa hat, came around the counter. "I heard you had an adventure last evening. So, Meredith, you say we have a wild wolf dog running loose?" He led them to a table and held Grandpa's chair out. Once Grandpa settled, Keith handed them menus and asked, "Is this something we should call the county sheriff about? Could someone get hurt?"

"The wolf dog was more interested in playing with Grandpa than eating him," Meredith said. "The odds of someone getting hurt are slim."

"Jimmy Murphy's sure taken an interest in what happened last night. He came in this morning and wanted to know if anyone had dropped off any Have You Seen This Dog posters."

"What for?" Why was Jimmy asking questions? He'd not even been overly concerned about the too-tight collar.

"He said something about recognizing a good story when one dropped in his lap."

Now Meredith knew exactly what she'd say

to Jimmy if he ever challenged her commitment to Bridget's Animal Adventure. She might be working with animals that would be happier in their natural habitat, but to her they were more than stories.

"What did you tell him? Has anyone been looking for a lost dog?"

"I sent him over to the library. If anyone had been asking around, Agatha Fitzsimmons would have heard about it."

"The library's still open?"

"Every day but Sunday from ten to three. What'll you have?"

Meredith ordered while Grandpa said, "The usual," before shuffling off to the bathroom, looking as if he could topple at any minute. Keith stayed close behind.

Looking around the Drug and Dine, Meredith noted that not much had changed. Keith stocked a little bit of dry goods and a whole lot of tourist paraphernalia. The only things completely new were all the cell-phone displays.

She wondered how much the Gesippi library had changed. It was housed in three rooms under the courthouse. It had half windows that started at the ceiling and that teased with just a little natural light. But Agatha Fitzsimmons, who'd once managed a library in Washington, D.C., had made it something special. During her teens,

Meredith had spent a lot of time perusing the young-adult section. Agatha had also made sure a good number of animal books were on hand for a questing Meredith.

Agatha had to be about the same age as Grandpa, if not older.

Unfortunately, while Meredith had been a favorite hometown girl, Jimmy had been a favorite hometown boy. Agatha, who'd not had any children of her own, had attended the high school's Friday-night football games just to cheer for Jimmy.

When Jimmy left and Meredith came in to show off her engagement ring from Danny, Agatha had called her a stupid girl.

That was the last time Meredith had traipsed down the stairs to the Gesippi library. It wasn't until many years later that Meredith realized Agatha had been right.

Grandpa returned. "Food not here yet?"

"No."

"Penny for your thoughts."

She couldn't tell him the truth, couldn't tell him that Jimmy's presence in town was making her uncomfortable and bringing forth memories she'd tried to bury for so long.

Memories of a love that wouldn't stay buried.

CHAPTER FIVE

THE MEDICAL CLINIC was the first house on a residential street. A big golden retriever was asleep on the porch. He, too, wore a big Santa hat. "That is Zeus," Grandpa introduced.

The living room was the reception area. "Each of the bedrooms functions as an examination room," Grandpa informed her. "I've been in all of them."

It hadn't existed during Meredith's youth. When she'd broken her nose, thanks to a horse merely lifting its head, she'd had to go to Adobe Hills, a good fifty miles to the east. When Grandpa was young, though, Gesippi had boasted a small hospital. It had also had a working copper mine. The old hospital, built in nineteen hundred and twelve, stopped taking patients in nineteen hundred and thirty-two and was now a restaurant, aptly named the Hospitable; the copper mine gave tours to tourists.

"This is a good place," Grandpa said. "You'll like Doc Thomas. Just eight years ago, he moved from Phoenix and retired."

"Only it's not so quiet and I didn't get to stay retired." Doc Thomas looked old enough to retire, thanks to a white beard and thick white hair. But he didn't act old enough. His smile appeared genuine and his eyes danced. He wore bright green tennis shoes and a T-shirt advertising The Rolling Stones. He was Santa on vacation.

"You should be a movie star," Meredith said.

"I get that a lot. Then people find out what I really do and the questions start coming."

"People want free advice," Meredith guessed.

"Yup. They'll say, 'Hey, Doc, I got me a cold,' or 'My sides been hurting, right here. Do you think…?' Or my personal favorite, 'I've been throwing up in the morning and don't want my coffee. You don't suppose…'"

Grandpa finished up, "So he decided to open a clinic and now he isn't quite so retired."

"Not when I have a fool like you for a neighbor," Doc Thomas agreed. "What were you doing chasing down a dog at your age?"

"Seemed like a good idea at the time," Grandpa mumbled as the doctor led him down the hall to one of the bedrooms.

There was no receptionist to hand Meredith a three-page form to fill out. She could sit on the couch and thumb through one of the magazines, read the Christmas cards taped to the wall or…

"Grandpa, I'm going to run an errand. Call me when you're finished."

"I want to be finished now," Grandpa called back.

JIMMY MURPHY SPENT his morning working with his dad and decided no way would there ever be a documentary about the plight of sheep. So he spent his afternoon researching wolf dogs and keeping up with what was happening at *Nature Times*. More to the point, who was getting the assignment that should be his.

No, not entirely true. Part of him was grateful when his boss suggested he take some time off, for Briana's sake. Now he could pick her up from school.

Just before three, he found a parking place outside Gesippi Elementary, where he could see Briana when she exited, and took out his notes about wolf dogs. Then he called his boss and gave an enthused three-minute spiel on his idea for a new piece.

"Wolf dogs would be a small draw." Thom Steward, Jimmy's editor, didn't even pause before answering.

"That's because not many publications even bother to mention them. We'd be one of the first."

"You're grasping at straws. I can't take this

idea to our producers. I'm glad you are taking a break, you can do better than this."

It had been three years since any of Jimmy's ideas had been turned down. He was good at his job, dependable, and had the kind of relationship with Thom that if the editor didn't give him an assignment, all Jimmy had to do was shoot off an idea. Thom had rejected Jimmy only once, and that was because someone else was already doing the story.

"I've been researching the problem, and wolf dogs suffer the same fate as big cats and monkeys. They're taken as pups, raised, and then when they grow into their own, many are abandoned."

"How is that a story?" Thom asked.

"No one I know of, in North America, would abandon their pet lion on public land. But, because these animals are part wolf, they've easier to walk away from. That's my angle."

Finally Thom hesitated. "Okay, it's Christmas and I'm feeling generous. Send me a proposal. I want to see some footage, though. You're gonna have to sell me on this idea."

Jimmy agreed and promised him a solid pitch before New Year's. It was the first time Jimmy had ever ended a conversation with Thom feeling less than talented.

And there was no one he could complain to.

His crew was in China, and while they liked and respected him, if they thought their bread and butter was with the new guy, they'd be polite at most if he called and did some digging.

His brother might have listened had the wedding not been in just over a week.

From his car, he could see the comings and goings of Gesippi's townsfolk. He watched as Meredith hurried down the street and went into the courthouse, most likely heading for the library. She wouldn't get anything from Agatha on wolf dogs that he hadn't already gotten.

He'd first fallen in love with Meredith because of an animal: a silly goat that escaped its pen nearly every day. Zack had been thirteen, Meredith twelve. The goat, aptly named Stupid by Jimmy, had a favorite fence spot, one that ran between Meredith's grandpa's land and Jimmy's uncle's. Stupid wanted whatever was on the other side. He'd stick his head through the railing, and then because of the way the fence was built, he wouldn't be able to get his head back out.

The first time that had happened, Jimmy'd been mad, especially when Meredith, all wild blond hair and know-it-all opinions, had easily helped Stupid get free.

The next time, he'd let Meredith help, understanding even at fifteen that it was better to have Meredith on his team than to try to compete with her.

Maybe a similar approach could work for him now....

GESIPPI'S COURTHOUSE WAS in the center of town. Meredith remembered her third-grade teacher marveling that it had been built in 1899. Apparently being built in 1900 just wouldn't have had the same distinction. The town's budget had been stretched too thin during the construction. There had been plans for a split staircase and an outdoor pavilion. Today, there was a single staircase and instead of a working clock, there was just a clock facing. The time always read six o'clock. Back then, that was when work started, and if one was lucky, it was when work ended.

Meredith took out her cell phone. It was two-fifteen. She had forty-five minutes until Agatha locked the door and turned the sign to Closed. But Meredith might only have ten minutes before Grandpa called her to come pick him up at the doctor's. She hurried up the front stairs and opened the door. The front entry was empty except for a sign that gave directions to the different offices and goings-on. Meredith turned left and went down some narrow stairs painted concrete blue. There were posters on the walls, some older than she was. All advertised books and some were signed by authors. Before she reached the bottom, she could hear voices. One she immediately recognized as Agatha's, the other voice sounded as if it belonged to a girl.

Stepping into the main room of the library was like finding a lost treasure, one you didn't realize the value of until you held it again.

Even the smell was magical.

"I'm telling you," an indignant voice declared, "she took a book without checking it out."

"It's fine, dear. I know her father. We'll get the book back."

"But—"

"It's more important that a child reads than it is for a book to rest on its assigned shelf just because of the rules."

It was a conversation Meredith might have had with Agatha back when she'd haunted the library.

"Someone's here," the young voice said.

"Good."

"But we're only open for thirty more minutes."

"Ah, Jessica, when you let go of your love for rules, you'll be much happier."

"Or not," Meredith said, stepping into the center of the room where a girl of about twelve was bent over a library cart. Agatha leaned on the cart, looking at a book that had seen better days. She hadn't changed at all. Agatha was about a foot shorter than Meredith and so slender she could probably nap on one of the library shelves and not fall off. Her hair was shoulder length and not even Grandpa could remember when it hadn't been pure white.

"Two old friends in one day," Agatha said. "Jimmy still emails me. You I have to keep track of on YouTube. I liked what your zoo did with Crisco the bear. That was quite a story."

"It was," Meredith agreed. "We suspect someone wanted to harvest his organs and that's why Crisco was taken from his mother. A dried gallbladder can sell for five figures overseas. The paws are worth money, too."

The young girl looked interested. "Really, why?"

"Mostly medicinal reasons. Some people believe the paw will make you healthy, while the gallbladder..." Meredith paused. The gallbladder was especially tempting to males in some cultures. But Meredith wasn't sure she needed to share that.

"What do you mean?" the young girl queried, obviously of a different mind-set.

"Jessica," Agatha said quietly, "since we're only open for a few more minutes, and since I have Meredith here to help, you can leave early."

"But this lady doesn't know what to do." Aghast at the prospect of leaving her job to someone ill-qualified, the girl forgot about the bear's gallbladder.

"Oh, trust me, she knows," Agatha said. "Meredith was you fifteen years ago."

"Has it been that long?" Meredith whispered.

"Yup. One day you were my helper. The next day you'd discovered Jimmy Murphy and suddenly the library was a distant memory."

"The man who was just here," the girl said.

"Yes, now scoot. Meredith and I have some catching up to do."

The girl wasn't happy, but she knew to mind Agatha. With a quick hug to Agatha, she was out the door and stomping up the stairs.

"Did you come by to see me or do you have the same question as Jimmy?" Agatha nodded toward the cart, and as if she'd never been away, Meredith took a stack of books and headed for the shelves. Though she used to recognize by title where they belonged. Now she had to use their call numbers.

"Originally, I just wanted an answer to the same question, but now I realize seeing you is more important."

"Glad you're finally starting to put your priorities straight." Agatha didn't sound convinced, not completely. Changing the subject, she added, "I'm also glad you're here to stay with Ray. He needs you. Something's been bothering him these last few years and it's not because he's missing his wife or his absent son."

"Yes, I'm seeing that."

"You take care of him. He's precious, you know."

Meredith did know. Her grandparents had sacrificed to help raise their grandchild, help pay their way through college, and more.

All without complaint. If they'd not been willing to help, her life would have been very different. She'd have married Danny and stayed in town, the dreams of her siblings more important than her own.

Grandpa had paid her tuition, every dime. She was paying him back but knew that he put her money right into Zack's and Susan's college fund.

It probably only helped a little.

"Ray actually got a library card right after you went to college. Did you know that?"

"I didn't realize he liked to read," Meredith confessed.

"It was only on the one topic," Agatha shared. "He went through all my books on Native Americans, especially those dealing with the Tohono O'odham and Akimel O'odham tribes."

"That's strange."

"I figured he must have watched a documentary on them or something and become interested. I enjoyed researching the subject for him. I'll miss that."

"What?"

"I'm retiring next year."

Meredith's hands stilled. The book she'd been shelving was stranded in midair. Too many things were changing in her life and too quickly.

"You'll hate it."

Agatha chuckled. "I'm sure I will, but it's time."

Meredith finally shelved the book and then quickly worked through the ones still on the cart. Finished, she started to move the cart but stopped when she noticed Agatha was using it to hold herself up.

"Let's sit for a minute," Meredith suggested.

"No, it feels better to stand. I sit and my butt starts to hurt. If I'm standing, it's my back, but I can handle that. Here, put this away too."

It was an aged copy of *Black Beauty*.

"You checked it out five times," Agatha said. "Remember?"

"I want to read it again. Maybe this time the fox will get away. Can I get a new library card today?"

"Just take it and make sure you return it. We won't tell Jessica."

Meredith's cell phone beeped. After checking

the screen, she tapped the answer key and said, "Grandpa, can I come get you now?"

"Better hurry before Doc decides to do any more prodding." Something distracted Grandpa, and he hung up before Meredith could ask anything else.

"Ray's gonna be okay?" Agatha asked when Meredith put her phone away.

"For now, he's okay. Just forgetful."

"Aren't we all," Agatha shared.

"Agatha, you never forget anything, so I do want to ask. Has anyone been looking for a dog, really a wolf dog?"

"No. Jimmy says he's called the sheriff, talked to the newspaper editor over in Adobe Hills, plus his cousin who publishes the tabloid here. He had to promise to be interviewed for an article. Then, he even went driving around to see if there were posters up anywhere. Together we did an online search for wolf pups for sale. We did find some nearby, but no one answered the phone when we called. And no one's reported a missing dog. I called a couple of librarians I know from Adobe Hills and Scorpion Ridge, but outside of a runaway Chihuahua, nothing."

Recognizing she was at a dead end for now, Meredith helped Agatha close up the library, turning off lights, locking up, just the way she had more than a decade ago. Agatha lived just three houses down from the courthouse, so Meredith waved goodbye as Agatha walked home.

Meredith fought the wind as she got back into her brown SUV. There was a storm brewing, and not just in the air. Just what did Jimmy think he was doing, researching the wolf dog? He was going to make this a mission. That's what he was going to do. Televise the plight of the wolf dog and the injustices it suffered. Get his stupid by-line and then take off again.

Well, she wasn't going to be his star of the month, and neither were Yoda or the wild wolf dog.

Grandpa and Doc Thomas were sitting on the porch when Meredith drove up. While Doc helped Grandpa down the ramp, Meredith opened the passenger-side door and took and stored the walker in the back. When Grandpa found his seat, she said, "Doc, I'd like just a moment."

Doc Thomas met her at the end of the car. She shut the hatchback and whispered, "He's not eating. Maybe four bites at breakfast and not even that at lunch."

"You hear that, Ray. Your granddaughter says you're not eating."

"I eat when I'm hungry, and she hasn't made me pancakes."

"You're going to need your strength during the next few months if you want to get better, Ray."

To Meredith, Doc Thomas said, "His ankle's fine. I took an X-ray of his spine, though, and I didn't like what I saw. You watch him close. If he slows down anymore—" both of them looked at Grandpa, who was still settling himself into a comfortable position "—I want you to get him into Adobe Hills and to a specialist. I know he has an appointment in January, but it would be good if you can get him in earlier. If he's to keep living on the farm in the middle of nowhere, he has to be able to walk—no matter how slowly."

Doc Thomas said a few more things, mentioned rehabilitation and even surgery.

"I can walk," Grandpa groused.

"At the moment," Doc Thomas said so softly that only Meredith heard. His expression told Meredith a diagnosis she wasn't ready to hear.

Yes, he was eighty-two, but, well, he was Grandpa. The thread that held the family together in so many ways.

As they drove home, he was quiet, too quiet, not even commenting on her driving. Usually he held on to the door handle and commented, "How fast are you going?"

Meredith kept shooting him glances, hoping he'd open up, tell her she was driving too fast or something. When he didn't, she tried talking to him. "Do we need to fill a prescription?"

He nodded.

"You want to do that now?"

He shook his head.

She'd been communicating with animals for years now—spent more time with them than people, really—and was used to figuring out problems without the exchange of words. But Grandpa was about as easy to read as a hedgehog.

Either he was overly tired or something had upset him. Or maybe it was a combination of both.

"I just want to get home, Merry."

When they finally got to the farm, she helped him out, opened his walker and then followed behind him as he walked unsteadily to the front door. Pepper came limping from the side of the house, greeting them with a wiggling body. Then, with doggy wisdom, he slowed down even more to walk sedately beside Grandpa.

Grandpa didn't even acknowledge him.

But she knew something was really wrong when he walked past the television and went into his bedroom and shut the door, leaving both Pepper and her in the living room.

Meredith tried to soothe Pepper. "Come on, boy. I really need you with me, and Grandpa wants time alone." She spent the rest of the late afternoon and evening walking Grandpa's land. She found the remnants of a tree house and an old shoe that had probably belonged to Zack. By the time she headed back to Grandpa's, melancholy had set in. She'd started off looking for the wolf dog but, if she were honest, she'd ended up looking for Jimmy.

She just wasn't sure which Jimmy she was searching for, though: the idealistic boy from her youth or the man from yesterday who asked too many probing questions.

CHAPTER SIX

"DADDY, I REALLY need a Rainbow Loom," Briana said Thursday morning as Jimmy drove her to school. "And not for Christmas. I have to get it before then."

He had no clue what a Rainbow Loom was. "You need it for school?"

His daughter looked at him in disbelief. She'd been in school for just a couple of weeks and already she had a list of things a girl simply must have. He should have waited until after Christmas to enroll her.

"No, it's this thing that makes bracelets out of rubber bands. I could make you a bracelet, maybe a million, and in your favorite color. You could wear them to work. I could even, if I hurried, make one for Aunt Holly and the bridesmaids for her wedding."

"We'll see," he said.

"The bracelets could be my wedding present to Uncle Danny's new wife."

Briana was the flower girl, and she was taking her role seriously.

"We'll see," he repeated.

Briana rolled her eyes in a very adult manner. She had quickly learned that "We'll see" meant her father had no clue what she was asking and was not about to commit.

Gesippi Elementary School was situated behind the courthouse. A two-story redbrick building, it housed grades kindergarten through eight. Briana was well aware that she'd missed out on some important first-grade girl fads as well as all the kindergarten ones. She'd been schooled, for the last year, by Jimmy and by his coworkers. All adults. Consequently, she could read and write and knew how many still pictures it took to achieve one second of video. She could also help out with a Foley session, use a pocketknife and climb trees like a pro. But none of these accomplishments helped her fit in with six-year-old girls, so she was making up for lost time.

"Grab your backpack," he told Briana as he entered the school circle. He might have only started doing this a few weeks ago, but he knew the drill. When it was his turn to pull up to the curb in front of the school, Briana needed to jump out and Jimmy needed to move on. There were cars behind him and slow parents were frowned upon.

Once Briana was safely dropped off, he headed to the diner. He wanted to sit by himself, drink coffee and do some more research on his laptop for his pitch to Thom.

The wolf dog photos he'd found so far on the internet made him want one; the stories he was reading convinced him not to.

It had been a long time since Jimmy had felt a real connection to the animal he was covering. For the last few years, he'd been more concerned about the set—be it studio or in the wild—than about the animal.

Hopefully, his passion for this subject would put him back on his game. Sometimes, late at night, he worried that writing articles and putting together documentaries was the only thing he was good at.

He'd not been the best husband.

He'd have to try a lot harder to be the best dad.

If he failed at this documentary, too... No, not happening.

What he needed to do to strengthen the proposal for his boss was to meet a wolf dog. He'd prefer to meet the one from Tuesday night. But first he had to find her.

No one had reported a wolf dog missing, at least not that he could find. Meredith had been optimistic when she'd speculated that the wolf dog had escaped by accident, but they both knew it was more likely that she had become too much of a handful for her owners and been abandoned.

As he drove through downtown Gesippi, he called the number he and Agatha had found for the man who sold wolf pups. No answer, no answering machine.

The Drug and Dine was busy. There was a line at the cash register, so Jimmy didn't bother Keith and headed for a table by the window. The please wait to be seated sign was for the tourists, anyway. The table closest to him was filled with mothers laughing over morning stories about children who didn't want to go to school. Jimmy was sure he heard the term *Rainbow Loom* bandied about.

At another table sat four old men drinking coffee, all wearing hats that proudly heralded their veteran status. They were discussing what Gesippi used to be like. A group at another table was in the midst of a feisty game of Scrabble. They weren't talking and seemed unaware of the noise surrounding them.

The dine portion of Drug and Dine had always boasted a rustic decor. There was a wooden Indian statue by the back door, lots of carved bears scattered throughout the room, as well as paintings of horses and deer. The stock hadn't changed since Jimmy's youth except for the cellphone display and a few kachina dolls sitting on the shelf behind the hostess stand. Jimmy fingered one as he went by, amazed at the cost.

Victor Lucas's name was on the tag—the man who owned the Crooked Feather Indian Trading Post next door.

Jimmy set his laptop at a table for four. Looking around, he spotted Meredith at a table in the corner. She, too, had her laptop open and was staring intently at the screen, oblivious to the people and noise of the restaurant. This morning her hair was loose, not in the usual ponytail. It was darker than he remembered and fell to her shoulders. He used to run his hands through that hair, bring those lips to his own and kiss her until her knees buckled.

For the last two nights, he'd wrestled with memories of Meredith and had decided to avoid her except when it came to the wolf dog search. The decision hadn't helped him sleep.

This morning as he'd done an on-line search about wolf dogs again, her name popped up over and over. She really was considered an authority. There was a YouTube video of her working with Yoda, as well as a presentation she'd given on wolf dogs at the university, and more than one journal article.

She was the last person in the world that he should be cozying up to, but she was the one he needed most.

For the story.

"I think I'll join her," Jimmy told the waitress as she gave him a glass of water and a menu.

He pulled out a chair at Meredith's table, and set down his laptop, instantly feeling the sting of her glare. She had a way of cocking her head to the left, her expression part perplexed and part annoyed, all the while sending a strong message with those piercing green eyes. Pretending he didn't notice that she was annoyed with him, he leaned over and looked at her laptop screen. A large photo of a wolf dog, glaring much the same way Meredith was, looked back at him.

"That's not our dog," Jimmy commented.

"Our dog?"

"The one we saw day before yesterday."

"You're right. It's not." Her tone suggested he had the intelligence of a gnat.

"That animal," Jimmy pointed out, "belongs to a wolf dog rescue called Aqui Lobos well past Tucson. I called them early this morning. They're not very chatty, but I did manage to find out that they're not missing any dogs."

For a moment, Meredith stared at him, looking as if she was contemplating swatting him away. He couldn't remember the last time a member of the female species had not only implied he had the intelligence of a gnat but had acted quite so willing to treat him like one, too. Then she let out a sigh before asking, "Have they turned away anyone wanting to give them a dog?"

"I didn't ask that."

"Who else have you talked to?"

He scooted his chair closer so he could see her laptop better, but also because he loved the way she smelled, like strawberry shampoo. "I've talked to the county sheriff department and the wolf dog rescue organization," he said. "I've stopped at a few stores and one rest area checking for missing-animal posters."

"Agatha said you came to see her, too, to ask about wolf dogs. Why?"

"Same as you, I'm following a story."

"I'm not following a story," she protested. "I'm following y—" She stopped, regrouped and asked, "What makes this a good story, that we have an animal that should be left in the wild or that we have an animal that should be a pet?"

"I'm not sure," he admitted. "This is a new area for me. Usually my documentaries cover the latest hot topic, animals that are either unusual or endangered. Animals that have or could have public sympathy." He paused. "I noticed you didn't give me the option wolf dogs shouldn't exist at all."

"Wolf dogs have been around for thousands of years and are somewhat endangered," Meredith emphasized. "They hunted dinosaur, and they lived with the Aztecs. They're not going away, especially since many people think it's cool to own a dog that is part wolf. But they are endangered because most people haven't a clue how to take care of them. They're gorgeous animals and owning one comes with a certain prestige. Certain breeders know this and cater to it, no matter what happens after the pup is sold."

"Most of my research comes to the conclusion that wolves and dogs shouldn't be crossbred."

"It's a matter of opinion," Meredith said softly. "There are owners who truly love and take care of their wolf dogs. If Yoda were mine, he'd—"

"Don't you work ten-hour days?"

"How do you know that?"

"I visited your grandfather last week. He told me the reason you don't come home."

It had been a while since he'd gotten to watch Meredith fight to keep her composure. He'd always enjoyed riling her. Finally, she said, "So a few visits with my grandfather and you know everything about me?"

"I didn't say that."

"You implied it."

"I didn't mean to."

"Why did Grandpa say I don't spend time with him? Did he say it was because I didn't want to run into Danny?"

"No, he says it was because you didn't want

to run into me. And after our conversation last night, I think he's right."

She went stock-still, so rigid she wasn't even blinking. This was a new reaction. She'd never been one to use calm as a response. As a teen, she'd used righteous indignation, foot stomping and even pacing to make a point. He'd loved each one because they showed her passion.

Finally, she said, "That's ridiculous. I've been building a career. You have too. We've both neglected our families."

He'd not *neglected his family*. His job didn't allow him the leisure to come home for every birthday or graduation. He'd made it to the important ones. "You're right next door in Scorpion Ridge, not even an hour away. I've been in Russia, China, Guam—"

"I came when I was needed," Meredith said calmly. "And all I said last night was that I didn't love Danny the way a wife should love her husband. And, if Grandpa were honest, he'd tell you that I didn't want to run into either your brother or you."

Her tone was even, but Jimmy reveled in the way her cheeks had turned red and her breathing had gotten faster. A part of him, a very primitive part, took satisfaction from the fact that he affected her. But the journalist in him needed her help, and he realized that meant he had to change the subject.

"Look," he said. "I'm intrigued by the wolf dog's plight. I spent hours online last night looking at videos, reading opinions, and quite frankly, I think wolf dogs are more wolf than dog and belong in the wild. What do you believe?"

"I believe every wolf dog is unique. While I'd rather they be in the wild, many experts say they don't belong there. A partially domesticated wolf dog like Yoda wouldn't live long in the wild."

He leaned forward, all intense. "So you believe they should be pets?"

"Are you going to quote me or something?"

"Not sure."

All indignant, she sputtered, "I don't want to be quoted. Not on this."

"Why not?"

"Because owning a wolf dog is controversial. I don't want people on either side of the debate sending me millions of emails telling me how wrong I am. Or, even worse, I don't want my opinion to be taken as the opinion of Bridget's Animal Adventure."

"The zoo where you work?"

"The *habitat* where I work," she corrected. "We need every dime that comes through the front gate. I'm not about to insult any animal lovers."

She wasn't committing, but he'd gotten what he wanted. He now knew she swayed more to the "wolf dogs should be pets" side. And he knew why. She believed that they wouldn't survive in the wild. Now probably wasn't the time to argue that the circle of life had worked for centuries and it was man's interference that caused more damage.

He'd always loved sparring with her, watching her hackles rise. Even after a decade, the desire to one-up her still existed.

"I'm going to visit the wolf dog rescue in the next day or so. Want to come?"

"If I want to visit it, I'll go by myself."

And she was still just as good at stomping on his attempts to win.

"Your grandpa's prescription is ready!" Keith called.

Meredith had almost forgotten why she'd stopped at the Drug and Dine. Now, after three cups of coffee and an irritating, but informative, chat with Jimmy, she put down two dollars for a tip and gathered her things.

"You need any help?" Jimmy asked, his voice a different kind of serious.

"No." She certainly didn't need any help with the prescriptions; she might, however, need a prescription to get rid of a very real headache named Jimmy Murphy.

"How is Ray?" Gone was the calculating journalist out for information any way he could get it. She'd dealt with people like that before. They had agendas; she had animals to take care of. They had deadlines; she had animals to feed. Still, it felt different when the one asking the questions happened to be the one who got away.

She must have taken too long to answer because Jimmy said, "I could kick myself. I've been interrogating you about wolf dogs when the real concern is Ray. The two times I visited he seemed distracted. Really, how is he and what can I do to help?" He stood, as well, picking up his laptop and following her out of the restaurant and into the store.

"Grandpa's not doing well," she admitted. "The family's gathering tomorrow for a big pow-wow."

"What did the doctor say?"

"He said to watch Grandpa, and if he's really hurting, I should get him to a specialist in Tucson. He almost mentioned admitting him to a rehabilitation center."

"Ray would hate that."

"Tell me something I don't know." Meredith checked her watch. "I'm glad the prescription's ready because I have to leave. I've been gone almost an hour. I really hope this makes him feel better."

"Why didn't he come to town with you?"

"After we got home from the doctor yesterday, he went to bed. Then he had a restless night. I heard him tossing and turning. One time he cried out. This morning he wanted to stay in bed."

"Have you seen him walk in the last twenty-four hours?"

"Not much, and he's stopping to rest often."

"Want me to come over?"

"No, there's nothing you can do."

She made her way to the pharmacy area, very aware that he walked right behind her. So close she could touch, smell, feel him. It was affecting her far more than it should have.

"Really," she assured him, speeding up. "We're fine. If there's something you can do, I'll call." Beside her, the door to the Drug and Dine opened and a bell that had welcomed customers for more than a hundred years dinged. A loud voice boomed, "Hey, Murphy, I've been looking for you." Followed by, "Meredith, is that you? Boy, this is like old times."

Meredith gave Joe Bailey a hug. "It's not a school break, not yet. Shouldn't you be in some premed class somewhere dissecting something? All my little sister does is talk about you."

"You always were jealous of my ability with

the frogs," he teased her. "I needed to come into town, take care of a few things. I'm flying out in a couple of days. Mostly because I can't bear to be away from your little sister."

Joe looked like a typical med student. His hair was longer than usual, probably because he didn't have time to get it cut. There were dark circles under his eyes, probably because he didn't have time to sleep. Well, she could blame that on Susan. Her sister had never needed much sleep and didn't know how to sit still. Joe had never looked happier.

Because there were no secrets in a small town, Joe next asked, "How's Ray? I heard he fell."

Meredith said. "Right now, he's curled up in bed, refusing to eat and complaining about the doctor, which is pretty smart for an old man who chased down a dog and took a tumble."

"Wolf dog," Jimmy corrected.

Meredith only nodded.

"I heard it was a wolf dog," Joe said. "I hope the animal's all right. Your sister showed me a picture of you, her and Yoda that she took last summer. You were talking to a group of people at what looked like a KOA camp."

Meredith remembered that talk. They'd sold a few memberships to BAA after and gained a sponsor. "Got a moment?" Joe asked Jimmy. Meredith took advantage of the distraction to pay for the prescription and inch toward the exit. If she hesitated, both men might be offering the "Want me to come over?" bit again. Meredith wasn't in the mood for company.

She shouldn't have worried. Joe had a serious look on his face as he spoke to Jimmy. He was up to something, and Jimmy seemed quite willing to go along. They both were trying very hard not to look at her. She didn't trust those two.

She hoped whatever they were planning had nothing to do with her, but with her luck lately, it was a very small hope.

CHAPTER SEVEN

"GRANDPA, I'M HOME."

Meredith put a small bag of groceries on the table, found the prescription and pill bottle in another bag and then went into her grandpa's bedroom. Pepper followed. Grandpa was sitting up in bed and watching a small television that sat on his dresser. Another judge show.

"You're supposed to take these pills with food, so what do you want to eat?"

"Just give me a handful of cookies."

"I'll give you a handful of grapes and maybe two pancakes."

He didn't say yes or no, just went back to watching television. She started to leave the room, but he stopped her. "Help me up. I want to step out on the porch for a minute."

"Sure, Grandpa." To her surprise, he got up easy enough. She'd expected to have to support him. The drugs the doctor gave him must already be helping. "I ran into both Jimmy and Joe Bailey at the Drug and Dine. Looked to be just as close as they were in high school."

"I saw a lot of Joe this summer. I'm not sure if it was because he wanted to make points with Susan or if he just wanted to practice medicine on me." Grandpa smiled. His first one of the day.

The smile continued as she helped Grandpa onto the porch.

She gave him a hug and settled him in his favorite chair before fixing him the pancakes she'd promised. He fell asleep before he'd finished even one. After feeding Pepper and checking on the chickens—after all, there was a wolf dog in the neighborhood—she pulled out the calendar from her purse and stared at the empty days.

She'd fill them by working on the house. The bathroom needed both a new rug and a new shower curtain. The living room needed a good vacuuming. The screen door to the backyard looked as if an animal had jumped through it. The hole was too small for Pepper, so Meredith would have to ask Grandpa what happened.

The exterior of the house and the shed would take a lot longer.

Pepper followed Meredith, poking his nose into everything and into the palm of her hand for a good petting. He wasn't much of a watchdog, not really. He certainly wouldn't chase off a bad guy. Meredith couldn't even imagine him going out of his way to dig up a bone. He was that laid-back. Or maybe he was just old and tired like Grandpa.

"You're worried, aren't you, boy? Me, too."

Too many things were out of her control. Her grandfather's health. The wolf dog. Jimmy Murphy. Heck, she couldn't even keep a lid on her own emotions.

She was supposed to have come home for just a short time, take care of Grandpa until he was back on his feet and make the world right again.

But she couldn't make it right, not with Jimmy making her remember what it was like to have support, to have somebody caring for her.

But he was only here until he got his next exotic assignment, and she and the wolf dog would be yesterday's news. She had best remember that.

MEREDITH SPENT ALL Friday morning searching the area for the wolf dog. Grandpa was none too happy about her adventures. He'd practically forbidden her to go. When she returned home, he relaxed so much he fell asleep. So she spent the afternoon cleaning. During the course of the day, she also managed to convince him to eat some pancakes, soup and, of course, cookies. The chickens still ignored her when she took care of them. Ungrateful things. Even Speckles, her favorite, acted as if she'd never seen Meredith before.

Still, she'd made progress, and in a way, Meredith was afraid to leave tonight. After the family get-together, she was driving back to her apartment in Scorpion Ridge so she could get up bright and early to work at BAA. Unless, of course, she tumbled over Pepper and wound up with a broken leg.

Then Zack could doctor both Grandpa and her.

When five o'clock finally arrived, the house was ready for the whole family. It would be a small gathering: Meredith and Zack, her mom and dad, and, of course, Grandpa. The only one not coming today was Susan. She was off at college and no one was filling her in on the day-to-day concerns. They didn't want her to lose focus on her studies.

Meredith's dad came right on time bearing three large pizzas. Meredith's mother, looking happier than she had in years, followed behind him.

If Meredith were being honest, once her mother had stopped practicing real estate, she'd stepped up to the plate with Zack and Susan. She'd helped with homework, driven them to swim meets and prepared homemade meals. Unfortunately, Grandpa had never withheld his opinion of her and her lack of parenting skills early on. Otherwise, maybe she'd be the one helping him.

But Meredith wished, more than anything, that she'd still needed all of that when her mother had decided to be a mother.

Her father settled in front of the television watching a reality show about Alaska. Before the first commercial, he got a cell-phone call and did what he did best. He disappeared.

He was a creature of habit. When the real estate market crashed, he'd gone out and found another job that took him away from home even more.

With Zack's arrival, Grandpa looked happier than he had since Meredith had first showed up at his door. With the exception of Susan, everyone he loved was here today. It was almost enough to put Meredith back on his good side. She'd dropped off his favorite-person list this morning when she'd gone exploring. She'd already dropped a spot yesterday when she had to make him take his medicine even as he claimed vehemently that it wasn't helping.

Then, late this afternoon, she'd had to scold him because she'd caught him walking across the backyard as if he had something to do, somewhere to go.

Tonight, though, he sat in the living room cushioned in his favorite chair watching the news and debating politics with Zack. He'd only eaten maybe two bites of a slice of pepperoni pizza, though, and everybody noticed.

"So, how is he, really?" Mom asked. "On Tuesday, after you found him alone and hurt in the desert, I called your father and told him to come home and talk to Grandpa. Maybe convince him to go into assisted living. Now I'm glad your father wasn't available. Grandpa looks…better since you've been here."

Meredith's father wasn't good with decisions that required emotional input. He was better with monetary input. But her mother had tried. Meredith gave her mom a hug, scolding herself for not taking the time to visit.

For not forgiving.

Her mother, in the last few years, had reached out more than once. Even apologizing. Meredith figured that being alone in that big old house finally opened her mother's eyes to how alone she'd left Meredith.

Alone with a younger brother and sister, that is.

Apparently she'd have to keep working on forgiving.

"Grandpa's better than he was on Tuesday, but he's not better than six months ago," Meredith said. "I'm hoping he turns around."

"His father lived to be a hundred and one."

"Great-grandpa?"

Meredith's mother sighed. "Let's hope Grandpa lives a hundred and one years." She looked over at Meredith. "I'm trying to make more time for family, for you."

"Thanks, Mom." It wasn't what her mother wanted to hear, but it was what Meredith could offer, for now. "Look at Grandpa. He's in his element, with all the family around. Maybe he just needs to know how much we love him."

"We could show him more often if he'd move to town. There's a group home right behind the elementary school. If you were here, taking care of the farm, he wouldn't worry so much."

Meredith put her own slice of pizza down. She'd been hungry, and pizza was a favorite, but now her mother was trying to guilt her into staying in Gesippi. Not happening. Turning the conversation back to Grandpa, she said, "All he wants to do is sleep, eat cookies and watch television."

"At least Zack's staying this weekend while you work." Her mother sighed. She'd never been comfortable with the fact that Meredith's job put her in contact with wild animals. It was a barrier they couldn't seem to cross. Meredith had grown up caring for animals. Her mom hadn't worried about her then. But now every time there was a story on the news about an accident with a zoo-keeper, her mom emailed with what-ifs. Not once had her mother visited BAA.

"Maybe Zack can talk some sense into Grandpa." Her mother looked around the room as if hoping to find an answer. "Where did your father go? I wish he'd talk to Ray, convince him to move into town, into assisted living."

Meredith scanned the room, too. Not for answers but taking in all the belongings that told Grandpa's story. He wouldn't be able to leave this place without some reassurance. "You were right," she said begrudgingly, "I think if one of us took over the farm, Grandpa'd be willing." But nobody wanted to move to the farm. Meredith was happy where she was. Oh, she loved Gesippi, loved the farm, but every time she stepped in the backyard she remembered the wedding that wasn't and the man that couldn't be.

"Ray always hoped you'd be the one to take over the farm," Mom said.

For years, Meredith had assumed the same thing. She'd pictured herself as a veterinarian with a rural practice while her husband—yes, Jimmy—wrote the great American novel. Then, for a brief time she'd tried to imagine turning the place into a working farm again with Danny growing crops and she caring for the animals.

But the thought of being a farmer's wife had scared her to death. At least that's what she'd told herself as she'd wrestled with so many doubts the month before the wedding. Really, it was the thought of being a wife to someone she didn't love. Something her grandfather had made her face the day of her wedding.

Meredith really didn't want to have this conversation with her mother right now, so she turned to Grandpa and urged, "Eat another bite of pizza." He stuck his tongue out at her, in jest, and did as she asked.

Just then, the front door burst open. Cold air seeped into the room and Grandpa muttered, "Close the fool door."

Joe Bailey, grinning from ear to ear, ushered Susan in. Meredith's father was right behind, and suddenly everyone was standing.

"I thought you weren't coming home until Christmas." Mom rushed across the room, enveloping Susan in her arms. "Will you be staying?"

"Joe convinced me to take the weekend off work and come home for a visit. He came early, leaving me to fly by myself." Susan pouted prettily, a skill Meredith had never mastered.

"I hope Joe's convincing you to get your Spanish credits done in summer school," Meredith said.

Nobody paid any attention to her.

"Susie deserved a break," Joe said. "And she needed to see her family."

Susie? Susan never allowed anyone to call her Susie. Just as Meredith didn't allow anyone to call her Merry except Grandpa.

"Joe insisted," Susan said. Her eyes went to Grandpa, but Grandpa couldn't have been the draw. Joe would have had to arrange the travel a whole lot earlier than Grandpa's fall.

Judging by the expression in Joe's eyes, the draw was something much happier.

More chairs were pulled into the living room.

"You might want to take a few photos on your cell phone," Meredith's father suggested to his wife.

Confused, Meredith glanced across the room to find Joe going down on one knee and holding out a blue velvet box to her sister. But Susan didn't even wait for the proposal. "Yes!"

CHAPTER EIGHT

UNTIL MEREDITH WALKED through the entrance to Bridget's Animal Adventure, she hadn't realized how stressed she was. Luckily, BAA always chased away the realities of life that kept her awake at night.

Meredith breathed in. Yes, there it was. The smell of popcorn and wild animal. All around was the proof that Christmas was alive and well at BAA. Colored lights in the shapes of animals. Christmas music played. The carousel animals wore Santa hats—somewhere there must have been quite a sale on Santa hats; everyone seemed to have made the purchase.

"Hey!" Katie Rittenhouse, Meredith's boss and friend, left the photography booth and hurried over. "We've missed you. My husband is exhausted trying to be as superhuman as you." How's your grandfather?"

"He's slowing down. Zack is staying with him this weekend. But look—" Meredith moved closer to peek in on the sleeping child attached to

Katie by a cloth carrier "—in the week I've been gone, Catherine's grown a whole inch."

There'd been a day when Meredith had sworn she didn't want children. She'd changed both her brother's and sister's diapers, helped them with their homework and babysat them from the time she was eight. By eighteen, she was convinced she never wanted to repeat the experience. But now that she was nearing thirty, she was starting to reevaluate.

Or was she reevaluating because Jimmy was around and Susan was getting married? Would Meredith be changing a future niece's or nephew's diapers instead of changing those of her own children? Could she see herself as Briana's stepmother? Meredith almost lost her breath at the thought.

"She's sleeping." Katie touched her young daughter's forehead, her fingers trailing down. "I'll let you hold her later. Right now, go meet Luke by the wolves' habitat. He needs your opinion."

Of all the people who ran BAA, Katie Rittenhouse probably knew the most about animals. She'd been caring for wild animals from the time she could walk. Yet she deferred to her husband on almost every decision. He was fairly new to the world of being an animal keeper and was learning by trial and error.

Meredith wasn't sure she'd be able to do what Katie was doing, play second fiddle when she could be, should be, lead. Maybe that's why she was still single. Not only did she avoid the "How many children should we have?" conversation, but she also had issues with "Do you promise to obey?"

It had been a year since Meredith's last "real" date. He'd been a local cowboy who trained horses as well as doctoring and branding cows. She'd hoped their proximity and shared love of animals would be enough to take them through dinner and a movie, but he'd wanted to pick everything from the restaurant, to what she ate, to what they watched. Meredith ended the date before dessert and was home before nine.

He'd not called again. Meredith had been glad. And until today, or maybe really this week and her run-in with Jimmy, she'd not thought about her stalled love life.

Looking back, her relationship with Jimmy had been a bit adversarial, too. They'd both enjoyed the sparring, but had Meredith's need to win, to control, ultimately cost her the love of her life?

Nothing to be done about it now, and she had better things to think about.

"Wait," Katie said, hurrying back to the photo

booth and reaching down. She retrieved, yes, a red Santa hat for Meredith to wear.

Last year, Meredith had been the lone holdout of the staff. This year she didn't have the energy to protest.

Today, it seemed to Meredith that people were a little nicer to her as she made her way to the middle of BAA where the wolves lived. Usually, she got a "Oh, it's Miss Bossypants" kind of greeting. Before she made it halfway to Luke, she'd gotten not only waves but also a half-dozen questions. She truly was needed here.

But she was also needed in Gesippi.

"Meredith, good to see you. You find the wolf dog yet?" Luke was in the habitat with two wolves that were chasing each other in a figure eight and paying no attention to him. He didn't look at her for a moment. Well-fed wolves weren't necessarily a danger, but any keeper worth his salt knew where to keep the focus of his attention.

"No, and believe me I've walked the perimeter of Grandpa's farm a dozen times. Sorry I couldn't make the morning meeting. Do you have my schedule?"

"I do. Give me a moment." He was moving some rocks, doing something to make the wolves' lives more comfortable. At one time BAA was home to eight wolves; now, they had just the two.

Three had been released back into the wild. Two had been traded to another habitat for breeding purposes. And then there was Yoda.

"Where's Yoda?"

"Prince here attacked him yesterday, another scuffle for leadership. One that Yoda can't win."

Yoda had just enough dog in him that he'd never win the battle for alpha wolf, but enough wolf to want it.

Meredith sighed. "So, where is he? Don't tell me—"

"It's the best place for him."

Yoda was once again living in the barn behind Luke's house.

"What's the best place for him?" The man who joined the conversation earned a smile from Luke. Jimmy, however, didn't earn a smile from Meredith. The fact that Yoda was sequestered in a barn was the perfect lead in some slanted documentary arguing that wolves—even the ones that were also dogs—belonged in the wild.

She introduced the two men. "Luke, this is Jimmy Murphy, from Gesippi."

"Murphy?" Luke straightened, looking tall and capable in his blue BAA shirt and khaki pants. "Not…?"

Meredith shot him a warning glare. Luke was the only one at BAA who knew all the sorry details of her past. About a month after she'd been hired, he'd found her crying while she was straightening up the bedding for their black panther, Aquila. When Luke had probed, she'd told him everything, about leaving Danny at the altar and about really loving Jimmy.

It hadn't been her finest moment.

"Ahem." She cleared her throat. "Jimmy was with me when we found both Grandpa and the wolf dog. He works for *Nature Times*."

Meredith expected a negative reaction, but Luke was better at hiding his opinion of *Nature Times* than she'd been. Or maybe, as he'd insisted more than once, both sides had right on their side.

"I was hoping to meet Yoda," Jimmy said after hoisting his camera and taking a few pictures. "I've watched the YouTube videos of him and Meredith."

"Hopefully," Luke said, "we'll have him back in the habitat soon. Right now we're having pecking-order issues and for his safety, he's been removed."

"Sequestered," Jimmy said. "Not much fun for a pack animal, especially one that isn't old or sick."

"It's in his best interest. Our second goal is to put him back with our wolves. Our first goal is to protect his welfare."

"What are you doing to assure his return? Is

there such a thing as behavioral training for wolf dogs? I've not read about a program that works with wolf dogs to run with a pack. If you were doing this, it would certainly make you unique."

Meredith stopped frowning at Jimmy and looked at Luke. She'd wanted more wolves, but maybe all along she should have been pushing for more wolf dogs so there would be a pack. Wolf dogs could be a draw. They'd be even better ambassadors than Prince and Penelope, the two wolves Luke was walking away from.

"Not a budget item," was Luke's response. "And we don't have the staff to give the training the time it would require. Yoda ran with the wolves before, he will again."

Meredith wished she could believe Luke.

"How long will that take?" Jimmy asked.

But Luke was already moving to the back of the habitat, away from Jimmy. He'd been polite, he'd answered Jimmy's questions, but he knew he'd be misrepresented. *Nature Times* would dwell on how much time wasn't being given to Yoda while neglecting to mention how much time was being given to Cheeky the camel and all the other animals at BAA.

"Why are you really here, Jimmy?" Meredith's good mood had evaporated.

"As I said, I was hoping to meet Yoda, take some pictures, watch and see if the zoo's visitors can tell the difference between him and the real wolves."

"Usually they can't."

Jimmy looked impressed. "He's that much wolf?"

"Probably more than eighty percent."

"And the wolf we saw in the wild, you estimated at about fifty percent, right?"

"Right, but I wouldn't want you to quote me on that until I actually find her and do a close visual assessment."

"I'm doing a story on wolf dogs."

"I figured that."

Jimmy stepped closer, so close that had Meredith wanted to, she could have touched his shoulder, his cheek. Any urge to do so evaporated when he said, "Maybe we could help each other. The article could help raise awareness for the plight of wolf dogs, and you could provide balance to the article. Even you have to admit the issue isn't cut-and-dried. I discovered an incident with Yoda. One time he bit Luke, in a public place."

Figured Jimmy'd do his research. "We were doing a talk, in a public venue. Yoda was one of our animal ambassadors. A civilian brought in a dog. Yoda was in a strange place and feeling territorial. It's a risk we willingly take. Luke got a big Band-Aid and lots of teasing for that."

"Yoda ever bite you?"

"No, but I've been bitten, scratched and peed on by other animals. One of your horses also broke my nose way back when. How about you, you tangle with any wild animals because you're on their turf?"

"A bearded dragon bit my ear."

"You got that close to a bearded dragon?"

"It was my first assignment. I was overexcited."

She almost smiled, picturing him in a new job, making a mistake, and all because of his love for animals. That was something they'd always had in common.

"I've never stopped being excited," she said.

Jimmy blinked, then gave a lazy smile. "Me neither." He looked around. "This is the first time I've been to a zoo in more than five years. Yours is different."

"It's a habitat, remember, not really a zoo."

"Will some of these animals stay here forever, like Yoda?"

"Yes, because of their histories. Many were taken out of the wild—not by us—and now are too old or too domesticated to return. Others have been wounded."

"So," Jimmy said, "there's not a single animal here that can be reintegrated into the wild."

Meredith paused. It was a loaded question. Yes, there were animals here that could go back to the wild, notably Rexette the anaconda. But the snake was a low-maintenance animal that was a huge draw and earned money that helped with the upkeep of the high-maintenance animals, like Cheeky the three-cheeked camel or Ollie the aging orangutan.

"I'm not privy to the story behind every animal. Prince and Penelope, the wolves you're watching, were picked up by hikers as pups and kept by them until they were over a year old. They've had too much human exposure to survive in the wild. Every bird in my charge came to us wounded. We've kept or traded the ones who cannot return to the wild. The birds that can have been released. Come with me, I'll show you one we're rehabilitating now."

For a moment, she thought he'd come, thought he'd let her take the lead the way he used to, intent on her every word. Instead, he said, "Maybe another time. By the way, nice hat."

Then he gave her a heartthrob smile and took off, leaving her standing in front of the wolf exhibit, annoyed because she hadn't been able to ask Luke enough questions about Yoda and frustrated because once again Jimmy Murphy had made an appearance that unsettled her day. An appearance that left her feeling frustrated and somehow exhilarated.

And a little pissed that he'd gotten the last word.

Two hours later, Meredith was sure of two things. One, a week off had softened her. Right now she hurt from all the physical labor a keeper's job entailed. Two, being the weekend keeper was different from being the permanent keeper. Meredith didn't care much for the temporary feel. She entered the birdhouse and checked the record chart, glad she was still lead person when it came to the birds' overall care. Feedings and diet seemed right where she had left them. The aviaries were clean. Next, she went to the enclosure of Ouch the eagle. She'd named him Ouch because that's the first word Meredith had said when the bird was brought in and she'd heard his story—the eagle had flown into a barn, gotten frightened and then tried to fly out a glass window.

The window won.

Fred, BAA's vet, thought there was no brain damage, but he was almost sure the eagle's vision was impaired. For the next few months, BAA would be keeping a close watch on Ouch. Meredith wished she could be here more often to do it herself. Ouch could be released back into his natural habitat if his eyesight corrected.

Wouldn't that be awesome?

Meredith didn't have a bird show until eleven so she finished cleaning one of the birdcages and looked at the schedule for her next assignment. As a weekender, she'd be a jack-of-all-trades.

Something she actually liked because she got to work with a lot of different animals.

Next, she got to work with the burros, mules and horses. Meredith radioed her intentions and continued on. The horse pasture and stables were near the back, by the petting zoo. Meredith had been opposed to the addition of the horses at first, that is until Katie had mentioned that a habitat with a wolf dog should be just as open to horses.

Now Meredith had to admit that the horses brought people in, not in huge numbers, but the ones who came were dedicated.

When Meredith first walked through the front gate of BAA four years ago, she'd known that this place needed her. But she'd needed it more. The BAA she'd been hired to work at had been small, understaffed and in need of tender loving care. She'd had big dreams for it, but she'd eventually learned that at BAA, dreams best came to fruition if the pack worked together.

It had been a hard lesson. She'd been used to calling the shots. But, really, she alone could do little. Working with the others, she'd helped turn BAA into the best little habitat in Arizona.

Meredith's thoughts went once again to Jimmy. Yes, she'd learned a lot about teamwork in the last ten years, but the idea of working with Jimmy now was a hard pill to swallow, especially since he seemed determined to disagree with her.

The fence surrounding the stable was a child's dream. Every few feet a wooden horse's head was placed on a plank at a child's level—right now, each head also had a Santa hat on, attached to the end. Some of the stick horses were placed in a way that kids could actually sit on fake saddles that jutted out of the wall.

A young girl—too young to be alone—sat on one today, all alone, her feet moving in giddyup motions and her hand formed in the shape of a gun as she shouted, "Bam, Bam, Bam." Messy brownish-blond hair streamed behind her. Thick glasses made her eyes huge. She wore jeans and a pink sweater.

"Hey," Meredith said, wanting to gain her trust and ask where her parents were. "You like horses?"

"I especially like their feet," the girl said seriously. "I could make Rainbow Loom anklets for them if my dad would let me have a Rainbow Loom."

"Rainbow Loom?"

The little girl held up her arm. Brightly colored rubber-band bracelets, about twenty in number, striped her arm from wrist to forearm.

"Pretty."

"I made them at school. Do you work here?

My dad says not to talk to strangers, but if you work here you're probably not strange."

"Probably not. I do work here."

"What are you going to do?"

"I'm going to clean some of the stalls right now, and then I'll do some grooming."

"Can I help? I like horses. I just know I could be a horse professional."

"Professional, huh? That's a pretty big word."

"My dad uses it all the time. So, can I help? Can I? Please?"

"The answer is no." But it was a woman's voice answering, not a man's, and Meredith immediately recognized it.

"Hello, Mrs. Murphy."

At one time, Meredith had called Jimmy's mom by her given name, Debbie. Debbie had driven all the kids to swim meets, church outings, and they'd made chocolate chip cookies together. Once, she and Meredith had addressed wedding invitations together. Nothing ruined a relationship quite as much as jilting a woman's son at the altar.

Regret swelled in Meredith's chest. She'd made a bad decision and it had cost her so much.

Worse, she didn't know if relationships, once so finely knitted, could be saved.

"I heard you were taking care of your grandfather in Gesippi." Debbie Murphy took a step back, clearly uncomfortable. "I didn't think you'd be here."

Meredith mentally added, *Or we wouldn't have come.*

"Zack's staying with Grandpa on the weekends."

"Briana," Mrs. Murphy said, the tone of her voice leaving no room for argument, "it's time we go find your dad."

"But, Grandma, I want—"

"You want to listen when you're told to do something."

The two walked away, Debbie's hand protectively on Briana's shoulder. Briana didn't protest. She kept looking back, though, longing in her eyes and defeat in her steps. So, this was Jimmy's daughter and she loved animals.

The dreaded and unwanted what-if returned, bringing along with it a melancholy feeling of if-only.

CHAPTER NINE

Jimmy took a picture of the information board in front of the wolf enclosure, which included Yoda's story. Next, he headed for the gift shop and purchased a few postcards that featured Yoda on them. He was huge, with a black face and black-and-white brushed fur. He had the legs of a wolf and the forehead of one. Maybe even the same ears. Jimmy would send a postcard to Thom to help convince his boss that this, indeed, was a story. He'd send a few more shots of Bridget's Animal Adventure so Thom could see what kind of place it was.

Yoda didn't look like the wolf dog they'd run into at Ray's farm. That one had resembled an oversize but underfed husky.

Still, if Meredith said it was a wolf dog, Jimmy believed her. The postcard he held showed Meredith holding on to Yoda's leash, looking strong and confident. She'd wanted to be a vet, he remembered, and wondered if becoming an animal keeper had been a "second choice" or an "instead of."

She was just as passionate as he remembered, be it about her grandfather's health or an animal in trouble. She used to be passionate about him. The thought made Jimmy smile. Meredith was the last thing he needed. Not only were they on opposite sides of the animal planet but they had a messy history.

He'd known that Meredith had loved him from the time she was twelve, a full year after he'd fallen in love with her. He'd been the one she'd sat next to at every outing. At fourteen, he'd been the one who'd pulled her out of the pool, dripping wet, and helped her with her towel, all the while thinking that maybe there *was* something to life besides football. At sixteen, he'd been the one who'd climbed up in the tree house with her and taken her attention off the horses waiting down below and the summer sun.

At seventeen, he'd been the one who'd chased her through the yard, who'd whistled every time she walked by and who she'd kissed in the back row of the movie theater.

He'd been the one she'd reached for.

Never Danny.

Closing his eyes, he remembered holding his high school diploma in hand and finding out he'd been awarded a football scholarship to Ohio State.

His dreams were coming true, and he and

Meredith had so many opportunities at their fingertips. She was a year behind him in school but had enough credits to graduate. So, he'd told her to come with him—they'd go to the same school, work and do it together.

Told her; not asked.

First mistake.

She'd said no, that she had some things to do. She wanted to wait a year.

A whole year.

He was still reeling from that declaration when she admitted that she might not even want to go far away to college. Not explore the world together? That she, meaning they, should consider attending one of the neighboring schools, either in Phoenix or Tucson?

He'd felt as if she was yanking the rug out from under him, crushing a dream. For a solid week, he'd pestered her, trying to get her to change her mind, but she wasn't budging. Sure, he knew that for most of her life, her parents had been MIA and she'd practically raised her siblings. But her mother was home by then, capable of taking care of Zack and Susan.

He'd been young, cocky and a little disturbed that the girl he loved didn't love him enough to come with him. And, in typical Meredith fashion, she'd been so mad at him that she'd refused to even speak to him. So he'd ended it, one early

June evening, and pretended he couldn't hear the sounds of her crying. The rest of the summer he'd made sure to be somewhere else when he knew she'd be around. His little brother, Danny, was confused, called him an idiot. They'd been a threesome. What was wrong with a state school?

Mostly that he'd not gotten a scholarship to one and might not make the team. Walk-on players who weren't recruited by the college seldom left the sidelines.

To this day, Jimmy wished he'd confided in Danny. Told his little brother that although he'd broken up with Meredith, he'd still loved her. Would always love her. Instead, he'd gone off to college and Meredith and Danny entered their senior year of high school together.

He'd been in his second semester, freshmen year, of college when Danny called with the good news: he and Meredith were getting married. They'd stay in Gesippi with their families. Who needed college?

Except Jimmy knew that Meredith's dream was to work with animals.

Jimmy had choked out the congratulations, unsure if the wretched kink in his heart was because he was sure Meredith didn't love Danny or because maybe she did love Danny.

Instead of Jimmy.

He'd been rash and hotheaded, and had paid

the price. Something he had to keep in mind if he was going to convince Meredith to help him with his assignment.

"You all right?" the woman working the counter at the gift shop asked.

"Fine." How long had he been standing there staring at a postcard photo of a very grown-up, very self-assured Meredith Stone? She'd changed immensely from the eighteen-year-old girl who'd innocently believed the world would do what she wanted it to do.

That he would do what she wanted him to.

He took his notebook from his field bag and sat down on a bench shaped like a concrete bear. There were a dozen stories waiting to be told at BAA, but he only had time for one and he needed to get started.

So he walked around, taking pictures and speaking to some of the employees: all friendly and happy to answer questions. All referred him to Meredith. All praised her abilities with animals. One even gave him directions to the neighboring location—referred to as the mini-manse—where Yoda, Meredith's beloved wolf dog, was being kept. He decided to stop on the way home, maybe get a few photos of Yoda, at least.

To his surprise, the hours passed quickly. Zoos usually made him unhappy. The sight of animals behind bars was wrong. It had only taken working on a documentary or two for *Nature Times*—orcas in tanks too small for a good swim; elephants chained so they couldn't stand on all four feet—to make him passionate on the subject. BAA seemed to be one of the better zoos, bent on education and rehabilitation.

But then, what else had he expected from Meredith? Her touch was everywhere. There was an honor roll of more than two dozen animals, complete with pictures—at least three that included Meredith—followed by the dates when the animals were released. There was also a work-in-progress board boasting ten animals all working hard so they could move to the honor roll and have a release date after their names.

Meredith said she was in charge of birds, and her name was next to one of the works in progress. A golden eagle named Ouch was in danger of losing his eyesight. Maybe Meredith was with Ouch now and he could convince her to go on the record.

He'd barely taken two steps before he spotted Meredith riding in a golf cart. He started to wave, but his cell phone sounded. Pulling it out, he expected to see his mother's name on the screen, but the word *ARIZONA* was there instead. He swiped the on button and said, "Hello."

"Dude," Joe Bailey said, uncharacteristically

jovial. "How are you? Where are you? I just went by your house. Your brother said you were chasing a story. Are you still in Arizona?"

"I'm in Scorpion Ridge at Bridget's Animal Adventure."

"Are you having an adventure?" Joe asked.

Jimmy looked around. Peacocks walked among the people and birds, not caged. The zoo had gone all-out on kid attractions. There were wooden cutouts for children to stick their heads through and become animals. There were pelts to feel. Every bench was an animal. The one he'd sat on had actually made a bear noise when he sat down.

Better than a fart.

Meredith's cart had stopped. She was on the phone, too, and hadn't noticed him.

"It's beautiful and unique, I'll give it that," Jimmy allowed. He wasn't really talking about the zoo.

"Meredith is there, right? You two together?"

"I spoke to her briefly about the wolf dog, that's what brought me here today. We're not together."

They couldn't be. Together wouldn't work.

"You talk about me?" Joe asked.

"Ah, you mean you popped the question and Susan said yes."

"I did! Her father gave me his blessing. I got

down on my knee right there in front of all the Stones."

"Congratulations."

"Thanks."

Across the way he saw Meredith smiling and nodding her head.

"You'll be my best man, won't you?"

The word *yes* left his mouth even as he nodded his head. At that exact moment, Meredith looked across the path and spotted him. Never had Jimmy felt such a pull.

He'd only been able to figure out what a woman was thinking when she came right out and told him. But by the expression on her face he knew without a doubt that he and Meredith had received simultaneous phone calls.

It didn't matter that she thought he was pond scum right now. They were going to walk down the aisle, dressed up, her hand tucked under his arm.

He offered a smile; hers disappeared.

MEREDITH GOT TO work at six o'clock on Sunday. It was catch-up day. At six-thirty, she sat in a meeting with Luke, Katie and a brand-new hire named Rick Sweden. Now that Meredith was only a part-time animal keeper, Rick had to be reconsidering his position on the food chain. He was so nice about it, though, that Meredith was finding it hard to be mad at him.

But the last time Luke had brought someone new on board, he'd wound up marrying that someone. Meredith hadn't been happy, but Katie had turned out to be exactly what BAA needed. She brought a level of professionalism that had been missing before her arrival. She was level-headed, and though her heart went out to every animal, she made good business decisions. Something her husband, Luke, was learning, based on his treatment of Yoda lately.

During the meeting, Katie gave out the day's assignments and spoke about which animals were a bit off schedule.

Yoda wasn't mentioned, which annoyed Meredith.

Because Luke was being so cavalier about Yoda's seclusion, Meredith followed Katie out the door and asked, "How long?"

"We've put him back in the enclosure twice. And both times Prince attacked him. They were vicious attacks and they scared a few visitors. Even more—" Katie held up her hand, effectively stopping Meredith from arguing "—it's for Yoda's safety. He's big for a wolf dog, but he's not in Prince's league."

"What happens if he can't return?"

Katie slowed. "We can't trade him to another

habitat. We might be the only one with a wolf dog. But right now, we can't afford a new enclosure."

"I'll take him."

"Really think about that," Katie advised. "A wolf dog isn't a pet that should be left at home for hours on end. You show up to work even on your days off, and you're also a bit confused about what time you're supposed to go home. Would that be fair to Yoda?"

"I never neglect my animals."

"No, you don't, but right now your animals all live here. You don't even have a fish at home. And, where is home? Your grandfather's feeble. Yoda could sneeze and knock the man over, right?"

Meredith wished she hadn't shared quite so much on her grandpa's condition and was glad she hadn't mentioned Susan's upcoming nuptials.

"I'll take him," she repeated, but Katie was already walking away.

Meredith rolled up her sleeves as she prepared to do her least favorite chore: cleaning the birdcages of floor litter, food remains and offal. When she finally finished cleaning the cages, she started for one of the outdoor aviaries, but her phone beeped before she made it. The screen showed Susan's name.

"I can't believe I'm engaged," Susan said for

about the fifteenth time since Friday night. "Are you sure you'll be okay with Jimmy being best man? I mean, you have a history and left his brother at the altar."

Susan hadn't been born with the diplomatic gene. She usually said what she thought and considered the consequences later.

"Jimmy's the best man...?" Meredith said slowly.

Susan ahemed. "I assumed you knew. Joe said Jimmy was at BAA with you. I figured you and Jimmy had already spoken."

"No, not about this," Meredith said with a sinking feeling that her objection wouldn't matter. "So, he's already been asked. If I say I have a problem with him as best man, are you going to unask him? Unask me?"

"You'll do it," Susan said confidently, and Meredith gave in.

In the next few hours, Meredith fielded about a half-dozen phone calls from Susan before her sister was finally convinced that Meredith was working. In between Susan's twittering about dates and dresses, Meredith also realized that not only would she be walking down the aisle with Jimmy—odd thought—but that Danny and his new wife would be in the audience.

Meredith's mother also called twice. And, yes, there was a subtle mention that Susan was a good decade younger than Meredith and getting married first.

"I work with animals," Meredith told Ollie the orangutan at lunchtime, "because human communication is overrated."

Ollie didn't appear convinced. He merely pointed at his stomach, a clear indication that he was hungry and looked at her expectantly.

"Were you ever in love, Ollie? No, well, you're lucky. Love has a way of bringing you to your knees."

As Meredith left Ollie's enclosure, she couldn't help thinking that maybe Susan was a whole lot smarter than she'd been at her sister's age. Susan had known to say "yes" and not "wait."

Later, when Meredith ended her shift, she stopped by the office to say goodbye to everyone.

And everyone had an opinion on Jimmy Murphy.

"He knows his animals." A compliment from Luke.

"He agreed that our black panther Tyre might do all right if we released him into the wild." Katie, no surprise, was there, too. "I'm going to research it a bit more. He gave me the name of someone to call."

Meredith wished she had the name of someone to call…someone who'd come and get Jimmy and take him back to California or Timbuktu—any-place far, far away.

Unfortunately, because Zack had to leave for his college classes early Monday morning, Mere-dith needed to get back to Gesippi and Grandpa's farm. She didn't have time to stop and visit Yoda.

Right now, time wasn't her friend, especially with Jimmy Murphy watching everything and ready to twist the smallest thing into an exposé.

It was just turning dark when she pulled into Grandpa's circular driveway. She found both Grandpa and Zack, and one dog, in front of the television.

"How are you doing, Grandpa?"

"He cooks worse than you do," Grandpa accused.

Zack pretended to be insulted. "I didn't cook. We ate cereal and peanut butter and jelly sand-wiches. He said all you would feed him was pan-cakes."

She rolled her eyes and carted her suitcase into the guest bedroom where her brother's belong-ings were spread out. Tossing his clothes onto a chair, she neatly put her own stuff away before joining them and asking, "What does our little sister, who's quickly turning into a bridezilla, expect of you guys for this wedding?"

"I'm one of the groomsmen and will drive the carriage after the I do's."

"Drive the carriage? She wants a carriage!"

Zack looked half guilty, half scared. "Susan already talked to you, right?"

"She did. I'm the maid of honor, but she called me at work and I had to stop talking because a little boy was chasing a peacock."

"Oh, sure," Zack said. "You'll give any excuse."

Meredith had no intention of letting Zack off the hook. Drive the carriage? What was their sister thinking?

But before she could query her brother, Grandpa laughed and said, "Make me a pancake or two, will you, Sandy?"

"What?" Meredith stopped breathing for a moment, all thoughts of her little sister gone. Sandy had been their grandmother's name.

"I'm hungry. Would you make me some pancakes?" Grandpa repeated his request as if nothing was out of the ordinary. Zack's eyes met hers across the room.

"Sure, Grandpa," Meredith said softly. "Anything you want."

Grandpa's kitchen wasn't much bigger than the one in Meredith's apartment. A table just big enough for three was shoved against the wall right where you entered the room. A refrigerator and old-fashioned sink stood against the other wall. Then came the counter and cabinets. The final wall was just big enough for a gas stove.

"He was fine all weekend," Zack said from the doorway as Meredith started the pancakes. "He's slower, but we watched television, played checkers, and except for not always hearing what was going on and constantly thinking someone was outside, there wasn't a problem."

"I've noticed him staring at the back door, too. Did you ask him how the hole got there?"

"He blamed Pepper."

"I don't think it was Pepper."

"Me neither," Zack agreed. "It looks more like someone put their foot through it. Do you suppose Grandpa did it and is too embarrassed to admit it?"

"Doesn't sound like something Grandpa'd do."

"No, it doesn't, but things are changing. He's changing," Zack said. "Maybe we should mention this to his doctor. He's slipping. That's all."

Twenty minutes later, Grandpa was slipping again—slipping into sleep in front of the television, his chin buckling and him sitting straight up.

"Five or six times a day he does this," Zack said.

"I must talk more than you do. He didn't fall asleep this much with me."

"Yeah, right."

"Or maybe you're boring."

Zack merely nodded before heading into the guest bedroom and packing his clothes and text-books into his overnight bag. A few minutes later, Zack went over all Grandpa's medications with her. As if she couldn't read the times and dosages—Zack was such a doctor in training. He left just before the nine o'clock news came on. Grandpa woke up in time to watch the coverage on a police standoff. "Hey, it's that cop from Adobe Hills," he hollered. "The one whose wife caused all those problems. Guess he's out of jail."

The segment ended before Meredith made it back to the living room. Together, using TV trays, they ate pancakes and cookies. It was the first time in a long while that Meredith stayed up late willingly. After all, tomorrow she didn't have a set schedule, which she was looking forward to more than she expected. When a late-night rerun came on, she helped Grandpa to bed, trying not to notice his weight loss.

Next morning, Meredith knew one thing for sure, being at Grandpa's would never be boring for her. She'd already done a sweep of the yard—no stray wolf dog to be seen—and had fed the chickens their morning pellets along with some old bread. The only one who remembered her was Speckles, who must have been at least twelve years old and whose feathers were no longer red but turning brown with age. The bird was ancient in chicken years and was definitely no longer laying eggs.

After assuring Speckles that mealtime would continue even without Grandpa at the helm, she stood in the front yard assessing the house. It needed a coat of paint and a little tender loving care.

A lot of tender loving care, and Meredith didn't want to have to be around long enough to complete the task.

She'd pretty much cleaned the inside last week, as much as she could with cleaning supplies and elbow grease. Surely the family didn't expect her to paint.

She was even more exasperated when a cloud of dust headed her way, heralding a visitor. She recognized Jimmy's SUV before it parked behind hers. He exited, looking good enough to eat in tight jeans and a green T-shirt that stretched across his chest. He walked confidently in cowboy boots that had clearly done a hard day's work.

"Meredith," he greeted.

She couldn't help herself and said, "Are you here to scold me because I've got chickens trapped in a coop and you think they should be free range?"

CHAPTER TEN

"HMM, THAT'S AN angle I've not considered. Free range definitely fits my way of thinking." He waited for her reaction. Was her mood this morning going to be defensive, or maybe, just maybe, could they could get things done?

She stood in the front yard in jeans and a black shirt. Her hair was just as he liked it— messy, loose and not in a ponytail. Truth was, her tousled-waif look was the most intriguing he'd seen in a year.

"What do you need?" She didn't move toward him at all. "Are you here to visit Grandpa?"

"I'm here to visit you. Didn't Susan tell you?"

Now he had her attention. She visibly tensed. "Tell me what?"

Jimmy tried not to chuckle. Meredith had no clue why he was here, which meant he'd get to break the good news to her.

Basically, two people who should avoid each other because of family, work and personal history now had to work together. His mother would have a cow. And Meredith...well, it would be fun watching her try to lead him around the way she'd done in high school. He was all grown up now and wouldn't make the same mistakes.

He wouldn't leave.

After all, the wolf dog story was right here in Gesippi.

Grinning, he said, "Susan talked to Holly last night. Susan and Joe are so in love, they've decided they can't wait until summer. They want a Christmas wedding. Holly's agreed to leave all her flowers, decorations and such at the church and keep it set up, if the elders go for it. So Susan and Joe will just use Holly's stuff."

"Christmas is less than two weeks away," Meredith protested weakly.

"You don't have to tell me. I'm not ready for my brother's wedding this coming Saturday, let alone another wedding two weeks later. Joe called me this morning, too. As best man and maid of honor, they've entrusted us to go through all the wedding stuff in Ray's basement to see what Susan can use."

"What?" Meredith paled. If there'd been a chair nearby, she probably would have sat down. "There's wedding stuff in the basement?"

"According to Susan there is. Ray kept it even though you didn't end up...using it."

Jimmy watched as Meredith pulled out her cell phone and punched in a number. Susan did most of the talking, but he was privy to scattered responses from Meredith, like "You've got to be kidding."

And, "He's the best man, not a wedding planner."

Then, "How do you know what's down there is any good?"

The conversation ended with a clipped "Fine, I'll do it."

He heard just enough to realize Meredith hadn't been able to come up with a good reason to turn down Susan's request.

But who could blame Meredith for not wanting to watch her little sister walk down the aisle using decorations from her own wedding that had never happened.

"The really bad thing about cell phones," Meredith said after she ended the call, "is that you can't slam down the receiver to let the person on the other end know just how you really feel. Did they mention what they wanted us to look for? I forgot to ask."

"Susan says you have more than a hundred bottles of bubbles."

"I wonder if there's an expiration date stamped on their tiny bottoms," Meredith bemoaned.

Good, she hadn't lost her sense of humor.

"Do we have a time line for this?" Meredith

asked. "Is there a reason you're here today, without calling?"

"No real time line for now. But soon I won't have any free time."

When she looked at Jimmy, frowning, he continued, "Come Friday, I've Danny's prenuptial dinner. Saturday's his wedding. Monday, I'm Skyping with my boss at *Nature Times*. If I get a deadline or—" he paused "—have to find a new job, time might be a problem. When Joe asked me last night, I figured I'd just get over here this morning, help you go through it, and then maybe I wouldn't need to think about it again until their actual wedding."

"Wow, Danny's getting married this Saturday," she said softly, more to herself than to him.

He nodded.

She frowned and said, "*Nature Times*. About your story on wolf dogs? You're worried they won't go for it."

"My last two stories didn't go as well as we hoped."

To his relief, she didn't dwell on the topic. Instead, she looked at her watch. "Grandpa's still asleep. I've already taken care of the chickens and Pepper. I even walked around a bit, trying to find that wolf dog."

"Nothing?"

"She's probably long gone."

"Someone will find her." Jimmy really hoped that someone would be him. Filming the actual rescue would make for a lead that would reel viewers in. If he managed to snag that footage, there'd be an opportunity for a before-and-after conclusion. Still, he needed Yoda for a comparison.

Maybe working together on Susan and Joe's wedding would give him an in with Meredith for the story. He just had to wait for the right time.

Otherwise, he might find himself looking for a job.

Turning, Pepper at her heels, Meredith walked into the house. He followed as she grabbed a notebook and some pencils before heading down the stairs. "Susan wants us to write down what's there and what's usable."

"Do you remember any of it?" he asked.

"Right now, all I remember is the bubbles."

The boxes were in an unfinished back room where Meredith used to find snakes to rescue. The boxes had Meredith's name and a decade-old date written on them in a spidery handwriting.

"Grandma wrote this," Meredith said. "I didn't even realize this stuff was down here. Susan told me right where to come. How did she know?"

"Maybe she helped your grandma pack it all up."

"She would have been about ten." Meredith

went down on her knees and pulled one dusty box toward her. "I never even wondered where it all went. I figured it had been given or thrown away."

He crouched down next to her and took out his pocketknife. Sliding the blade through the yellowed tape, he opened it.

"Napkins," Meredith said, pulling out two large packages, the plastic intact. "Those are still good."

"Nope, they have Danny's and my name on them. Plus the date."

They also had, Jimmy finally noticed, a horse and carriage imprinted on them.

"You loved horses," Jimmy remembered.

"We all did," Meredith pointed out. "I wanted to be a vet. You wanted to be a writer. Neither of us were thinking about wild animals then." She pulled out three giant baggies filled with napkin rings in the shape of horses.

"Do you have any regrets about your career choice?" Jimmy asked.

"No, working at BAA has been amazing. You?"

He shouldn't have asked her the question if he didn't want to answer it himself. "These past two weeks have been the first time I've been without an assignment. Its really given me a chance to consider my options. The only offer I have on the table has to do with the wolf dog, and my editor's not excited about it. For the first time, I'm not sure my boss will give it the go-ahead."

Meredith didn't answer at first. No doubt she knew getting the go-ahead would be a mixed blessing for her. "Well, whatever happens with the story, you deserve to keep your job. You're good at it." Wisely, she then changed the subject. "I hope using this stuff doesn't bring bad luck."

Jimmy laughed. "I'd forgotten that you were superstitious. What did your grandma always say?"

"A watched pot never boils. She said that every time I stood at the door waiting for you to show up."

"I always came."

"Not always," Meredith reminded him.

"I asked if you had any regrets about your career choice," Jimmy said. "Any other regrets?"

Her hands clutched a bag of napkin rings and it spilled open, tiny horses scattering over the floor.

"Tell me why you wouldn't leave with me," he pressed.

"Why?" she whispered.

"I should have asked years ago."

"Why didn't you?"

"I was young and stupid."

"Really?

"Really," he admitted. "You used to tell me everything. I never betrayed you—"

She started to interrupt, but he held up his hand.

"I never betrayed anything you revealed to me in confidence."

It was true. He'd always been a good listener— except when it really mattered. He'd also been the one to pitch in and help her when Zack needed someone to teach him to throw a hardball or Susan was scared of a school bully. "You remember my parents were never there?"

"I remember."

"Your senior year, Grandpa and Grandma were getting older, slowing down. Zack was having a hard time in math. Susan was hanging around some girls who only knew how to find trouble. Mom was home, but struggling to help them— Plus, we were about to lose the house. They'd not saved a dime."

"Did you tell Ray?"

"A little bit, but honestly, I thought I could take care of it. Should take care of it."

"Why didn't you tell me?"

"It was your senior year. You were riding high. Plus, I was embarrassed. The night you asked me to go with you, our electricity had been turned off. No way could I leave. No way."

He could only shake his head. "You should have said something."

A tear formed in one eye. She'd not appreciate him noticing.

"What would you have done?" she said. "Think back. You were all of eighteen. It was easier for me to be angry with you."

"So when I left, you started dating my brother?"

"Nothing changed after you left except you weren't there. Danny came around, just like before. He started helping Zack with math. He'd go with me to Susan's school because she was being bullied and we'd walk her home. He was always such a big guy. Soon, the girls left her alone. All it took was one look from him."

"I understand now." And he did.

"It was so easy to believe that everything would work out. Danny was easy to love, like a brother. There was no money for me to go to college. I didn't manage to earn a scholarship, and I was too busy helping Zack and Susan to spend much time pursuing grants. So when Danny asked me to marry him, all I could think was that at least I'd be in Gesippi. I'd be where Susan and Zack needed me. And Danny would help me, he'd be there for me."

He reached out, touched her knee and nodded. "Makes sense."

"But the morning of the wedding, I woke up terrified. A fear like nothing I'd ever felt. I ran into Grandpa's barn and started to cry. Grandpa found me. I told him I didn't love Danny but that I needed to marry him."

"And Ray said not to do it."

"He did. He apologized for not being more aware of what was going on. He asked me what I wanted to do and promised he'd help. I just wanted to run. It's the only thing I could think of. Grandpa gave me his money from the pickle jar. It was enough to get me started."

"And Ray sent everyone home."

"And pitched in again with Susan and Zack, and even helped out my mom and dad. I'm pretty sure it broke him."

Tears spilled, dripping down her cheeks like rain on glass. He took his hand off her knee and scooted closer. He wanted to kiss her. Wanted it so bad it hurt. Instead, he took her in his arms and rocked her. His shirt soon grew wet, but he didn't care. It was about time Meredith Stone let go of the secrets and guilt she'd been holding.

After a while, she stopped, pushing him away, her cheeks turning a cute shade of blush. He knew she wanted to run, get away from him, so he got back to business.

"Let's start by throwing away anything that's

no longer good. Things like the napkins can be donated to a shelter or the local church."

Meredith sniffled and raised an eyebrow. "Oh, really, the local church? I'm sure Danny's future wife would love to use one of these napkins during the next potluck."

"You're probably right."

For the next hour, they sorted. There were candles, silk flowers, a guest sign-in book. One box held twenty disposable cameras.

"You'd certainly thought of everything."

Meredith sneezed and surveyed all the stuff they'd unpacked so far.

"But we didn't spend much money at all. Probably the biggest expense was the barbecue meat we were going to serve the few guests after the wedding. I wasn't even getting a dress."

"Plus, you were going to do it without bridesmaids and groomsmen, right?"

"We didn't have any money and didn't want to ask our parents for it."

Back then, his parents had been channeling all their money into helping him with his schooling. Danny hadn't wanted to go to college, but Jimmy's parents had kept track of what they'd spent on Jimmy and planned to give the same to Danny to help him get a start.

He hadn't needed much; he wanted to take over the family's cattle operation as well as farm beans, squash and corn. He wanted to be his own boss and work the land.

"I don't think we were hurting for money," Jimmy said. "Why didn't Danny—"

"The only thing the groom's family is supposed to do is pay for the prenuptial dinner." Meredith continued, "My aunt sent me two hundred dollars to spend." She nodded at the boxes. "We spent it on food and on the stuff in these five boxes. Why would Susan want any of this? It's not her style at all."

"Maybe Susan got the same two hundred dollars and knows that combining what you had with what she has, the money'll go further."

Meredith stared at him as if he'd lost his mind.

"Hey, I don't know about all this. Regina and I got married in Las Vegas."

He, Regina, their family and friends had waited in a foyer while another wedding took place in the chapel. Then they'd been hustled into the chapel and the wedding had started right on schedule even though his father had been in the restroom. Last, they'd been hurried out so the next wedding could begin on time.

Regina had loved it. The chapel had looked out on a golf course and neighboring casino.

Jimmy would have preferred wearing jeans and being outside.

He pulled out the decoration that should have

stood on the top of Meredith and Danny's cake. A tiny plastic likeness of a blond female gazed up at a dark-haired male dressed in a suit. "This doesn't really fit your motif."

"I searched everywhere for a cowboy and cowgirl. The internet wasn't quite as advanced as it is today."

"Well," Jimmy said, laying it next to the bubbles, "this is something they'd be willing to use."

Meredith didn't answer. She was staring at the cake topper, a funny look on her face, her eyes shimmering.

"You all right?"

She didn't answer, but he knew she wasn't all right.

"Look," Jimmy offered. "This is really your stuff. If Joe needs money, I'll…"

He hesitated. Until a year ago, Jimmy could have lent the money without a second thought.

But now his well-paying job was iffy. In fact, his future rested on a wolf dog documentary that this woman would fight to prevent. If his boss ever approved it.

"I'll find him some," he finished.

Meredith shook her head. "It's all right. Just bringing up some memories."

Jimmy sat back on his heels, studying her and the sadness in her eyes. She'd answered his questions and now she was done, finished, spent.

But what she hadn't said, what he now realized he'd wanted to hear, was that she hadn't been able to marry Danny because she'd still been in love with Jimmy.

He couldn't take away the pain of the past, but he could do right by the wolf dog story, and right by her. Hopefully, that would be the same thing...

EXHAUSTED, BOTH PHYSICALLY and mentally, Meredith stood up, wiped the dust from her hands and pushed the boxes they'd not gotten to over to the wall.

"We've done enough today." She hadn't expected this rush of emotion about the past, hadn't realized how much she'd missed the easy friendship she'd had with Danny, or how much she'd missed the man across from her—how drunk with love she'd felt in those long-ago days.

Upstairs, Grandpa rang the bell Zack placed on the table by his bed.

"I'm being summoned," Meredith said, grateful. She needed some time away from Jimmy to think over the conversation they'd just had and to remember the pain he'd caused her—and would cause her again if he went through with the wolf dog documentary. "We can probably combine the stuff Susan can use into one box and I'll write her name on it. There're only three more boxes to go through. I can finish them tomorrow on my own."

Then she wouldn't have to see him again until the wedding rehearsals.

Jimmy pulled out his phone and checked his calendar. "Tomorrow morning I'm going to the Wilcox Livestock Auction with Danny. They're having some sort of special stocker feeder sale."

"Spoken like someone who's never been gone from Gesippi," Meredith tried to tease.

The bell sounded again. Meredith headed for the stairs; Jimmy followed right behind her. When they got to the top, she headed for Grandpa's room, saying to Jimmy over her shoulder, "I've never been a maid of honor before."

"I've never been a best man. But I'm in Danny's wedding next week."

Meredith felt a rush of emotion. Guilt that she'd hurt Danny; relief that she hadn't married him; joy that he'd found the right woman.

"Tell me a little about the girl he's marrying."

"Her name's Holly. They met online."

"Danny had an online courtship? You're kidding."

"No. Holly's really sweet and kind of a free spirit. She's got all kinds of ideas about growing her own food and even making her own clothes. I think they'll be great together."

Meredith laughed. "Because Danny's really sweet and a free spirit?"

"I wouldn't say that. He's just a homebody. He has everything he needs right here in Gesippi. He's just not comfortable anywhere else."

"Hey, Jimmy," Grandpa greeted. "I wanted to thank you again for helping Merry find me the other day. I don't think I could have made it out there on my own much longer. I couldn't get up."

"You're a stubborn old cuss. You'd have eventually gotten on your feet." Even as he said the words, Jimmy started to help Ray out of bed so that Meredith didn't have to. Grandpa wore the light-blue-and-white-striped cotton two-piece pajamas that he'd worn ever since Meredith could remember.

Grandpa smiled, but it didn't reach his eyes.

"So what you are doing here?" Grandpa didn't mince words. "You sniffing around my granddaughter again?"

"Grandpa!" Meredith handed him his robe and then bent down to help him with his slippers.

"No, I'm not sniffing around." Somewhere along the way, Jimmy Murphy had gained patience. He'd not had that trait when she'd dated him. "I was helping Merry—" he gave her a sideways look full of glee "—go through all the wedding stuff downstairs. For Susan."

"Sandy and Susan packed it all up. Lord, we

had barbecue meat for a year afterward. Today, anyone offers me a barbecue sandwich and I tell 'em no."

"I didn't know all that, Grandpa. Someone should have told me. I'd have packed it up."

Grandpa merely smiled. He'd been the one to pack up her clothes and drive them out to her because she'd been too busy looking for work and registering for school. She'd found an apartment, and for the first time, hadn't had to worry about anyone else.

And slowly, she'd found herself.

"Someday I might actually like barbecue beef again," Grandpa said. To Meredith's surprise, Grandpa headed for the kitchen instead of for the television set. "I think I'll take some pancakes," he said. "You hungry, Jimmy?"

"Sure, I've worked up an appetite." Jimmy sat down across from Grandpa. Meredith started making breakfast while Grandpa talked. "Both Sandy and Susan cried when they packed all that stuff up, especially Susan. She always wanted to do whatever you did, Merry, and she thought your wedding was going to be storybook."

"You're getting romantic in your old age, Grandpa."

"No. I'm quoting her."

Meredith had the batter all ready. She set plates

in front of Grandpa and Jimmy and got out the syrup and butter.

"Susan spent a lot of time here after that, especially when Sandy was sick."

Another thing Meredith hadn't known. She'd assumed her grandpa had done most of Grandma's caregiving. She'd not in a million years considered that Susan had done the mature and sensible thing.

"I think that's why Susan's decided to be a nurse," Grandpa said. "She did a real good job helping your grandma. She seemed to know what Sandy needed before Sandy even asked."

Meredith blinked, heavy tears forming. By the time she'd realized just how sick Grandma was, so many things had been left unsaid.

Seems she'd also missed out on her baby sister growing up.

Five years ago, Meredith had been a new hire at a big zoo in California. All she'd had was debt and determination. When she realized Grandma was really sick, she'd called home every night. "Do you need me?" she'd always asked.

Come to think of it, usually it had been Susan who'd answered the phone, saying that everything was okay, and that Grandma was resting comfortably. In the end, Meredith had made it home just in time to say goodbye.

"Sandy'd be pleased that this time you're the

one taking care of me," Grandpa said softly. "You always were my favorite."

"You're not supposed to have favorites." Meredith sniffed.

"You were my favorite, too," Jimmy said.

She ignored him, because if she didn't, she might say something she regretted, something exposing her heart even more. After serving both he and Grandpa, she pulled the step-stool chair up to the table so she could join them.

"Merry's a great cook," Grandpa said conversationally. "She makes excellent pancakes. Better than Zack."

"She does a lot of things well," Jimmy agreed.

"We need a wedding." Grandpa waved his fork in the air. "It's nice to have some upheaval, besides Merry here doing the unexpected all the time."

"I don't—" She was interrupted by the ring of her phone. Pulling it from her pocket, she checked and saw that it was Susan.

"Hey," she answered, mouthing to Grandpa and Jimmy who it was. "We're having breakfast. Jimmy's here. He helped me go through some of the boxes downstairs this morning. I'm not sure—"

His cell sounded. He pulled it out, checked it and said to Meredith, "I've got Joe on my end."

"I'm so glad Jimmy's there," Susan said. "Because Joe and I have been up all night talking."

Meredith almost said, "Now you call to tell me," but she'd never heard her sister sound this excited, this in control.

"Jimmy may have already spilled the beans, but we can't wait for summer," Susan went on. "Getting married over Christmas will save us time and money. Plus, well, we don't want to put it off any longer."

"You're right, that's old news," Meredith said.

"I'm glad you got a head start because with school, I need you to help plan the whole thing," Susan gushed. "I can do some of the last-minute things, but you're in Gesippi now. I'm not. You can arrange the food, help gather everyone for dresses and such."

"When's your last final?"

"I'm done on the twentieth, but Joe has to work until the wedding. I'm using the extra days to move my stuff into his apartment. So we won't get there until a day or so before the wedding. Holly's leaving me almost everything from her wedding, so you don't have that much to do, really. Jimmy will be right beside you. After all, he'll be doing the same thing for me and Joe that he's doing for Danny."

Across the table, Jimmy suddenly sat up straighter and looked at his phone with horror.

Then, his words etched with disbelief, he slowly said, "You want me to plan your wedding?"

Meredith felt the same shock. It was one thing to go through a few leftover baubles, but quite another to plan someone else's wedding, and the last person she wanted to do the planning with was the man she'd always wanted to marry.

CHAPTER ELEVEN

IT WAS ALMOST noon when Jimmy made it home. Despite the news, breakfast had been good. Afterward he'd helped Meredith with her chores, including fixing the back door screen. Ray insisted that Pepper had jumped through it, but Jimmy and Meredith both agreed it looked more like someone put a foot through it.

Jimmy had wanted to press Ray about it, but Meredith just shook her head, clearly not wanting to upset her grandpa.

Danny was out stacking hay, and Jimmy thought he should really be helping him since he'd be taking over the farm duties while Danny was on his honeymoon. Dad was out shearing sheep. Jimmy would have preferred to speak to either of them and share what was going on with Susan Stone and Meredith. Instead, when Jimmy closed the door behind him, he heard his mother in the kitchen. Dishes clinked and the smell of freshly baked bread surrounded him.

Since their visit to the zoo two days ago, his mother had been touchy. No, not a zoo. He needed to follow Meredith's lead if they were to work together. It was a habitat.

He looked across the living room and into the hallway, noticing the floor had been waxed to a high gloss. There were no old newspapers by the couch, no shoes on the floor, and Briana's brand-new Rainbow Loom and baggies of color-coded rubber bands were placed artfully in a decorative bowl on the coffee table.

When his mother was irritable, she cleaned. She claimed it was a stress reliever. She'd been cleaning steadily since Saturday night.

Maybe after Danny said "I do," she'd calm down.

Maybe after Danny said "I do," she'd forgive Meredith.

After she heard about Susan's wedding plans and Jimmy's part in them, the attic would probably soon be acquainted with a broom and dustbin.

Perhaps Jimmy should join her in the cleaning frenzy. He was certainly stressed. Going through boxes in your ex-girlfriend's basement and finding out why she'd canceled her own wedding was one thing; planning an actual wedding with her quite another. Not to mention his job troubles.

"I'm in here," his mother called.

So much for sneaking out the back door and finding Danny.

"Hi, Mom."

She stepped from the kitchen, wiping flour from her hands. "You took a while coming home from town. Did you stop and talk with Joe again?"

"Joe's already back in New Mexico at school."

"He should have gone to college right after high school. He'd already be practicing."

"I'm not sure he knew what he wanted out of life then."

His mother started to say something but she stopped. "So, what took you so long in town then?"

Jimmy had the sense his mother already knew.

"I was over at Meredith's. Joe asked me to be his best man and he said there were things in Ray's basement that maybe they could use for their wedding."

"And Meredith is okay passing it on?"

"Yes." He thought it an odd question.

"She really hasn't changed. She was always way too practical for her own good. Her grandma used to say Meredith was a thirty-year-old trapped in a kid's body."

He really didn't want to think about Meredith's body...

His mother sighed, loudly. "Can't you leave things be until after Danny's wedding? It's just five days away."

"Leave what be until after our wedding?"

Holly poked her head out of the kitchen door. She had red frosting streaked across one cheek. "Hi, Jimmy. We're making cupcakes in case we run out of wedding cake."

"I didn't know you were coming today," Jimmy said.

"I couldn't sleep last night. Guess I'm too excited. When I called here this morning, your mom answered. We're both feeling antsy and decided baking together would take our minds off everything we should be doing instead."

"Like what?" Jimmy couldn't imagine that his mother or Holly had left anything to chance, and now that he had to plan Joe's wedding, he should ask about the ins and outs.

"I'm afraid we've left somebody off the invitation list," Holly said.

"I'm afraid people who have not been invited will show up and we'll run out of food," his mother added.

"We'll make more cupcakes," they said together.

"Then, too, I still need to find tablecloths for the tables." Holly didn't look excited about the prospect. "Every store I've been to has been out of Christmas colors. Please say you'll look for some, Jimmy. You've got time."

Right. Because he wasn't really working. Might not have a job.

His mother had a few more worries. "And I'm afraid we'll show up at the Hospitable and they'll have forgotten we're having the rehearsal dinner there."

"But I'm getting away from my question," said Holly. "What do you want him to leave alone for five days?"

Jimmy's mom shook her head subtly, but Holly noticed and said, "It can't be that bad. Does it have to do with Meredith?"

"Now see what you've done," Jimmy's mom accused. "You'll get Holly all upset."

"Oh, please," Holly said. "Do you think Danny and I haven't talked about her being here and the timing of it all? Really, I'd like to meet her. I want to thank her."

"Thank her!" Jimmy's mom looked ready to faint.

"Sure. If she hadn't backed out of their wedding, I'd not be marrying Danny. In fact, I think I'll go over there now."

"Are you sure—" Jimmy began.

"—I'm sure," Holly interrupted. "While I'm gone, you can help your mother make cupcakes."

"HELLO, ANYONE HERE?"

Meredith didn't recognize the voice. Never mind that, she'd been in and out of Grandpa's shed for the last hour and was covered with sweat, cobwebs, old leaves and dirt. Opening the door a crack, she peeked out at a redheaded woman who looked young and happy.

An unfamiliar bicycle leaned against the house.

"Can I help you?" Meredith asked, opening the door all the way.

"Probably," the woman answered. She stepped closer to the shed and glanced inside. "Wow, is that a bicycle built for two? I've always wanted to ride one."

Meredith actually had to move back as the stranger pressed inside. Following the other woman's gaze, she noted the old brown bike, its front tire not just flat but destroyed, and said, "I don't think this one would get you far."

"Then it's a good thing I won't need to go far. I'm Holly Whittaker, soon to be Holly Murphy. I've come to say thank-you and personally invite you to the wedding."

Meredith opened her mouth, closed it and finally said, "Thanks, but I'm not sure that's a great idea."

No, no, no.

"Sure it is. Wow, is that an old Maytag wringer washer?" Holly was clearly enthralled with the treasures inside Grandpa's shed. She looked at Meredith, eyes beaming. "I want to try the old homestead approach when Danny and I get married, go as green as possible. Grow vegetables, maybe buy a loom. I've been watching an old Maytag wringer on eBay. So far, it's outpriced me."

Meredith thought of the piles of bedding she washed at BAA and how grateful she was for a commercial washer and dryer. This woman was crazy.

Meredith stepped all the way out into the sunlight and studied Holly. The young woman couldn't have looked more different from Meredith. Holly's hair was bright red and curly, falling way past her shoulders. Her expression was open and honest, and she had a face as round as the sun. It just didn't have a myriad of freckles. She stood at maybe five foot two, so Meredith—at five foot six—felt oversize next to her.

"Nice to meet you." Meredith couldn't stop staring. This woman—girl, really—wore white capris and a red-and-white gauzy shirt. Her open-toed sandals were white.

She was put together and confident.

Like Meredith was at BAA.

Holly chuckled. "I brought you something." She reached into her back pocket and pulled out some folded papers. "I made a list of everything I needed to do for the wedding. Thought I'd give it to you. Planning Susie's wedding should be a breeze. She's so easygoing."

Meredith wasn't sure they were talking about the same Susan. Susie?

"I've wanted to meet you ever since Danny showed me the tree house," Holly said. "It was during my second visit with his family, and we rode the horses over to meet his aunt and uncle. Then we went for a ride out behind your grandpa's land. Wow, you guys had some childhood memories. I was feeling all jealous of you until I saw *MS* loves *JM* carved on the wall."

"That's still there?" Meredith figured the tree house might indeed be the one place where she'd be hard pressed to erase the memory of Jimmy Murphy—especially a memory chiseled in wood.

"Pretty faded but holding on. Kind of like this wringer."

Meredith gazed down at the chipped, white Maytag wringer washing machine. She didn't remember Grandma using it. Funny how many items were in the shed that she'd never noticed before. As a kid, she'd been more interested in grabbing wood, nails or anything that she and the others could use to build forts, ramps and such. "Grandpa told me he had paint and brushes out here. We need to do some painting. Fix the place up." Meredith didn't add they had to do it because they'd either be selling the farm, and all these memories, or hosting lots of wedding events.

Holly stepped into the shed and Meredith followed. Inexplicably, dirt did not immediately attach to her pants and shoes the way it would have to Meredith had she been wearing white.

"Want some help?" Holly offered.

"No," Meredith spoke the word too quickly, with too much force.

Holly looked both disappointed and relieved. "I'm almost glad you said no. Sometimes I forget that I'm getting married on Saturday and have a ton of things to do. That's why I'm here, actually." She held out a Tupperware dish that Meredith hadn't noticed. "This is for you."

Meredith was almost afraid to take what Holly offered. But when she opened the container, she found four Christmas cupcakes. "Uh, thanks."

"They're for the wedding reception. Debbie and I have spent the whole morning baking. I'm pretty sure we're doing it because we're stressed."

"And being stressed made you think of me," Meredith joked.

"No, listening to Debbie and Jimmy talk about you made me think of you, and it made me realize I had to meet you."

Jimmy and his mom were talking about her?

"Great," Meredith couldn't help the sarcasm.

But Holly quickly said, "It really is. During the two years I've been dating Danny, your name has been taboo. At first, I thought the breakup must have been recent. Like right before Danny and I met. But, then, finally Danny admitted it's been almost a decade."

Meredith looked to the porch and wished Grandpa would come out and yell, "Make me some pancakes," or if he were intuitive, "Can I have one of them cupcakes." Anything to get her out of this conversation.

"The fact that your name is being bandied about," Holly said, "means they're letting go. And I'd prefer it if Debbie completely let go of you before the wedding on Saturday."

"Not Danny?" Meredith asked, more concerned that the groom still held on to a grudge.

Holly smiled, the smile of a woman who knew she was loved. "Danny forgave you a long time ago. I don't think he even realized when it happened because by then it was part of the family dynamic not to mention you."

"Psychology major?" Meredith guessed.

"Childhood spent in foster care."

Meredith blinked. She wasn't an emotional female. And she didn't even know Holly. But for nine years she'd felt as if she'd wronged Danny, somehow needed to apologize to him and his family, make things right. And here was Danny's future wife, offering cupcakes and sharing a piece of her past.

A past where things obviously hadn't been perfect, a past that didn't necessarily nurture a person to be put together and confident.

"I'm sorry," Meredith finally offered.

"Don't be. Everything led me to the place I am now. Right where I need to be."

So, Holly not only didn't look like Meredith, but her personality was the polar opposite, too. Meredith would never share the guarded secrets of her past with a stranger.

Meredith was saved from responding by a disturbance at the side of the house, a side she couldn't see. Just as Meredith and Holly stepped out of the shed, Speckles came jumping and flying by squawking like crazy before finally taking flight—chased by the wolf dog.

In a moment, the dog plowed Holly down, not even pausing in his quest to capture a loudly cackling lunch. Holly's sandals were spotted red.

"Are you all right?" Meredith quickly dropped to her knees, examining Holly. "You're bleeding."

"Not me. And I didn't know chickens could fly!"

The spots of blood on the ground guided Meredith to the back of the shed where Speckles had dashed in between trash cans. The wolf dog wasn't deterred. She was up on her hind legs trying to climb over the trash cans and get to the chicken. A large gash on her right front leg dripped blood.

"How can I help?" Holly, now looking not so put together but still confident, was at Meredith's side.

"Make sure my other chickens are safe!" Meredith started to turn toward the coop, thinking to save the remaining chickens, but faltered. If the wolf dog had been injured breaking into the coop, Speckles might be the only one left to save.

At that moment, Speckles found a broken board on the shed that allowed her to squeeze inside. The wolf dog growled her rage and scrambled over the trash cans, heading first right and left, sending the silver canisters rolling toward the two women. Then the dog turned to circle the shed, but the trash cans were in the way. Dust went flying along with everything in the wolf dog's way. Something rolled against Meredith's foot.

For a moment, she thought it was a feather, then realized it was a bone. She picked it up and rolled it between her fingers. Had the wolf dog had gotten to the chickens and already gnawed one down to the bone? But the bone in her hand was clean and dry. With no time to examine it further, she stuck it in her pocket. The wolf dog jumped over the trash cans, crashing into both Meredith and Holly. Meredith managed to stay on her feet and pursued the animal. Holly, however, landed amidst the trash cans.

Ten minutes later, Meredith, covered with dirt and grass, had the wolf dog tied up, thanks to a trail of dog treats she'd used to lead the animal away from the chickens and toward the shed.

Speckles was harder to round up, but she finally managed to urge the hen back into the coop. The other four chickens, looking slightly worse for wear, clucked a terse welcome to Speckles. They were all shedding feathers and visibly shaking.

But the chickens looked better than Holly.

The slight limp probably would be gone by Saturday. If not, four aspirins could possibly save the day. It was the puffy eye that had Meredith worried. Unless she missed her guess, Holly Whittaker would be sporting a black eye—one too pronounced to hide with any amount of concealer—when she said "I do."

If Jimmy's mother had anything to say, Meredith figured she'd now be uninvited to the wedding.

Funny, she'd not been aware until this moment that she wanted to go.

"THIS CAN'T BE GOOD." Jimmy stepped over a small tumbleweed and nudged aside a sheep that was in Danny's way.

Danny was too busy concentrating to look up. "What?"

"That's Meredith Stone's brown SUV coming up the road, and she's not alone."

Now Danny glanced up, squinting. By the time Meredith parked, Jimmy knew that the day was about to get a whole lot more intense.

Danny dropped the pliers he'd been using to fix the kinks in the drip system.

"Is that Holly?"

Jimmy hoped not. However, Gesippi was small, and there weren't that many short, curly-haired redheads in town.

Danny took two steps toward the SUV, stopped and then started again. "What did Meredith do to her?"

Both men headed to Meredith's SUV. Strangely enough, Holly didn't look unhappy as she got out. She was, however, limping, sporting a puffy eye and there was blood on her shoes.

Danny passed Jimmy and got to her first. "Honey, are you all right? What happened? Meredith…" The last word was spoken in a growl.

Meredith opened her mouth, but Holly spoke right up. "Guess what?"

Jimmy was still getting used to Holly asking questions or making comments that had nothing to do with the topic at hand. It drove him nuts.

Meredith also looked a little disheveled but nothing like Holly.

"We found the wolf dog!"

Meredith nodded. "Actually, the wolf dog found us."

Jimmy glanced back at the truck, but no wolf dog face was in the window.

"I've got her tied up in Grandpa's shed. She's too upset for me to go near. She's hurt and hungry. I wanted to get Holly here so you can—" Meredith grimaced "—so she can get cleaned up."

"Meredith's coming to the wedding," was Holly's response.

Both boys nervously looked at the house. The only thing that could make this moment worse was their mother coming out.

"I didn't say yes," Meredith protested, her eyes also on the house, but Jimmy's mother was nowhere in sight. "I work weekends. I'll be in Scorpion Ridge."

"Do you really want to miss Danny's wedding?" Holly pressed. "You used to be best friends." Almost as if they'd known each other before, as if *they'd* been friends, Holly put her arm around Meredith's shoulders.

Meredith looked at Danny, but Danny only had eyes for Holly. Meredith switched her gaze to Jimmy. He shook his head helplessly and shrugged.

"And you can bring a date," Holly said brightly as Danny guided her up the sidewalk toward the house.

"I work weekends. I'll be in Scorpion Ridge," Meredith repeated weakly.

But Holly didn't hear. The door was already closing behind her and Danny.

"Holly's a powerhouse, all right," Jimmy said.

"That's putting it mildly." Meredith headed back to her truck, not looking to see if Jimmy followed or even watched. He'd always admired that about her. The muted devil-may-care attitude that had made him question if he really mattered to her.

"So, will you be attending?" he asked.

"Sorry, got things to do." She climbed behind the wheel and put the car in Drive. Then she paused. "You wouldn't have any dog treats, would you? I've already used all of Pepper's."

"Most girls want diamonds," he teased. When she didn't smile, he said, "How many do you need?"

"How much do you have?"

A moment later, he handed over all the dog treats they had—and *that* earned him a smile.

As she drove away, he realized he should have asked for something in return for that kibble.

A kiss maybe?

No! He wanted footage!

Hurrying back inside, he found Holly sitting at the kitchen table while Danny put a frozen bag of green peas to her eye. Jimmy's mother leaned against the sink shaking her head. "It's like you're teenagers again, getting hurt at the worst possible times."

"She's got an old Maytag wringer washer in a shed."

"Makes the grandfather clock Danny's father and I got you for your wedding gift suddenly seem inadequate," Debbie Murphy said dourly.

"No," Holly protested, "not at all. It's just, well, think of the history of that old thing."

Jimmy met Danny's gaze. Holly didn't have a history. She was going to have to make one with Danny. No wonder she was mesmerized by Meredith. "I'm heading over there. I need to be filming the wolf dog." The poor animal was tied up in a barn, bleeding and somewhat out of control. Now, *that* was a story.

And, good journalist that he was, he knew to go bearing gifts. All his research emphasized how much a wolf dog ate. Along with kibble, shelters fed them venison, turkey and beef. Fresh meat, according to his research, wasn't the best and only choice for the wolf dog—or for Meredith—but would do in a pinch.

Really, who needed diamonds?

It only took him five minutes to gather up all the food. But by the time he pulled into Meredith's drive, she was sitting cross-legged on the dirt in the front yard—away from the chicken coop—just staring at the gorgeous black, gray, and white wolf dog from last Tuesday.

Had it really been just a week since Meredith sashayed back into his life and he'd seen this wolf dog for the first time? Everything had happened so fast that day, he'd not had a chance to appreciate the natural beauty...

Jimmy ordered himself to stop looking at Meredith and focus on his next assignment. Thom had to say yes.

Jimmy got out his camera. Through the lens, he could see how magnificent this specimen would be once she put some weight on. But right now, sitting on her rump and staring back at Meredith, her ribs were showing through her fur, and her tail, which should be full and lifted, was thin and drooping.

Jimmy knew enough to keep still.

Finally, after what seemed at least thirty minutes, the wolf dog settled down on its haunches, whined and put its nose between its paws. Jimmy got his shot. Thom would have to acknowledge the story's potential now. And seeing this wolf dog, thin and starving made Jimmy even more determined than ever to do the story. He could make a difference.

Meredith stood slowly and gracefully. Her jeans were coated with dirt. The button-down blue shirt she wore fit snugly. She used to be all elbows and knees and smile. But he was enraptured by the woman she was now.

If only she'd smile. He loved her smile, and he hadn't really seen it much this past week.

Without acknowledging Jimmy or making a sound, she headed up the porch stairs and into Ray's house. After a moment, she came out with a plate of food and a water dish. She placed both where the rope would end. Then, turning her back on the dog, she walked over to Jimmy.

"I can't believe I've walked and walked this area looking for her, and then she just shows up this morning."

"Holly said she was more than interested in your chickens. You need some help fixing the coop?"

Meredith rolled her eyes. "That's next on the agenda."

He followed her to the coop where a good three-foot hole had been ripped from the bottom of the wire. She'd blocked the hole with some old lumber and bricks. The chickens, four of them, were huddled nervously in the corner.

"I brought over some more food for the wolf dog, just in case."

"Thanks."

There was a lull in the conversation. He filled it with, "I don't need to pick up Briana for another hour, so I can help you with whatever you need."

"Your little girl is beautiful, by the way."

"You met her?" That surprised him.

"At BAA on Saturday. She was playing near the horses."

That didn't surprise him. His daughter loved animals. She was quite content at his parents' house and had already started naming the sheep.

His dad, who'd never allowed him and Danny to name the sheep, didn't seem to mind.

"I wonder why Briana didn't tell me."

"I doubt she knows who I am or how I'm connected to your family. Your mother quickly snatched her away when she realized who Briana was talking to."

Avoiding the subject of his mother, Jimmy went to his knees, moving away the boards Meredith had used to block the hole. She went to the shed and brought out a section of chicken wire. Together, they wove the new into the old.

"I can't believe you caught the wolf dog," Jimmy said.

"I think she wanted to be caught. She's starving."

When they finished, Jimmy stood, reached down and helped Meredith up.

"I need to check on Grandpa, make him some food." She separated her hand from his.

He didn't move. "I need to pick Briana up from school."

He stood so close to her that he could see her chest moving as she breathed.

She stepped back again, shoving her hands into her pockets. The expression on her face suddenly shifted, and she pulled something from her pocket.

"The wolf dog found a bone," she said. "It can't be one of the chickens', they're all safe."

He took the bone from her, rolled it around in his palm and finally said, "No, it's not from a chicken. I think it's human."

CHAPTER TWELVE

TUESDAY MORNING, MEREDITH got close enough to remove the collar. The wolf dog still wasn't happy about her situation, though. She backed away from Meredith, growled, whimpered and tried to run between Meredith's legs even though the animal was tied up. Meredith stayed patient, spoke soothingly and never wavered from her mission.

On the back porch, just a slab of cement with a small railing, Grandpa hollered advice. "Look in his eyes. Let him smell you."

Meredith let the wolf dog smell her while filling the food bowl and providing fresh water. All the while, talking to the animal. She knew the way to a wolf dog's heart.

Grandpa held on to the railing and shouted more advice. "Show him who's boss!"

At the moment, the wolf dog didn't care who was boss, she wasn't going to sit still long enough for anyone to look her in her eyes, and as for smell...she'd recently rolled in something vile.

She'd also managed to cave in the side of

Grandpa's shed. Good thing Meredith had tied her to a hitch secured in concrete.

"You sure he was someone's pet?" Grandpa asked.

"She," Meredith emphasized the gender, "had on a collar."

"You going to fix the shed?" Grandpa finally suggested—a half order, really—when he realized that Meredith had no plans to continue working with the wolf dog.

She looked at the shed and groaned. Besides the messed-up side, the ground was dug up as if a dinosaur had needed traction. The Maytag wringer washer was on its side. The bicycle built for two was now missing a wheel. Meredith was half convinced the wolf dog had eaten it. The mess was the chicken coop times ten. It looked as if the dinosaur had leaned against the shed, decided to take a step in and then backed out.

Great, something else to add to the to-do list. Good thing Susan wasn't getting married in Grandpa's backyard. But still, family would be staying here—and soon.

"Yes, I'll fix it, but probably not today."

Grandpa glanced at the sky. There was one cloud.

The wolf dog yelped a few times. Meredith turned and noted that the canine was looking at her, wanting her to pay attention. Funny what a full stomach, fresh water and a kind voice could do.

"Grandpa, I need to head into town. We made do yesterday, but I've got to get a lot more kibble and some fencing, plus a sturdier rope and—"

"What you going to do to keep the chickens safe?"

Good question.

After taking a quick shower and then making sure Grandpa was fed and everything he needed was nearby, Meredith headed for her truck and into Gesippi.

Meredith had been back just over a week. She'd really hoped to avoid going into Gesippi and just stay with Grandpa, but already she'd been to town three times. And she'd been to Jimmy's house once! So much for a low profile.

Her phone sounded and soon she was dealing with the next issue that was keeping her from a low profile. Her sister's wedding.

"I've already called Cathy, Libby, Connie and Marina," Susan gushed. "They'll be bridesmaids. I'm going to head for a Dillard's and pick out a black dress, something classy enough for a wedding but simple enough for everyday wear." If anyone could do that, it would be her sister. "Once I tell you the dress I've decided on, you can take the girls to the store in Tucson to let them try on their size. Make a day of it."

"The odds that the Tucson Dillard's will have four of the same dress in the right sizes is slim to none," Meredith pointed out.

"Call ahead, then. Figure out if you should go to Tucson or Phoenix. There's a dozen Dillard's within driving distance."

"Are the guys going through all this?"

Susan laughed. "Of course not. They'll wear either black suits or black tuxes. All Jimmy has to do is find silver ties."

Jimmy had the easy job, Meredith thought. "Okay, what else do I need to do?"

"I'm going to text Mom some ideas for my wedding cake. See if…" Susan's voice trailed off. Their grandmother had been the cook. Mom had made cupcakes, but only once she figured out they just required cake mix. Of course, she'd not known that until Meredith pointed it out to her.

Meredith sighed. "And did you settle on the date?"

"The day after Christmas. It's a Saturday. People will either stay longer if they're visiting for the holiday or they'll have time to clean up after their own Christmases and head to Gesippi."

Someone, probably Joe, said something in the background. Susan giggled and said, "I've got to go, Meredith. Wait. I forgot to ask. How's Grandpa?"

"He seems better. We've had some excitement. I found the wolf dog."

"Oh, that's good. Joe's hurrying me. Tell me more next time I call." With that, Susan disconnected, leaving Meredith wondering what chores she'd be given the next time her sister phoned.

"And I thought I'd be bored in Gesippi," she said to herself.

Nope—between Grandpa, Susan, Jimmy and now the wolf dog, there was plenty to do.

None of it boring. Especially not Jimmy, who'd called her this morning to let her know he'd taken the bone to the sheriff, and he too thought it was human.

On Wednesday, Meredith headed for town again. She found a parking spot just down from the Drug and Dine and fielded a dozen or so greetings—all from people who knew everything about a past she only wanted to forget.

Or did she? It had been good to finally talk things through with Jimmy. But it was also unsettling, as she wasn't sure where things stood between them. She'd thought he'd been to kiss her, once that morning in the basement and again by the chicken coop. And she'd wanted him to.

She slipped into the Drug and Dine, purchased a few Christmas presents and then picked up a copy of the tiny *Gesippi Gazette*. Sitting at the counter, sipping a soda, she leafed through the pages of the paper feeling as if she'd gone back in time.

There was a review of the movie playing at the Gesippi Theater, which boasted seating for forty viewers. Meredith had seen the film two months ago. The Bowl Game offered two-for-one off-hour bowling and free shoe rentals on Monday nights. The Corner Grocery had a few coupons. Human-interest stories filled most of the rest of the pages. Meredith read a brief paragraph about her return to town to care for her grandfather. The words *single* and *no children* were used. Danny and Holly's upcoming wedding got a much longer paragraph. Next week, it would be the announcement of Susan and Joe's wedding. Then there was a story about a family who'd decorated a giant Christmas tree in their front yard only to have it break quite a few bricks in their walkway when it fell. Another story told of a ten-year-old Gesippi boy finding a wallet with two thousand dollars in it but not a single piece of identification.

Meredith wondered if that story had anything to do with the conversation she'd overheard her first day back in Gesippi.

But it was the next-to-last page that truly got Meredith's attention. A feature story on Jimmy not only told of *his* return, but had a picture of him and his daughter. From their one meeting, Meredith knew Briana to be inquisitive and cute. She hadn't reminded Meredith of Jimmy until his mother had showed up.

Thinking about Jimmy's mother made Meredith hastily put the paper down. She hadn't stuck around long enough to see Debbie's reaction to her soon-to-be daughter-in-law with a black eye and limp, but Meredith was certain it hadn't helped the older woman's opinion of her.

Time to think of something else. Meredith picked up the paper again and realized that the words *single* and *with only one child* weren't mentioned in the article. Instead, Jimmy was described as "well-traveled" and "renowned."

She tried to throw the tabloid down in disgust, but the word *wolf dog* jumped out at her.

The article went on to say that Jimmy intended to write a story about the unfortunate plight of the wolf dog. On the next page, there was one more paragraph about Jimmy and another photo—of Yoda.

Jimmy had found his way to Meredith's boss's house and had taken photos of her wolf dog. The way Jimmy had shot him, Meredith's favorite animal in the whole world didn't look like a dog at all. He looked exotic, wild and poised for action. Dangerous.

And he'd made sure no reader would be able to

ignore the fence keeping Yoda from actually ex-
periencing any of the action he was so ready for.

The caption read: Trapped by Man's Manipulation.

Anger, white hot and painful, pooled in the pit
of Meredith's stomach. She felt violated and used.

Luke knew how much Yoda meant to her. He
knew why Yoda was at BAA, and she doubted
he would have allowed this. Meredith pulled out
her phone to call Luke and find out if Jimmy'd
asked permission and gotten the proper releases
signed. She'd almost hit the call button on her
phone when Keith, the owner of the Drug and
Dine, leaned forward, filling Meredith's cup with
more soda.

"I hear you caught the wolf dog and found a
bone?" Keith said.

She flipped the phone off. If she made the call
here, she might as well relay the conversation
during the Sunday-morning announcements at
the Gesippi Church.

"Good news travels fast," Meredith quipped.
"The wolf dog is somebody's pet. I need to find
the owner. The sheriff says the bone's probably
human but old, probably not anyone you knew."

Keith laughed. He was joined by his wife, who
sometimes helped at the restaurant, especially on
Wednesdays. "I hear," she said, "that you decked
Danny's fiancée."

"I did not. It was the wolf dog who pushed her down!"

"Should we be worried?" Keith said. "Could the animal hurt a pet or small child?"

Somewhere, Meredith had heard the question before. "No, the wolf dog's happy I caught her. Now she'll have regular meals and tender loving care."

"You talking about Ray?" It was one of Grandpa's cronies, sitting at the end of the counter, and who'd only managed to hear the last six words.

There was a sort of poetic justice about the wolf dog and Grandpa needing the same kind of care.

"Yes. No." Meredith wished she hadn't stopped at the Drug and Dine.

"Jimmy was in here earlier," Keith said. "He wanted to mail something." The town's post office was in the back of the drugstore.

"Why are you telling me that Jimmy was here? I don't care," Meredith protested.

"Just passing the time. Looked like the two of you were getting pretty cozy last Thursday." Keith went back to stocking headphones on the wall behind the cash register. Meredith put down two dollars and left before anyone else could inform her of what Jimmy Murphy was up to.

The man would get what was coming to him, but first she had to care for the wolf dog.

After stocking up on lots of kibble, peanut butter and begging a few bones from the Corner Grocery's butcher, Meredith headed home.

She had two more days to get through before she could head back to BAA—her real job—and relax. Maybe she'd even take the wolf dog with her, see if Luke would fall in love with her and maybe agree to put together an enclosure for Yoda and... Should she name this wolf dog? It was probably premature to give her a name. She might still be able to integrate into a wild pack.

She pulled into Grandpa's driveway, parked and grabbed her grocery bags. She easily got them up the steps and into the house.

"Dog's been digging a hole ever since you left," Grandpa said from his favorite spot in front of the TV in the living room. "Got me kind of worried, but I'm not about to go near her. I—"

Meredith interrupted, "Let me put the groceries away, and I'll check on her." She didn't want Grandpa to worry. "I'm going to call the Aqui Lobos Rescue later on this afternoon. Check if they know anything about her or have space for her. If not, I'll see about moving her to BAA this weekend."

Grandpa didn't look appeased. "Since you've been gone, all she's done is destroy the shed and dig a hole."

"She's bored."

"When you kids were bored, I told you to find something to do. You didn't tear down whole buildings." Grandpa was making light of the situation, but he didn't quite manage to smile.

"I promise I'll take care of it."

"Today might be the perfect day to fix the shed," Grandpa remarked, peering around her and taking his attention away from the television for a moment. "Looks like you'll have some help."

Once again, Jimmy's vehicle was turning into the driveway. The truck skidded in the dirt, coming to a stop fast and hard, no messing around. Like the man. As he stepped from the truck, Meredith noticed that this time he'd came with filming gear, lots of it.

Making it clearer than it ever had been that she wasn't his friend. She was his story, whether she wanted to be or not.

MEREDITH DIDN'T SMILE or wave. Great. Every time Jimmy thought Meredith was ready to thaw toward him, something new gave her reason to chill. He decided to ignore her mood and jovially said, "Hope I didn't miss the show."

"Hey, Jimmy, good to see you." Grandpa failed to notice Meredith's discomfort.

"There is no *show*," Meredith said. "Right now we're just getting the wolf dog acquainted with her new surroundings. I've not had time to fence her in…or should I say *trap* her in."

Okay, she'd read the article in the *Gesippi Gazette*. He'd worried some about that and then gotten mad at himself for worrying. The reporter, one of his cousins, had done a good job. Nothing was misquoted or sensationalized. The photo of Yoda had been purchased and approved. Every word was the truth, and because of Meredith, Jimmy hadn't gone into the detail he usually would have. But Jimmy knew Meredith wouldn't appreciate any of that.

"I only stated the truth in the article."

"'Trapped by Man's Manipulation'," Meredith quoted.

"You know they're just going for a catchy title," Jimmy hedged.

"We're talking about the *Gesippi Gazette*. Their titles are more along the lines of Wolf Dog Woes. You wrote this one."

"You're taking this too personally," Jimmy insisted. "We could work together. Then you could be the one to answer the questions, make sure both sides of the issue are addressed, make sure no other wolf dog is abandoned and half starved like this one."

"I don't want to answer the kind of questions you would ask."

Deciding to take a different track, Jimmy took

out his camera and focused on the new wolf dog. "So, you're going to keep her?"

"No." Ray grumped.

Jimmy paused. He hadn't noticed Ray had come onto the back porch. Now, he watched as Ray held on to the railing, carefully maneuvered down the steps, and pointed to the shed. "Look what that animal did to my shed. Give me a minute to get my cane. I'll show you."

"Wait—" Meredith started to say, but Jimmy was already starting for the yard. Never mind that he'd seen the damage yesterday. If he gave Meredith too much time, she'd figure a way to get him off her grandfather's property, his questions unanswered, his camera unused.

His meeting with Thom was in just a few days. He needed more footage of the wolf dog.

It didn't hurt that more days with the wolf dog meant more days with Meredith.

She quickly headed inside the house to put away the groceries and grab Ray's cane. And by the time she made it to the yard, Jimmy had made a wide arc around the wolf dog.

She was spectacular. No wonder people wanted to make pets of the species. Her glare, however, told him why she shouldn't be a pet.

"You named her yet?" he asked.

"No."

"Why not?"

"I'm afraid to name her. I'm not sure where she belongs. It might not be with me. My first priority is to rehabilitate her."

Meredith had changed a lot since the girl who'd named everything, including the ducks in Gesippi Pond.

But, Jimmy knew her, knew her well. What Meredith was really saying was *I'm afraid to name her. I'll get attached, and I might lose her*.

Instead of saying what he really thought, he asked, "What kind of rehabilitation does Alice need?"

"Alice?" Meredith gazed at the wolf dog. "No way. She doesn't look like an Alice. If anything, she's Princess Leia and needs to—"

The wolf dog gave a short howl and nudged toward Meredith.

"Leia it is then." Jimmy chuckled, then finished for Meredith. "—who needs to fight the evil empire to ensure her freedom."

Jimmy moved closer to the shed, adjusted the lens on his camera and started taking pictures.

Meredith followed. "Shouldn't you be asking me or Grandpa to sign a release?"

"You're right. I should do that. I'll bring the papers over tomorrow."

"Don't. I won't sign them."

"It's not your shed. It's your grandpa's, and I already asked him."

"What?"

"Yup, I called a little while ago. I suggested to trade the photographs for my help repairing the shed. He thought it was a great idea."

"I tried to tell you," Grandpa interjected, "but you kept interrupting me."

Jimmy simply starting snapping pictures again. He was well aware that she watched his every move—unhappy, tense, ready to pounce—very much like the wolf dog.

After a moment, she said, "I've never seen you work. When we were…" She paused, regrouped, continued, "When we were friends, you were a cocky football player who rode horses for fun and avoided homework because you had me to do it for you. Back then, I doubt you even owned a fancy camera."

"I owned a cell phone which had a camera, and I have quite a few pictures of you." He grinned, knowing he had the upper hand. "The only reason they're not of both of us is I took the photos."

"Pshaw." She hadn't forgotten for a moment what he wanted to do, who he represented and his beliefs.

So different from hers.

"Hey," she spoke up.

He pretended he didn't hear her or even notice her nervous pacing.

He leaned forward for another shot, putting

his body into it, bending down, backing up and looking at the sun—not paying attention to anything but the scene in front of him. He loved the world his words and photos portrayed.

When he paused, she asked, "What's your angle?"

"What do you mean?"

"With the wolf dog story. Are you going to write how cruel I am to capture her, stick a leash on her and think to domesticate her? Will you mention that she's half starved and not making it on her own?"

He didn't answer her question. Instead, he asked one of his own. "Why did she come so close to your house? Did hunger drive her? Why wasn't she more scared of you and Holly? And why couldn't she make it on her own? She's bred to hunt. Surely instinct kicks in."

"What makes you think I know all of that?"

Jimmy laughed. "From the moment you said your first word, you were a know-it-all. And don't forget, I sat by you in junior-year history."

Because he'd failed it the first time he took it and needed the class to graduate. She'd gotten him through it. "Back then, we were on the same side," she reminded him.

"What side was that?"

But he knew. She'd believed they were both working toward a future together, one that involved animals and a good life. One that didn't involve him suddenly walking away from her—one day a best friend and a boyfriend, the next a man with his bags packed and no backward glances.

"The side of right," she muttered.

"We can still be on the same side. That's why I want your help. Maybe you could start by telling me about Yoda's background? How did BAA acquire him?"

Meredith cocked her head. "Yoda's story might make good reading. And if nothing else, I'm sure you'll do your research. Do you know what happens to wolf dogs when they're no longer wanted?"

"They're either let free or…"

"Or put to sleep. Someone tried to drop Yoda at an animal shelter by tying him to a fence outside one night. The shelter didn't accept wolf dogs, but luckily an employee called my boss. Yoda had been a pet his whole life. Do you think we should have driven him out to Rail X Road and dropped him off so he could wander free?"

"Maybe," Jimmy said.

Meredith stomped her foot. "Yoda was little more than a pup and already timid. Leia, here, was barely making it on her own because somewhere she learned to be dependent on a human. And, yes, her instincts did kick in. She probably was able to capture small game, but I'm guessing by her weight and her easy acceptance of me that she's not as aggressive as a wolf needs to be."

Meredith turned and looked at the wolf dog. Leia was on her stomach, nose between her paws, staring at Jimmy as if he was to be avoided at all cost.

"Yoda would do better in the wild than this girl," Jimmy mused.

"Why do you say that?"

"Because Yoda's at least been with real wolves."

"Only at BAA. And those wolves bully him to the point we have to separate them."

"Leave him with them. See what he can do. Quit rescuing him."

"Like I'm rescuing this half-starved animal?"

Jimmy tried to think of a comeback, but with Leia looking at him as if he was the enemy and with Meredith obviously changing her plans for the day in order to work with Leia, he knew he was on the losing side. As usual.

Meredith drove the point home. "Did you come here to argue?"

He glanced from the shed to the wolf dog to her. "No. I came to work on the story. I've got a call with my editor on Monday, and I'm worried he's not going to go for the story."

"Can't you do some other story? Go someplace far from Gesippi."

"You're kidding, right? Besides helping with the wedding between my best friend and your sister, I'm supposed to take over for Danny on the farm while he's on his honeymoon. My beloved Canon's going to gather dust while my palms harden thanks to tossing bales of hay onto the truck."

"How's Briana taking to farm life?"

He sighed. "She loves it. She's going all girlie on me and has her grandparents wrapped around her little finger. When it's time to leave, she's going to balk."

"Kids adapt." That's what people had always said to her about her parents working so much. Funny, she'd not believed it then, didn't believe it now.

"Any chance you'll stay here?"

"If I get the wolf dog story, I'll stay for a bit longer. It would be an answer to a prayer. Not only is it a story I can sink my teeth into that will allow me to prove myself to my editor again, it allows me to stay in Gesippi and be a more hands-on dad."

"No matter what happens, you're a good father. And I figure you're already pretty hands-on." She pointed to his left wrist.

The Rainbow Loom bracelet was bright red.

"Briana made it for me last night. I forgot to take it off." He made no move to remove it. "She made one for Danny and Holly, too."

"How is Holly?" Meredith asked.

"Experimenting with thick makeup and thinking about wearing white tennis shoes with her dress."

The wolf dog stood, inched her way toward Meredith and gently put her nose against her knee as if trying to comfort. Or maybe she was looking for food. Seizing the moment, Jimmy quickly took some shots of Meredith gazing down at the wolf dog, already committed to her; the wolf dog gazing up at her, already devoted.

"You've made this much progress in one day?" Jimmy asked.

"I'm surer and surer she was someone's pet. This morning she was talking to me. I don't understand a word she says, but if I had to guess, she's telling me she never wants to be alone again."

"It's no fun being alone," Jimmy agreed.

"When have you ever been alone?"

Funny, he'd never thought about being alone until Regina died. Then, as he packed away their life together, he realized that they'd never really been together: not like his parents had, or his grandparents.

Or like he and Meredith had.

Two people, two different goals that led down the same path.

CHAPTER THIRTEEN

IN THE END, Meredith let Jimmy keep his pictures. He stayed to help her board up the shed and move Leia to a more secure location. Grandpa's barn hadn't been used in more than a decade, and both the entrance and exit doors were missing hinges and the wood was rotting so that neither closed properly.

Between the two of them they managed to drive metal posts into the ground beside the rims of both doors. Meredith held the posts and Jimmy pounded the hammer. They'd spent many a summer mending fences for both her grandfather and Jimmy's relatives. Back then it had been hold, hammer, kiss.

Today's way was faster.

Leia, for her part, seemed content to follow them, butting their knees with her head and acting as if she wanted to be chased. Unfortunately, the rope Meredith had secured her to only went so far.

"She'll have a little more freedom in the barn,"

Jimmy said after the third time Leia almost knocked him down.

"And hopefully, I'll be able to convince Luke to let her stay at BAA until we find out who she belongs to. When I spoke to him last night, I almost got a yes."

Meredith hesitated, not sure how much she should share. This was Jimmy Murphy, renowned animal-rights reporter. The last person she should be talking to.

Yet, for all her misgivings, she still found him the one she wanted to talk to.

"Whatever you say right now is off the record," Jimmy said. "It's just the two of us, working together, friends."

Friends? Could they ever really be friends?

No, probably not, but Jimmy did understand animals, and he was right next to her researching wolf dogs, especially the wolf dogs in this area. And he did have a point about her being able to influence the story better if she was a part of it.

"I convinced Luke it would be beneficial to see how the two wolf dogs fare together with the wolves. It could be a win-win if Yoda was finally able to stay in the habitat full-time and Leia found a home. Or I may soon be looking for homes for two wolf dogs instead of one."

Together, they unrolled field fence—left over from who knew how long ago—and Jimmy began to wind and staple wire across the barn doors' openings while Meredith aligned the mesh so it was even with the metal posts.

Few words were needed and each understood their role. At first, Meredith's job was to assist Jimmy, but when it came time to double stack, she was right next to him, so close she could smell his sweat, feel the heat of him. Had he reached out for her, he could have captured and held her with little or no effort.

Part of her wanted him to.

Wanted him to reach for her now, while she was so near. His hands had always been her favorite part of him. She remembered how strong his touch had been, whether it had been a caress under her chin or his palm cupping her cheek, drawing her close to him for a stolen kiss.

Hold, hammer, kiss.

Tucked up beside him, holding the fence taut, she wondered how his touch would feel today. Were his hands rougher? Would he give up so easily when she giggled and moved away, or would he grab her toward him and give her a kiss that—

Hold, hammer, kiss.

She stepped closer to him, leaning, something magnetic guiding her toward him—something he obviously didn't feel because he merely handed her a clip, and for a moment she had to think hard to remember that they were working.

Against each other, not with each other.

Then his hands tangled in her hair and he pulled her toward him. Her heart started hammering. Then his lips were on hers, kissing, consuming, reminding her of those long-ago days and how it felt to be cherished, to be alive.

She pulled away first, a little short of breath, but knowing if she didn't stop, she'd be lost. "We have to get this done," she said.

"Yeah," he agreed, reluctantly.

It took four hours to block the barn's entrance and exit. Luckily, every other opening either had a working door or a shutter. They didn't kiss again, but the anticipation was there, the dance, the acceptance. But not quite the trust.

Just before suppertime, Jimmy left and Meredith went inside the house to convince Grandpa to eat. It was Wednesday evening, and after a tough day shouting directions at her and Jimmy, Grandpa should have been extra tired.

"How about ham and eggs?" Meredith suggested, expecting refusal.

"Sounds great to me. If we eat now, we can get going. I want to go to church."

Meredith almost dropped the plate she was holding.

"Come on, Grandpa. It's late. You're exhausted. It's not a good idea."

"Used to be I didn't miss a service. I've not been on Wednesday night in more than two years. Last Wednesday I'd planned on having you take me, but I hurt too much. Tonight, there's no excuse."

"You still hurt too much."

"No, today's a different type of hurt."

Meredith tried to think of a few more reasons why they shouldn't go, but the only one that was completely true had to do with her not wanting to attend because the Murphys would be there. It would be Danny's last time attending church as a single man.

"According to the *Gazette*, Herb Taylor's in town. I'd like to see him."

Herb Taylor was Grandpa's age. He'd sat in a kindergarten classroom with Grandpa when Arizona celebrated her tenth year as a state.

He'd been in a wheelchair for the last twenty years.

"We'll go, Grandpa. If you eat."

It was the first time since she'd been with him that Grandpa dug into his meal with gusto.

An hour later, they arrived at the church. Her grandfather passed over his handicapped-parking decal. "A fringe benefit of getting old," he said.

She parked, helped him out and followed him

in, one hand behind his back in case he stumbled. His walker, getting less and less necessary in the week since the fall, skidded a bit on the black tar of the parking lot.

The inside of the church looked smaller than Meredith remembered, but everything else was the same, from the brown pews, to the bulletin board showing members' photos. Leaving Grandpa to deal with the minister—a new man since Meredith's day—she stood in front of the bulletin board and found her family's photo.

It showed only her mother and father.

Meredith's photo was missing. Grandpa and Susan stood alone. "Grandpa looks good," her father said from behind her. "Your mom and I have been trying to get him to come to church for months."

She greeted her father and said, "He wanted to see Herb."

"Herb's been here for two months. We offered to fetch your grandpa and bring him to church, and he said no."

Maybe, Meredith thought, Grandpa'd just changed his mind. She followed her mom and dad into the auditorium and sat between her father and Grandpa. Across the aisle, Danny and Jimmy sat with their parents.

Meredith opened the songbook and tried to calm her nerves. Maybe tonight she could just relax, be happy to see old friends, and yes, that included Jimmy and Danny Murphy. Before the first words were sung, her cell phone vibrated. She removed it from her purse and glanced at the screen.

Luke's name appeared.

Standing up, she made her way to the foyer and answered. Her boss didn't waste any time on pleasantries.

"Yoda's chewed a hole through the wire we had fencing him in. Near as I can tell, he's been missing for maybe three hours."

THE FIRST HINT Jimmy had that something was amiss was Meredith's exit from services. More than a few people frowned, even though Meredith wasn't so uncouth as to actually hold her cell phone up to show that she had a call.

Meredith came back in, whispered something to her father and then slinked out—further proof. Her father followed. It only took Jimmy a few minutes to realize Meredith wasn't going to return. Grandpa didn't seem to notice. He stayed in his pew, content, drifting off to sleep.

Stepping over his brother and mother, Jimmy made his way out to the foyer in time to see Meredith running out the door.

"Everything all right?" he asked her father.

"That wolf dog of hers is missing."

"The one we're keeping at Ray's?"

"No, it's the one at BAA. Yoda. He escaped from the barn and has been missing for more than three hours. Meredith's heading to Scorpion Ridge now."

It was six-thirty, already dark, and Scorpion Ridge was a good hour away.

"She's…" Jimmy was about to say nuts, but then he realized that she had no choice.

And neither did he. After all, he couldn't let Meredith go alone, and he had a story to follow.

He tiptoed back into the church, whispered to his mom that he was leaving and why, and crept out to the foyer. His mom had agreed to watch Briana, who, luckily, was in a Wednesday-night children's bible class or she'd have wanted to come with him. His daughter was already annoyed that he'd gotten to meet the wolf dog and she'd been stuck at school. Homeschooling her on location had taught her plenty of things. One of them had been that school came second to animal adventures.

Now that she was in Gesippi, that philosophy was no longer proving true.

He hurried to his truck, stopped for gas and then drove down the dark, dirt roads toward Scorpion Ridge. He half expected to catch up to Meredith, but she must have been flying. He'd forgotten how velvet the Arizona nights became, the intense blackness offset by the myriad of stars.

He wanted to call Meredith, offer to help, but she'd question his commitment. And she'd be right to do so. The fact that her "pet" wanted to escape didn't support her "he needs to be in the zoo" beliefs.

When he finally got to Scorpion Ridge, he drove to what BAA zookeepers called the mini-manse. He didn't know the story behind the too-regal home, but he'd learned that today it belonged to BAA's owner who let Luke and Katie Rittenhouse, BAA's director and head keeper, live there. The front had a circular driveway that seemed to imply a valet would appear. The elegant steps made him think that a tux was necessary in order to enter.

He didn't head for the steps. Instead, he went around back where the barn and other pens were. Just a few days ago, he'd been back here watching Yoda chase a butterfly, running up and down a kennel attached to the barn. Floodlights bathed the area now, but only one human was visible: an old man who Jimmy hadn't met.

"Excuse me," Jimmy said. "I'm looking for Meredith Stone."

"She's not here." The man who turned had to be eighty if he were a day. He was bent, gnarled and spoke in a soft voice. "And you are?"

"I'm James Murphy, a friend of Meredith's. I've come to help. What can I do?"

"You're the writer for *Nature Times*." The man didn't look impressed.

"Right now I'm one more set of feet willing to travel and find Yoda."

The old man didn't respond at first but finally nodded. "Luke and Katie headed south. Ruth and Janie went north. We've got two policemen searching behind BAA. As for Meredith, who knows in what direction she went. She's got a sense when it comes to Yoda. I just wish she wasn't out there alone. Me, I'm Jasper Dunbar, and I'm here watching the little one and waiting to see if Yoda returns on his own."

That's when Jimmy noticed the stroller. A sleeping baby, wrapped in pink, was next to the pen.

"You think Yoda might come back?"

"Nope. He wants to find Meredith as badly as she wants to find him."

It was a thread that didn't work well in Jimmy's documentaries. Human interference with wildlife left a disruptive thumbprint that was often too hard to measure.

For example, both Yoda and Leia.

But, really, Yoda couldn't survive without Meredith and BAA. He'd never been on his own. And look at Leia. She'd been half starved.

So, who was right? Meredith or Jimmy?

A week ago, he'd had an answer. Yesterday, he'd have said the same. Today, he didn't want to think about it.

He blamed the kiss.

"That dog loves her," Jasper said. "He's been upset since she's been gone. He's not crazy about how slow I am to walk him, and everyone else is so busy. We need to build another enclosure."

Next thing Jimmy knew, Jasper'd written down his phone number and handed Jimmy a flashlight, leather gloves and a leash. "Yoda's got his collar on. Be careful if you catch him. He tends to favor females and gets his hair up over males."

"Which way should I go?"

Jasper was already reaching for a clipboard while talking on his cell phone to figure out where the searchers were. He made an X on two spots and then pointed to an area just north of the mini-manse.

A few minutes later, Jimmy's truck was parked on the side of a desert road, and he was maneuvering through loose gravel and cacti.

He'd thought the drive over to be a study in darkness, his photographer's mind searching for light. Now, alone in the middle of nowhere, blackness took on a whole new dimension.

"Yoda!" He wasn't sure if calling the wolf

dog would inspire it to come or scare it away. His voice echoed in the night, and a cool breeze, smelling of animal and sweat and something burnt, made him wish he'd brought a warmer jacket. Christmas was around the corner, but this part of Arizona rarely grew too cold.

Speaking of this part of Arizona, he wished it had been Leia who'd gotten loose around Ray's place. Jimmy knew the Gesippi area and how to best hunt for the dog and who to call to help. Scorpion Ridge, however, wasn't his territory.

Oh, he'd traversed plenty of strange land. He'd camped in the Australian bush once, filming and writing about the northern quoll, an animal that reminded Jimmy of a squirrel.

The quolls were yet another example of man's interference leading to an animal's demise. Sugarcane farmers had introduced the cane toad to help control pests. Turned out, the toad liked to kill the quolls, too.

One thing about the places he'd explored in Australia and China and South Africa, he'd always had a film crew and they'd always carried plenty of light. He'd never meandered alone more than a few yards from the tent, never needed to pack a jacket.

"Yoda!"

Did Meredith know every hidden place in the barren land of Scorpion Ridge? Somehow Jimmy doubted it. And boy was Scorpion Ridge flat. There wasn't a single place he could climb in order to scan the area for bobbing lanterns or flashlights.

He thought about calling Jasper on his cell to see if Yoda had been found, but truthfully, Jimmy had only been searching for maybe thirty minutes. No time, really.

A flock of birds suddenly burst from the dark, leafless trees and flew overhead. Their wings echoed in the emptiness. A coyote howled, then another, and another. For a moment, Jimmy wished he had a compass. Then he realized he had one on his phone.

Fat lot of good it did him. He had no clue in which direction he'd parked his car. The rate he was going, Meredith would be out hunting for *him* after she found Yoda.

Jimmy hoped she was willing to search as hard for him as she was the wolf dog.

He stumbled over an embankment, almost went to his knees and gritted his teeth when the spine of some type of cactus spiked into his boots. Boots were supposed to block cacti!

Ahead, he saw lights. He took a step but stopped when the cactus stabbed him. Pulling off his left boot, he used his flashlight to find the offending cactus. He carefully removed his sock and peeled away the cactus's spiny joints before putting his sock and boot back on and heading for the lights.

Up ahead loomed some type of dwelling. Probably a farm or ranch, based on the smells drifting past. He hit a dirt road, narrow, with room for only one vehicle, and turned toward what looked like an oversize shed, which was where the light was coming from.

Checking his cell phone, he noted that it was just after ten. Early enough for the family to still be awake. But maybe the lights were a safety issue.

His walk became a trot when he detected four figures. What looked like a man, old and bent, was bathed in the light shining from inside the shed. Jimmy could see the outline of a tractor inside. Another figure stood by an old truck. This one was younger, standing tall, with a cowboy hat. Near as Jimmy could tell by the noise, there was a chicken coop on the other side of the truck. That's also where the third figure was standing—a female.

Meredith?

The man by the truck was moving, slowly, toward the chicken coop where the chickens were cackling and a dog barked. He raised something—a gun!

Jimmy's trot turned into a full-out run.

He heard Meredith shout, "No!"

The gun's report drowned out anything else she might have said.

And then Jimmy couldn't see her; she was gone. The night was now silent. No barking dog, no Meredith.

Had she run for cover? Or had she been shot?

CHAPTER FOURTEEN

JIMMY'S FIRST THOUGHT was to protect Meredith as he stumbled to a stop right in front of the man holding the rifle. His heart raced, the scent of alfalfa cloyed in his throat and adrenaline almost pushed him into doing something he'd regret. His goal had been to tackle the man. Then, he got a look at the old gentleman, gray faced, perspiring.

Instead of a hero's welcome, Jimmy heard a young man say, "It's a good thing you're a lousy shot, Dad."

"Next time don't move when you see a person aim a rifle." The older man's voice was shaky, and he wasn't moving from the truck. When he realized the older man had actually grazed his son with the bullet, Jimmy figured it was the only thing holding him up.

"Leroy, you all right?" Luke Rittenhouse said to the older man. Jimmy hadn't realized that Meredith's boss was also there.

"Soon as my heart stops pounding."

Leroy didn't so much as move when Jimmy, making sure his flashlight beam announced his every move, went to stand by him and gently took the rifle.

"You just nicked me, Dad. Don't worry. I do worse when I'm shaving."

"He's all right," Jimmy said. "Everything's fine."

The old man, Leroy, shot him a dirty look.

Meredith, holding on to Yoda's collar, yelled, "You could have hurt someone, seriously, your son or Yoda."

"I did what I needed to do. I got that dog away from what's mine."

"Who knew that old rifle was loaded," the son muttered.

Jimmy carefully put the gun on the ground and made his way to Meredith, ears still humming from the rifle's report. Yoda, still subdued in Meredith's grip, had his hackles up.

Luke Rittenhouse, who Jimmy'd met just last week at BAA, was helping the son hobble over to a bale of hay so he could gingerly take off his sock.

"My dad barely broke the skin of my ankle," the son was saying. "As for your dog, I think he managed to put a small hole in my little finger. I should have known better than to interfere. But Rambo was whining and running with your dog in pursuit, and I just didn't think."

Jimmy wasn't sure who Rambo was, but figured it was one of the many dogs running around. Leroy was still leaning against the truck. His face was no longer gray; it was red with anger. Jimmy figured it was probably because his evening had been ruined, his farm compromised, not to mention his son hurt.

"I hope you can work tomorrow," Leroy said. "We've got two semitrailers to load with alfalfa. They're due in Texas by the end of the week."

"Don't worry, Dad. I can walk."

"You have others here to help you load?" Luke asked.

"Only one," Leroy answered in a clipped tone. Anger was evident in his every movement, from the way his hands opened and closed while he talked, to the way he snapped his boots down on the ground as he walked to the barn and bent low to look under an old bench.

"You see Rambo?" the son asked.

"No, figures that once the problem ends he does the sensible thing and hides."

"He was protecting us."

"And the beast was only doing what beasts do." Leroy gave Yoda a half-admiring look.

Meredith apparently took that as a get-out-of-jail sign to put Yoda in her SUV. Yoda protested with a few tugs and a low growl, but Meredith firmly ordered, "Go." After a moment, she returned, wiping her hands on her pants. Jimmy moved next to her, touched her arm and pulled her close. She didn't protest.

He didn't feel lost anymore. He felt as if they were working, together.

"I'm so sorry," Luke said. "We work hard to ensure that our animals don't get loose. He chewed through wire."

"Wolves don't take well to confinement," Leroy said.

"Thank you for not shooting him," Meredith said, softly.

She didn't move away from Jimmy, and he wondered if Meredith was aware that the old man had just been firing a warning shot.

The son's ankle had stopped bleeding. "I'll have a story to tell for weeks. Could the dog have rabies or something?"

"What are you going to do to make sure this doesn't happen again?" Leroy added.

"Put him back in the wolf enclosure," Meredith suggested hopefully.

Luke shook his head. "Third time's a charm. We tried again yesterday, but Prince and his mate are definitely taking a stand against Yoda."

"Back to the barn, then. I'll fix the fence, get stronger wiring, whatever it takes."

"And I'll pitch in," offered Jimmy. He'd already helped her once today with a wolf dog.

To Leroy, Luke said, "You said you had some

loading to do tomorrow. I'll be back tomorrow afternoon along with two more men. Plus, we'll pay for your son's doctor bills."

"It wasn't anything but a flesh wound," the son said.

"Good enough," Leroy agreed. "I'll probably convince him to go see a doctor tomorrow morning. It'll hurt more then."

Luke looked at Meredith. "You know what this means."

"They'll be an investigation. Yoda needs to be quarantined. It could be bad."

"I won't press charges," Leroy said. "My granddaughter's having her birthday at your place next month. She comes to all your summer activities."

Luke's expression didn't change. Neither did Meredith's. Jimmy wondered how he'd deal with this in his article. If Yoda had been a wild wolf dog, Leroy might not have missed.

Meredith stepped up. "I'm just curious. Is Rambo a dog?"

"You sure the wolf's secure?" Leroy asked her.

"He's locked in the car."

Leroy whistled.

A tiny white poodle strutted from the barn. She ran right to Leroy's son.

Never had a dog looked less like a Rambo.

"Rambo probably has a high-pitched bark,"

Meredith said. "The sound would have set Yoda off."

"Made his instinct to go after prey kick in," Jimmy agreed.

"Still shouldn't have happened," Luke said, "because Yoda shouldn't be able to get loose."

Judging by the expression on Meredith's face, the truth wasn't always welcome.

"We can secure the barn's enclosure," she said. "Make it so Yoda can't escape."

Luke wearily responded, "The barn was only supposed to be temporary lodgings anyway. For Yoda, too often of late, it's been his home. He doesn't belong in such a small area. He needs more room. He needs more attention."

Meredith didn't hesitate. "I'll take him."

Luke didn't appear to hear. "No, the barn's not a solution. We've talked about finding Yoda a home with other wolf dogs."

"Near Gesippi there's a place called Aqui Lobos. It's a rescue for wolf dogs," Meredith suggested. "I called the other day but only got a recorded message telling me their mission and a P.O. box number if I wanted to donate money."

"Agatha says they're full and turning animals away," Jimmy said. "She managed to speak to them yesterday. I keep getting the answering machine, too. They're referring people to a rescue facility in New Mexico."

"I'll take him in myself then," Meredith said. "I'll give him a home."

Finally, Luke nodded. "It's for the best. We'll fill out the paperwork this weekend."

Meredith spun around and headed for her SUV. Jimmy followed, listening to the murmurs behind him as Luke apologized once more to Leroy and his son. The farm, a big one, had outside lights, so parts of it were as bright as daylight. If not for that, he might not have noticed Meredith's shoulders quivering.

She'd stood up to a man holding a gun. Had run toward the man, in fact, just to make sure Yoda stayed safe. Hurrying, he caught up to her, taking her by the arm and turning her so he could look in her eyes.

They shimmered.

"You did good, Merry."

She didn't even notice him using the endearment from the past, only said, "I thought he was going to shoot Yoda. I thought I wouldn't get there in time."

"He shot past Yoda. It was his dumb luck that he grazed his son. While he didn't want his son or Rambo hurt, he wasn't willing to shoot your wolf."

"Wolf dog."

"What can I do to help?"

She leaned against the side of her SUV. Inside, Yoda put his head against the window as if knowing she needed to see him. Jimmy's hands went to her shoulders and gently massaged. The sweater she wore kept him from feeling her skin, and only the adrenaline of the night's events kept him from bringing her mouth to his.

But the adrenaline was ebbing; her face was upturned. Her eyes said she wanted him to kiss her. His head was dipping, almost without his permission.

But her words stopped him cold. "You still writing the story? You still think these animals belong in the wild?"

"I…" He wasn't sure what to believe, what to do. He only knew he was glad that both she and Yoda were safe.

"We're more than a story," she insisted. "Happily-ever-after can only happen if Yoda's with me, not in the wild." She looked at Leroy, who held his gun again.

"Not all stories have to end in the wild," she said softly.

He'd come to Gesippi for a change, mostly for his daughter. He'd not expected to change his way of thinking.

But his job was the only thing he did well. Who was he if he wasn't Jimmy Murphy, reporter for *Nature Times*?

THE SMELL OF pancakes woke Meredith, and for a moment she kept her eyes shut tight trying to orient herself. Something was wrong. Her life was off-kilter. Her control was slipping.

It wasn't that she had been up rescuing Yoda for half the night or that she was staying with Grandpa. If anything, it was calming to lie in this soft bed, smelling the laundry detergent that Grandma had always used, tucked under a quilt made by a great-grandparent Meredith had never met. So calming that she'd slept until the sun shining through the window woke her up.

It was Yoda.

She'd had to bring Yoda to Grandpa's house.

It was Jimmy.

He kept popping up every time she turned around and too easily becoming a fixture in her life. She'd given him a ride to his truck last night after they'd walked away from the ranch, and he'd not asked any probing questions on the way back to the mini-manse. He'd just sat in the passenger seat, talking calmly to Yoda, who wasn't too pleased about Jimmy's presence. Before he'd exited her truck, he'd only paused, put his hand on top of hers and said, "Everything's going to be fine."

His hand had felt warm, rugged, solid. His words, however, had been flat, without their usual forcefulness.

She'd driven home to Grandpa's, scolding Yoda for causing such a ruckus, and then she'd gone to bed still feeling Jimmy's touch, still thinking about their kiss earlier that day. She'd slept better than she had in years.

But she didn't want to think about the way he made her feel. She didn't want to think about him at all. His priorities right now were the story and the weddings of his brother and best friend.

Not her.

Opening one eye, she checked the clock. Nine o'clock! She was a get-out-of-bed-at-five kind of girl. Didn't matter if there was a middle-of-the-night rescue. Usually by nine o'clock she'd not only chiseled through a good portion of her to-do list, but she'd usually set others on course, too. At BAA, that would have been the employees she supervised.

And the animals. She always had plans for them.

Here in Gesippi, it was Grandpa she intended to organize. Speaking of Grandpa…

"Grandpa, are you cooking?" she shouted, flinging back the covers and sliding from the bed. The man was supposed to be taking it easy, supposed to be the one oversleeping and watching the dreadful judge shows on television.

"Yes," came a muted reply. Then Grandpa

must have cleared his throat, because the second part of his was louder. "We're hungry."

We're hungry? Hopefully, he was talking about Pepper, who did eat too much people food. She'd have to really educate Grandpa when it came to taking care of Leia and Yoda.

But then, would she be with Grandpa long enough for him to have to know how to care for them?

As Meredith headed to the window, her morning got a whole lot more unsettled. Jimmy Murphy's truck was parked behind her SUV.

Oh, that man. Lately, she just couldn't shake him. Absently, she rubbed the hand he'd touched last night. How silly was she? She'd already been wooed and put aside by Jimmy Murphy. She wouldn't make the same mistake twice. Especially since it seemed she was going to star in his newest documentary, whether she wanted to or not.

She took a pair of jeans from her suitcase—maybe she should go ahead and switch her belongings to the dresser—and tugged them on. Then she grabbed a sky-blue ribbed sweater, a pair of socks and her boots. She had them on before she got to the door.

Jimmy had always inspired her to be a quick dresser. At one time she'd not wanted to waste a moment that could be spent with him.

She almost left the bedroom and confronted him without brushing her hair. Had it been Luke, her brother or any other male, she'd not have paused. Because it was Jimmy, she turned around, went to the dresser and quickly captured her blondish-brown hair in a rubber band.

She stopped by the bathroom and brushed her teeth for good measure.

"What do you want now?" she asked, entering the kitchen. Jimmy sat at the small table looking big and handsome and comfortable. He had his laptop open—Grandpa grumbled at her if she had her laptop out at breakfast time.

"Two more pancakes," he answered easily. He nodded toward her grandfather, his expression contrasted with the ease of his words.

"You know what I me…mean." Meredith grumped. Grandpa stood at the stove, the bottom of his pants dusty. His shirt, always tucked in, was loose. Not his usual look.

"Grandpa, are you—"

"I'm fine," he snapped, giving Jimmy a somewhat guarded stare.

Grandpa never snapped.

Jimmy took the conversation in another direction. "How'd Yoda do last night? I should have followed you home, seen if you needed any help."

"So you'd have more fodder for your documentary?"

He didn't deny it. At least honesty was still part of his makeup. The trait made him both appealing and dangerous. "This morning I called one of my cameramen. He was glad to hear from me."

"You've always been good at what you do."

"Yeah," Jimmy said. "But for *Nature Times*, I've been the idea man, scriptwriter, photographer, and acted as the spokesperson. The cameraman said there's a dozen wannabes after my job, and one of them is already doing the assignment I was pitched."

"Why?"

"Because I came here to be in Danny's wedding."

Something about his voice clued Meredith in to the fact that he wasn't telling the whole truth.

Jimmy continued, "And now he's been given another assignment. Which means my idea about the wolf dog is either not on the calendar or has been pushed back."

"Sorry." Meredith opened the fridge and took out the milk. "You're not going to get sympathy from me. You want a real story. Do a documentary about how zoos and habitats are constantly striving to breed tigers in order to save the species."

"But—"

"No buts. California did it with the condor.

Believe me, animals in the wild is wonderful, but until we successfully eliminate poaching and stop tearing down habitats, places like BAA are necessary. Instead of focusing on a species, focus on an animal."

"But—"

"Do Leia's story, not the wolf dog story."

"Would you trust me to do her story?"

She didn't answer, and instead turned her attention to Grandpa, marveling that an eighty-two-year-old man who'd recently taken a fall out in the middle of nowhere could bounce back so quickly. "You seem to be feeling better," she said. "Were you working outside this morning?"

"Yes, I *was* working outside, and yes, I *do* feel better," Grandpa agreed. "Enough so you can go back to Scorpion Ridge and your work."

"You trying to get rid of me?"

His answer was no, but his eyes said yes.

Curious.

After pouring herself a glass of milk, Meredith opened the back door, leaned against the frame and gazed toward the barn. Last night at 2:00 a.m. she'd been exhausted as she'd led Yoda from the SUV and introduced him to Leia. Thank goodness wolves were pack animals and usually welcomed company.

Leia had been awake. The wolf in her wanted to be nocturnal while the dog in her understood human time. Yoda, however, had been more interested in where he was than in who he was with. He'd inspected the barn, seemingly unimpressed. Leia followed for a moment, then, satisfied that he wasn't an usurper, stayed curled up in an empty stall.

"That barn seemed bigger yesterday," Jimmy said, coming to stand next to her. She took a long drink of her milk, and then stepped away from him on the pretense of needing to set the milk glass on the counter. It bothered her how her body wanted to react to him, wanted to lean closer, to touch him.

"Two wolf dogs take up a lot more space than one," she answered.

"How'd they do last night?"

"I'm not sure," she admitted. Like a magnet, Jimmy drew her back to the doorway. "Yoda spent a good fifteen minutes exploring. I finally left him to it and went to bed. I'm not sure Leia cared."

"They seem okay now."

The two wolf dogs stood next to each other outside the barn. Leia's head was bent, sniffing something. Her muscular body was at attention. She knew where she was, where Yoda was and what was going on. Yoda stood next to her, all his focus on her.

"She's going to be the alpha," Meredith said.

"What?"

"Alpha," Meredith explained. "It means—"

"I know what it means," Jimmy said. "How can you tell by just looking at them? I thought there was always a dominant male and a dominant female."

"That's when there's a pack. Here we just have the two. I can tell because she's more confident and Yoda is standing a bit behind her."

"She's also been here a few days and had a chance to acclimate," Jimmy pointed out. "He's had a traumatic night and needs some time to adapt."

"Wolves don't think like that."

"How do you know?"

Meredith hesitated. "I know from working with Yoda and from working with Prince and Penelope."

Jimmy raised one eyebrow.

"The wolf couple at BAA. They're the ones who bullied Yoda so much that we had to remove him from the enclosure."

"Is that going to happen here?" Jimmy asked.

"Probably not. With just two, she'll tolerate him just fine as long as he lets her have her way."

"Sounds like somebody else I know."

Now it was Meredith's turn to raise an eyebrow. Then she asked, "Don't you have somewhere you have to be today? Danny's getting married in two days. Surely you should be trying on your tux or some such nonsense."

Jimmy put his hand over his heart. "Nonsense? You wound me. My tux fits fine. When you see me in it, you'll probably decide you want to spend more time with me, help me understand Leia and her kind. Will you work with me, Merry?"

Looking back at his open laptop, Meredith sighed. This was a battle she couldn't win. He was a beloved hometown boy, at one time also beloved by her. He wanted this story badly, and he was already fully vested in it—he would do the story with or without her. And hadn't she just been thinking a few days ago that she should try not being so competitive with him?

"Okay, what have you found out so far about wolf dogs?"

There was little she didn't know about what was happening in Arizona's wolf dog community, but years in the field had taught her that just when she thought she'd heard everything, something new came along.

He smiled. "First, there's still no one advertising for a lost wolf dog that fits Leia's description. So now I'm taking my search in a different direction. I've started looking for wolf dog owners, rescue organizations and even breeders."

"It's not the right season for puppies. High-content wolf dogs are born in the spring. December would be about the last month to expect a litter."

"Yes, but the people who sell the puppies can lead us to the people who *buy* the puppies."

"Do we absolutely have to find where Leia came from?"

"No, but it would be a nice part of the story. Come look at the people I've found so far."

Against her better judgment, she sat down next to him at the table. On the screen, he brought up a spreadsheet of names of people, the towns where they lived and the number of wolf dogs they owned.

Most owned one, a few owned two, the rest owned in the double digits. Meredith only recognized one name, the butcher in town.

"Grandpa, did you look at this list?"

Grandpa came over, squinted and groused, "I can't read print that small."

"Email it to me," Meredith suggested. "I'll make the font larger and then print it."

A moment later, Grandpa thrust the list back at her. "I don't recognize a single one."

Meredith was surprised. Her grandfather used to know half the county.

"I'm going to take the ones who have advertised puppies for sale and start visiting them. I'll be asking about Leia…" Jimmy held up his camera. "But I'll be looking for anything else I can document."

"I think that's a good idea." She wished she could go, but at least he'd share what he found.

"I'm also going to the Aqui Lobos Rescue to learn more about wolf dogs and what's been happening in the area."

She bit her lip. She wanted to visit the rescue, too. She might need to check it out as a possible home for Leia.

"I'm going there today, why don't you come?" Jimmy said.

"Why?"

"It would be interesting to hear how your opinions differ from that of the owners," Jimmy admitted.

"We both rescue," Meredith pointed out. "The difference is they rescue one animal—the wolf dog. BAA rescues many animals."

"BAA also encourages the animals to perform," Jimmy said. "And they rely on ticket sales, whereas the rescue is dependent on donations for most of their operating costs."

"Their operating costs are nowhere near ours. Wolves are," she hesitated, "somewhat low maintenance."

Jimmy looked at Grandpa, concern on his face. "Ray, what are your plans for the rest of the day.

Why don't you and Meredith both come with me. Let's find out about Leia."

"You go ahead," Grandpa urged. "I'm going to rest. I'm already worn out. You, you're young pups, and it's a beautiful day. It will do you good, Merry. I'm fine."

Meredith wished she were sure about Grandpa. Although he was his usual self, he moved too slow to be called "fine." His hands also shook. Of course, she'd noticed that a few years ago. Since then, every time she sat next to him, she'd put her hand on his, wanting to stop the proof that the years marched on.

"Merry." Jimmy said. "I've always thought that name fit you."

The kitchen got quiet as Meredith and Jimmy looked at each other. The years dropped away. A decade ago, Jimmy had been a boy sitting at this table, all energy and dreams. She'd been full of energy and dreams, too, but tied to Gesippi by an invisible cord.

Grandpa's fork slid to the table and his head bowed in slumber. Lately, the man could fall asleep anywhere.

"I found him on the side—"

Grandpa snored, woke himself up and looked at Jimmy as if Jimmy had suddenly sprouted two heads. Standing up, Grandpa went to the stove and started scraping a pancake off the griddle.

"I also," Jimmy said, too easily changing the subject, "called ten veterinarians this morning. One of the things I love about small towns is how accessible everyone is."

Growing up, Meredith hadn't always considered that a plus. What it really meant was those same people had too many questions about her family and she had too few places to hide.

"I asked about wolf dogs," Jimmy continued, "and two vets mentioned the name Paul Livingston. He's one of the multiple wolf dog owners on our list. You ever heard of him?"

"No."

"The vets didn't sound impressed with Livingston. I can't figure out who he is or where he lives. Paul Livingston is a popular name, but the only hit I get on a Paul Livingston in this area is for a two-year-old. I'm fairly sure they're not one and the same."

Meredith nodded.

"Something else, and the vets I spoke to want this off the record, but I'm sharing it with you. Victor Lucas also has wolf dogs that tend to die young."

"The man who owns the Crooked Feather Indian Trading Post? I went to school with his daughter."

Behind them, something crashed.

Meredith whirled around to find Grandpa

holding on to the sink. A plate as well as two pancakes were on the floor.

"You lose your grip?" she asked.

He was pale, paler than he should be for just a simple slip of the hand.

"I don't like this," he stated.

"It's no fun getting old," she quipped. "Good thing you're not." She was trying to cajole him into a better mood.

Jimmy led Grandpa to the table while Meredith cleaned up the mess. This was the grandpa that had Zack running scared.

"Maybe we should call Doc Thomas?" Meredith suggested to Jimmy.

"I don't need Doc Thomas," Grandpa said. "I need people to leave me alone and let me do what I'm supposed to do."

"You've never liked being alone," Meredith said.

Jimmy was a bit more direct. "What is it you're supposed to do?"

Grandpa said firmly, "I'm supposed to take care of myself, not impose on my grandchildren."

"Who's imposing?" Meredith asked.

"You should get back to Scorpion Ridge and work."

"I'll be working for the next fifty years. Spending time with you right now is more important."

Grandpa merely shook his head.

"Want me to call Dad?" she asked.

Grandpa kept shaking his head.

So, acting as if nothing was wrong, together they ate breakfast. Grandpa only ate half a pancake. Clearly, his appetite was gone. So was his stamina. He headed for the porch and his daytime television shows before Meredith had even begun to clear the table.

"I'm not sure what to do," Meredith said softly to Jimmy. "One minute I'm convinced he should be in assisted living, the next I'm convinced he should be here."

"You've only been back a little over a week. You don't have to make up your mind yet."

"I don't need assisted living," Grandpa groused, returning to the kitchen. He picked up a magnifying glass from the table. "At my age, a bad mood and bad choices just mean I'm too tired to pretend."

"Grandpa!" Meredith scolded.

"And if the only thing I drop today is a pancake, then I'm doing good. I'm fine. You go on to the wolf dog rescue. I just didn't sleep well last night. I could use some peace and quiet."

With that, Grandpa shuffled off. Meredith followed and watched as he used the magnifying glass to check the TV guide. He looked tired, frustrated and old.

"I want," he grumped, "some time alone in my own house."

Since there was no changing his mind, she decided to go and to take Leia along, too. The rescue had told Jimmy they weren't missing any animals, but maybe they'd seen her before. It also gave Meredith the opportunity to find out if Leia was leash trained and if she would challenge Meredith's authority or go berserk when she saw all the other wolf dogs.

So she fed Leia and Yoda, changed their water and put a collar and lead on Leia. The wolf dog wasn't happy about the hindrance but didn't act as if it was the first time she'd been leashed. Jimmy followed Meredith, watching every step but not questioning her actions.

"Have you decided on your angle for the story now?" she finally asked. Part of her didn't want to know, didn't want to remember about that side of him, but she needed to be prepared when the story came out.

"I'm going with the theme of the misunderstood."

Meredith wasn't impressed. "Do you think any animal is understood?"

His expression became thoughtful. "No, especially not the American male."

"You still talking animal?"

His eyes darkened and he leaned toward her. "Oh, yeah."

Meredith was familiar with this game. "You don't deserve to be understood," she quipped.

"You used to understand me."

"And then you went away."

He looked ready to say something, but she didn't want to hear it. Her life was already out of control.

"If we're going to the rescue, we should go now. I want to be home in time to make Grandpa supper."

"I can take care of myself," Grandpa shouted. So much for him being hard of hearing.

"And I need to pick up my daughter at three o'clock," Jimmy added.

Meredith led Leia to her SUV and gently guided her into the back area, which she'd retrofitted to accommodate big animals. "Go ahead, get in, girl."

"You know," Jimmy said, "I've changed my mind. You should have taken Yoda a long time ago. You're great with these animals."

"No, Yoda should be at BAA. He's an ambassador for his breed. The greater good, if you understand what I mean."

"The greater good," Jimmy said slowly. "But should the greater good serve the animal or people?"

Meredith turned to face him. She knew the answer to this question. She'd thought about it almost every day since Jimmy announced his intention of writing about the wolf dog.

"I work one-on-one with animals. The greater good for both animal and people is the survival of all species. Unlike you, I don't walk away when filming is done. I'm there the next day and the next."

Unsaid was the implication that he was an expert at walking away.

CHAPTER FIFTEEN

THE FIRST FEW minutes they drove down the road, both Jimmy and Meredith were quiet. Jimmy wondered if she was thinking about him walking away or about yesterday's kiss.

He hoped it was the kiss but doubted she believed he deserved such consideration.

Finally, she cleared her throat. "So, what's with Grandpa? Why were you at our house this morning? I was afraid to ask you earlier because he might have overheard. Why does he look so scruffy?" she continued.

"This morning I dropped Briana off early at school and then headed to Uncle Matthew's. With Danny's wedding so close, Uncle Matt wants to make sure I know what I'm doing on the farm."

"I never pictured you as a farmer." And she'd pictured him as a lot things: writer, father, husband.

"I'm not a farmer, I'm just helping until Danny gets back from his honeymoon. Believe me, this wolf dog story is a godsend. I'd be going crazy if I didn't have it to pursue. Setting out seedlings puts me to sleep. Anyway, I found your grandpa walking along the road."

He hadn't believed it possible, but her fingers tightened even more on the steering wheel. "You're kidding. Grandpa was walking along the road? Did he have his walker or at least a cane? How early was it? I can't believe I slept through all this."

"We'd only been in the kitchen a half hour before you woke up, so it was about eight. He had the cane, but he was limping. I stopped and opened the passenger-side door. He didn't want to get in, but I threatened to call you. He tried to get me to promise not to say anything to you."

"I'm glad you didn't promise that."

Her lean fingers eased their grip. His eyes traveled from her hands to her arms to her neck to her face.

She'd been his first love, and if he was honest, his only love. He'd never met a woman more passionate in what she believed and in who she loved.

She'd loved him. And he'd blown it.

He reminded himself to stick to the important issue at hand. "Something's going on with Ray," Jimmy commented. "He was agitated when I picked him up, and it wasn't because he was hurting, I don't think. I got the idea he was expecting something or someone. He was trying to cut through the field, but he couldn't find an even path."

"That's so odd. I wonder what he was looking for."

"You said last time that he was searching for Rowdy. Could he still be trying to find that old dog?"

"I don't think so. He told me he just used Rowdy's name because he'd heard a dog and just figured he needed to call a name."

Jimmy shrugged. "Sounds strange to me, but I agree that it probably wasn't what he was after this morning. Could he be looking for your grandmother?"

"No." She let out a long breath. "Something else is going on. There's also the hole in the door. He blamed Pepper, but Zack and I both thought it seemed the right size for a foot. Then, there's how he read that list of names."

"Of people who own wolf dogs?"

"Yes. He said he didn't recognize any of the names, but I'm sure he did. I even recognized one, the butcher at the store."

Meredith tried to smile. Her grip released a bit more, and she stretched her fingers.

"I have no idea how all of that connects, but I'm afraid that what it adds up to is that he should be in assisted living."

"He'd hate being cooped up in a tiny apartment."

As if agreeing, Leia let out a woof.

Jimmy looked back at the wolf dog. "Most animals, especially males, need a whole lot of attention and shouldn't be caged."

This time it was Meredith who gave him the once-over, starting at his boots and ending at the top of his head. "Some males," she said, "deserve exactly what they get."

A HALF HOUR LATER, Meredith turned onto an obscure dirt road and slowed down so she didn't miss the entrance to Aqui Lobos. In the back of Meredith's SUV, Leia was chewing on one of Yoda's bones. Jimmy was on the phone, texting and talking to himself.

She'd forgotten that he liked to talk to himself when he was working. She used to find it endearing.

If she were honest, she still did.

"How long's this place been here again?" Meredith asked after Jimmy put away the phone.

"About three years. Their website says they started with a few strays, and that wolf dogs just keep making their way to them. What's odd is they don't list their address on the website." Jimmy pulled a map from his pocket. "We're almost there, though. Turn at the next stop sign."

Three years was a good start. Meredith had been called for advice by a few people interested in starting wolf dog rescues, but she'd told them that the cost and time often brought the ventures down, usually within a year. She was amazed that one so close had proved successful without her knowing about it.

The first thing Meredith saw after finding the driveway for Aqui Lobos was an expensive-looking adobe house. One thing all animal sanctuaries seemed to have in common was someone with money able to fund the facility.

For BAA, it was a woman named Ruth Moore, now Ruth Dunbar. She'd inherited money along with a million-dollar home from her late husband. She owned a geriatric lion and had held BAA together for more than twenty years. Only recently had the habitat come into its own, attracting attention from all over the state. And only in the last year had it managed to be self-supporting.

The sign directing them to the rescue didn't indicate the house as a destination, though. Instead, the road took them to a small trailer. Behind it, Meredith could see miles of empty land, most of it fenced in. Two quads were parked by the trailer's front door. Even before they stopped, Meredith could hear the howls. They started, then stopped, then started again as the next set of animals joined in, an echoing chorus heralding their arrival. Five dogs, one of them a wolf dog, came to investigate the newcomers. In the rear of the SUV, Leia rose, backed up, huddled down, and cowered.

"It's okay, girl," Meredith tried to soothe.

Leia didn't calm down. Meredith was still a new human in the wolf dog's life—a life that probably hadn't featured the best of human contact.

A woman came out of the trailer carrying a pail. She called the dogs, shooed them away and examined Meredith and Jimmy with a guarded expression before half smiling and starting their way. Meredith recognized the look. The woman had a long list of things to do and they weren't on the list. But any visitor was a potential donor.

"You called to say we were coming, didn't you?" Meredith hissed.

"Well, no, not really. Plus, I don't want to give people a chance to prepare for me. You get a truer picture that way."

Meredith shot him a dirty look and exited the SUV, moving to greet the woman. "You must be Lily King. I'm Meredith Stone."

Lily glanced at the SUV. Leia's doggy face was smashed against the passenger-side window. "That your wolf dog?" Lily asked, disappointment underscoring every word.

"Yes."

"You don't want him anymore?"

"She's a girl and she's not really mine."

Jimmy exited the SUV, careful not to let Leia escape. He leaned against the hood.

Lily said, "We're not able to accept any more—"

"I'm not in the habit of giving animals away," Meredith interrupted briskly. "I work at Bridget's Animal Adventure, and all we're doing today is trying to find out some information."

Lily's whole demeanor changed. "What did you say your name was?"

"I'm Meredith Stone."

With the guarded look gone, Lily appeared a lot younger, younger certainly than Meredith, because Meredith couldn't remember being this excited about meeting someone.

"I'm so sorry," Lily said, putting down the bucket and coming to give Meredith a hug—not a handshake. "I can't believe I didn't recognize you. The first time I worked by myself with a wolf dog, I watched your video on YouTube over and over again. My husband said if I watched it once more, he was hiding the computer."

"Wow, that's quite a compliment." The video had been Luke's idea. He was a master marketer. Meredith had been amazed by how many hits the YouTube video had received. Now, at least, she knew that most of them came from this woman. "Why didn't you call me?"

"Really, you'd have talked to me?"

"When it comes to saving an animal, I'd have talked your ear off."

"Animals she gets along with," Jimmy said. "It's people she has trouble with."

Nothing he said could diminish Meredith's good mood. Her video had made a difference! "Hush," she scolded Jimmy.

"Have you come to look at what we've done?" Lily asked, "Or did someone tell you we needed help? We're trying to get more government funding. It's not easy. And I've still got two wolf dogs that could dig a swimming pool if I let them. I'm filling holes in their enclosure at least twice a week. I'd love some advice."

"Actually, I need your help. I've got Leia with me—" Meredith motioned to the wolf dog whose face was pressed against the back window "—because we found her on our property in Gesippi. I wanted to see if you knew her."

Meredith walked to the SUV and lifted the hatchback. Taking a firm hold of the leash, she guided a trembling Leia from the SUV.

"She's beautiful," Lily said.

Behind Meredith, the howls started again, a swish of noise that crescendoed through the rescue, started again and finally tapered off.

Leia was all ears.

The five dogs Lily had shooed away started moving closer. The one wolf dog among them paced back and forth while the others used a more stealthy maneuver.

"How many do you have here?" Jimmy asked.

"We're at thirty-five already. We've taken in dogs from as far away as Nebraska. But we really only have room for thirty."

"Why so few? You've a lot of property." He nodded his head toward what must have once been a horse pasture.

Lily looked at Meredith as if mentally saying, "Your boyfriend's not very smart," and said, "If we allowed them loose on the field, most of them would escape. They're high-content. They'd dig or chew their way out in five minutes max."

Considering all the research Jimmy claimed to have done, he should have known that.

"Plus," Lily added, "there're only two of us doing all the care, and there's the cost. Because of hierarchy issues, we keep the individual packs down to groups of three to five. We'd don't want our wolf dogs injured or dead because of order disputes. Tigger—" she pointed to the pacing wolf dog "—is the only one we trust enough to run loose. We think he's mostly German shepherd with a sprinkling of gray wolf."

Before Meredith could point out that Jimmy

should have read all of this in his research, Leia dived under the SUV, timid and shy.

Lily positioned herself much like a baseball catcher, crouched and alert, so she could study Leia, look right into her eyes and allow Leia to do the same.

"We have three here that could be from the same bitch and sire as your girl, based on her coloring and markings. Can't be sure, though, without a blood test."

"More than half of wolf dog pups die before they make it to puberty," Jimmy said. "The odds of having four from the same litter..."

His words tapered off and Meredith knew he wanted Lily to answer.

Why?

"Those are stats for wolves in the wild," Meredith answered before Lily could. "Wolf dog pups born to a breeder wouldn't be exposed to the same dangers as pups in the wild."

Lily straightened after realizing Leia wasn't about to come out from under the SUV. "I'll get you a bone. Try to coax her over to the barn. I'll go find Trixie, our vet, and ask her to examine Leia. I want to see if she agrees that Leia is probably related to the others."

"You have a vet?"

"One morning a week she donates her time.

You picked the right day. She owns two wolf dogs."

"Could you ask her to take a look at Leia's right front leg, too? I cleaned it, but she wouldn't let me put a bandage on it."

"Sure."

"Why isn't your address on the website? How do you support yourself?" Jimmy pushed himself away from the SUV and came forward with his hand held out to shake.

Lily took it. "We can't take in any more wolf dogs, which is why we don't publish our address. How'd you find us?"

"I'm Jimmy Murphy. I work for *Nature Times*. I'm writing an article on the wolf dog. The little lady under the SUV in particular. We're trying to find out how she wound up dehydrated and wounded near Mailbox Mesa."

Lily pursed her lips. "Jimmy Murphy, huh. You're the man who called last week. I told you I wasn't interested in talking to you."

Now she understood why Jimmy had been so eager to have her along. Anger and betrayal churned Meredith's stomach. Again. She watched Jimmy's face, hoping her gut instinct was wrong. From his expression, though, she knew she was right. Part of the reason Jimmy had brought her along to open doors for him. For his story.

She'd trusted him. And he'd used her.

A YEAR AGO, Jimmy wouldn't have made such a mistake. He'd have known to wait to introduce himself until the right moment. He'd have also known that misrepresenting himself always led to chaos.

Losing his wife and now possibly losing his job had made him take risks that only a rookie would take. And he'd probably just destroyed any hope he had of reconnecting with Meredith. Right now, he was between two women who both looked as if they'd willingly feed him to the wolf dog.

Leia growled at him.

He'd inadvertently stepped too close to her bone.

"Not even the die-hard conservationists oppose rescue facilities," he defended himself, amazed that he felt the need to. He'd often had to defend what he wrote and what he filmed, but he'd never felt guilty about it.

Until now. What he'd seen and done over the last few days with Meredith had changed everything.

"Unless they happen to have a thing about noise," Lily said, "or possibly a thing about land use."

"I owe you both an apology," he said. "I figured out your address using Google maps. I basically scanned the area until I found a yard with lots of dogs. Then I waited until I could convince Meredith to come with me."

Meredith merely rolled her eyes. She had that right. On this venture, she was the good guy and not him.

"I don't like Jimmy's tactics," Meredith said to Lily, "but I'm glad I found you. I'll let BAA know you exist and what kind of help you need. Sometimes we get donations, like kibble, that we can share."

Meredith was clearly enthralled with Aqui Lobos. Both women, pretty much ignoring Jimmy, walked toward the back of the property.

"Picture a pizza," Lily said. "Each of our enclosures is a slice. The middle here—" she opened a door to a round adobe building "—is our base." Jimmy assumed they were entering a shed; he was wrong. Inside were a few items— food, tools and blankets. Six more doors were inside, each sported Christmas wreaths adorned with dog biscuits, and each one opened to an enclosure. Jimmy stepped closer. The dog biscuits had names written on them: Max, Tigger, Fritz, Bandit and more.

Lily snatched a handful of dog biscuits from an oversize bag and waited until Jimmy closed the door they came through before taking them to the "first slice," as she called it.

Inside, five wolf dogs were weaving back and

forth, curious about the humans but cautious. The howls started again, lasting a good five minutes.

Yes, Jimmy could see how the noise factor would disturb most neighbors. Luckily none were close.

"This chain-link fence is at least eight feet tall," Meredith gushed, petting each wolf dog as it came to sniff her. "At BAA, we only went to six feet. I'm wondering now if we should have gone higher."

Lily handed out the dog biscuits. "We've got some escape artists. I'm not willing to take a chance."

Meredith wasn't done admiring. "I also like this chain-link overhang. You went a step further with that, too. Is the line electric?"

"No, but it's barbed. We believe in being pro-active. If we don't keep things up to code, we could be slapped with fines up to a thousand dollars."

Jimmy gazed down the line of pens. This was not a moneymaking venture. This rescue location wasn't catering to visitors who wanted to gawk at the wolf dogs. This was a rescue mission to take care of the wolf dog.

He followed Meredith and Lily as they went in all the slices but one. The two wolf dogs in that one had been abused. "My husband doesn't believe they can be rehabilitated. We'll settle for keeping them fed and sheltered," Lily said.

Jimmy was starting to see the wolf dog through Meredith's eyes—not just their beauty, but their personalities, their needs. He was beginning to understand why a wild animal, even a half-wild animal, might not belong in the wild. This story would be different from every other story he'd ever done.

Each wolf dog came with a story. Some had been dropped off because owners couldn't care for them anymore, others had been found wandering, and the last two had been rescued from an abusive situation. Finally, Lily took him and Meredith back through the base and toward the house. The five dogs she'd shooed away earlier had roamed off except for the wolf dog Tigger. He was lying on the ground a good distance from Leia, as if guarding his territory.

"Tigger, retreat."

Tigger tossed his head and trotted off to bother one of the other dogs.

As if realizing she was in a safe place, Leia came out from under the SUV and sidled toward Lily. Lily hunched down and grasped the wolf dog on the side of her face. Then she practically rubbed noses with Leia. It reminded Jimmy of Meredith's action the day they'd found her grandpa in the field, the first time they'd encountered Leia.

In Jimmy's adventures filming and writing about the wild, he'd thought mostly about the proper way to document the animals. It had been a long time since he'd thought about the proper way to treat the animals.

After a minute, Lily looked satisfied that she'd bonded or at least befriended Leia. Standing up, she said, "She's walking with a slight limp. Let's get her to the barn and figure this out."

Meredith didn't even glance at Jimmy. He was still persona non grata.

Side by side the two women walked down the dirty road, away from the trailer and toward what looked like an old, weathered barn. The outside didn't represent the inside. It was a first-aid station for animals.

Jimmy stopped in the doorway to watch, as there wasn't room for him to enter. Trixie, the vet, came up to his chest. Her hair was roughly the same color as Leia's and equally streaked with gray. He pegged her at about sixty. She, too, knew her wolf dogs, and in a matter of minutes had introduced herself to Leia by rubbing her face and had gotten Leia up on the table to examine her.

"She's had pups," Trixie said, "and I'd say this past spring. She looks to be two, maybe three years old. She needs a few more pounds on her. When did you find her?"

"I've had her just two days, and she found me." Meredith quickly told the story, only this time it didn't sound as entertaining as when Holly had recounted it.

"I don't think she'll require stitches. You did a nice job cleaning this up. You have any idea how she injured herself?"

"She was going after my grandpa's chickens. When I found her, the wound appeared recent, but I didn't find an area near the coop that had her blood on it."

Jimmy took out his camera and snapped some pictures, already revising the story in his head. Instead of a "wild" animal that should be released, he was documenting a "tame" animal that shouldn't be. This would not go over with his readership. Or his boss.

Yet, he'd never wanted to do a story so badly.

As Lily led them through the maze of pens, she apologized that her husband, Tom, was unavailable. He was a long-distance truck driver and wouldn't be home until the next day.

"The rescue was his idea. He bought a wolf dog from a breeder who told him it would be just like raising any dog, but more fun. Not true. When Tom took Brute to one of the shelters, they wouldn't take him."

"Maybe he shouldn't have named the dog Brute," Jimmy suggested.

Now, instead of two women giving him the evil eye, he had three.

Lily continued, "The man he spoke to at the shelter said they'd had another wolf dog dropped off that morning, left outside tied to a post. They were going to put him down that night. Tom, who'd thought he couldn't handle one wolf dog, came home with two."

"What did you think when he came home?"

Lily laughed. "We weren't married then, hadn't even met. I never would have let Tom name him Brute." She stopped in front of a pen. "This is Brute."

For a wolf dog, Brute was small.

"He loves ice cream," Lily said, "and up until three years ago I would have warned you not to let his smallish size fool you. He has Napoleon syndrome. We couldn't put him with a pack."

They left Brute's enclosure and went to the pen that housed the three wolf dogs that looked like Leia. Jimmy could see the resemblance.

"How'd you get them?"

The three wolf dogs ran toward the fence, tumbling against it and rolling in good-natured fun, tongues lolling.

"A forest ranger named Jake Farraday brought them to us. Some professor from Adobe Hills went and got herself arrested. Seems these three were barely more than puppies, and she had them penned up in her backyard."

"They were underfed," Trixie added indignantly.

"How old do you think they are?" Jimmy asked.

"Right now," Trixie said, carefully opening the gate and letting herself into the pen, "I put them at about three years of age. Their teeth—" as if to demonstrate, one of the dogs gnawed on her leg, his teeth glistening in the Arizona sunshine "—have tartar around the canines. They also have smooth skin and good muscle tone. Their vision is excellent."

One thing for sure, these gals were passionate about their work. The way Jimmy used to be.

The way he wanted to be again.

He pulled the list of wolf dog owners from his pocket and handed it to Trixie. "You recognize any of these names?"

"Most of these are decent owners—except for him, he's the worst."

The "worst" was Paul Livingston.

"The veterinarian I spoke to mentioned him," Jimmy reminded Meredith. "He was less than impressed with Livingston."

"He sells puppies," Trixie said. "He's not exactly a puppy mill, but it's how he earns his money."

For the next hour, Jimmy followed the women as they showed the facility off to Meredith. They reminded him somewhat of salesclerks at an upscale store. Each wolf dog was perfect. And Meredith was the front-row spectator at Fashion Week. She looked as if she was willing to adopt them all.

At two, Jimmy nudged Meredith and said, "I have to pick Briana up from school."

"She should come here," Meredith said.

Jimmy wasn't sure. His daughter would surely want a wolf dog, and unless they left behind their nomadic life, they couldn't even have a goldfish.

"Next time," he said.

They rescued Leia from the holding pen and were soon on their way back to Gesippi.

"Don't think I've forgiven you," Meredith said. "You used me to get into Aqui Lobos."

Jimmy defended himself. "It worked out, and we both needed to go there."

"But they'd have welcomed me no matter what. You're the enemy."

"That really makes no sense. As I said before, I'm not against rescue facilities."

"Zoos are often rescue facilities."

"No, they're not."

"Yoda would be dead without BAA."

"He's an exception."

"How about Ouch, my eagle."

"*Your* eagle? Eagles shouldn't be owned."

"You know what I mean."

"Zoos can't afford to focus on rescue. And if they were truly rescue facilities, they wouldn't skew their resources toward the cute and cuddly."

"What?"

"Big cats are mostly what draws crowds to zoos. You advertise a new tiger cub, run a contest to name it and you've got a crowd coming through the door. That makes the zoo director happy."

"Sure it does. That crowd pays for the food the tiger eats. It also pays for the vet who works on the eagle about to be released. It pays for the type of fencing that will keep the wolf dog from escaping and eating the chickens at a neighboring ranch."

"Paying for such things is not the tiger's reason for existence. Not until man interfered, anyway, like man interfered with the breeding practices of the wolf and dog."

"So, if one man interferes, the next man shouldn't strive to make things right? Shouldn't follow his heart? Because I gotta tell you, the day we release that eagle back into the wild, I'll know I've made a difference. Just as I've known it a dozen times before." She looked at him, anger no longer in her gaze. Instead, he saw something else, something that made him realize he was the one lacking.

"Can you say the same? Give me an example of one animal that's personally benefited from your documentaries."

Jimmy didn't answer. Truth was, he couldn't.

He wanted to tell her that she and Leia had forced him to reexamine his assumptions, that he was going to do a different kind of story. Only it was one that could spell the end of his career.

CHAPTER SIXTEEN

ONCE AGAIN, MEREDITH had managed to one-up him. She'd ignited feelings he'd believed long dead—not just feelings about her, but feelings about that wrongs and rights in the world, and about his role as a journalist.

As he got into his vehicle, he tried to think as he used to, tried to convince himself he was taking her reaction to his questions at the Aqui Lobos too personally. So what if he'd piggy-backed her name and used her to gain entry to the rescue. So what if his history with her had opened a few lips at Bridget's Animal Adventure.

If what they were doing wasn't a secret, they should have welcomed him the first time he'd asked to visit.

But as he started the car, he admitted to himself that he owed his livelihood to Meredith. He'd followed Meredith to the Gesippi Library many a time and listened as she and Agatha had talked about extinction.

She and Agatha had not only discussed dinosaurs, but everything from wild horses on the reservation to the way javelinas no longer feared man.

When he'd applied at *Nature Times* after college, he'd been looking for a way into the world of making and writing documentaries. He'd not been searching specifically for a job that had to do with animals, but during the interview, he'd found himself sharing tidbits from those long-ago conversations between Meredith and Agatha. It had made him appear knowledgeable, exactly the kind of candidate they'd wanted.

So, he'd figuratively clocked in and discovered that he loved his work—and that he was great at it. His only regret was he was more of a voice than a participant. He told people he wanted to be Jacques Cousteau, and listed explorer, conservationist, filmmaker, innovator, photographer, author and researcher on his resume. So far, he'd really only managed six of the seven.

He'd done nothing innovative.

The most innovative thing he'd done lately was to help Meredith put up a fence to keep Leia contained. Once again, Meredith had helped him to get his hands dirty, but it had all been to help an animal, not to help his career.

He drove past his uncle's farm. He spotted Matthew walking out of the barn and toward the house, a half smile on his face. Matthew loved being a farmer and could tell you anything you wanted to know about beans, squash, corn... the list went on. He remembered the crops he'd grown ten years ago and he loved to consider the crops he'd be growing tomorrow.

Jimmy could tell you the research he'd uncovered about the rhino back in 2010. He could recount every word of the documentary's script.

What he couldn't recount was the rest of the story. Once the segment had finished filming, Jimmy had been onto the next piece. But this one would be different, no matter what it cost him.

It was still too early to pick up Briana, so he went home. His parents' house was empty when he got there. Dad had left early that morning, heading to Wilcox, Arizona, and hoping to come home with a White Dorper sheep to crossbreed.

Until Meredith and the wolf dog, Jimmy hadn't given too much thought to crossbreeding.

His mother was probably in town doing some last-minute shopping. She was convinced they needed two of everything for the wedding in case something went wrong.

If Jimmy ever got married again, he'd elope.

Where had that thought come from?

That reminded Jimmy. He'd gotten an email from Joe this morning. Joe and the preacher had agreed that the 26th, the day after Christmas, was a good date for the wedding. The church had allowed them to keep up Holly's décor. But

Joe wanted Jimmy to take a few photos of the inside of the church so that he and Susan could plan a few personal touches.

He still had about thirty minutes before he needed to drive to the school and pick up Briana. Heading for the kitchen, he made himself a sandwich and poured a glass of milk. Sitting at the kitchen table, he looked out the three-pane window over Murphy land. Some people, like his boss at *Nature Times*, believed Arizona was a barren desert. But the Murphy place was green, with trees and even a tiny stream that flowed at the height of monsoon season.

He'd always loved this kitchen. It wasn't like the one back at his condo. That kitchen was tiny, just a refrigerator, stove, sink and counter. Regina hadn't cooked, so they hadn't needed much.

His mother's kitchen, though, had a table that sat eight. Usually, by this time of the year, there'd be a Santa cookie jar in the center, and Christmas placemats at each chair. Danny's wedding had made Christmas into an afterthought this December.

With less than two weeks to Christmas, Jimmy really should get busy shopping. He had a list from Briana, but no idea what to get for his family.

And Meredith? It had been ten years since he'd bought her a present.

It hadn't been a Christmas present, though.

It had been an engagement ring.

No, don't go there. Take a different path down memory lane. Forget the ring, never worn, tucked away in your room.

The three-pane window looked out over a backyard filled with memories. He and his brother had once dug a hole so deep that they could stand in it up their necks. Did his daughter have such good memories? From being in Dallas with her mother while he traveled? Being with him, later, when he was on location?

That really wasn't a fair question, though, as Briana had been in mourning during her time with him.

She no longer acted like she was in mourning, though. She'd been raring to go to school this morning, had even gotten dressed without him having to nudge her. She'd been chattering about the other girls, what they were doing, wearing and playing. He was even starting to remember some of the names she kept sprouting.

His daughter was putting down roots; she'd not like it much when it came time to leave. Funny, he'd never questioned how Briana might feel about their vagabond life, he'd just assumed she loved it as much as he did.

He took a swig of milk, still gazing out the window, the past and present battling. He'd had so many dreams. Most had not come true. He'd wanted to play football. Instead, he'd discovered that he was a small-town hero and not a big-city contender. He'd met Regina and been drawn to her. She'd been exciting enough to distract him when his football career ended and when he started to miss his friends and family. She'd been a little like Meredith, always reaching for her dreams. But her dreams hadn't been quite so authentic. They'd been married a year and with a baby on the way when he'd realized that Regina liked the connections he made in his job, rather than the causes he took up.

"My husband's a filmmaker and writer," she'd say. She'd come to two shoots. Both had involved well-known Hollywood actors who'd helped sponsor an animal.

He'd built a name for himself. That was something. For a while.

Gathering his dishes, he headed for the sink and cleaned up. His mother had left the day's mail on the counter. *Nature Times* magazine was on top. Of course his mom subscribed. This might be the first issue he didn't have a byline.

He leafed through the magazine, looking at the animals in their natural habitats and skimming the words. Each article listed the numbers—how many remained in the wild, how much of their habitat was left. The writers always used the words *endangered, vulnerable* and *threatened.*

But the words and the articles were empty. Thanks to Meredith, he realized he'd been a short-term expert with no long-term commitment. He had to change that—for Meredith, and for himself.

The front door opened and a moment later his mother entered. "You're home," she said as she lay her purse on the counter and picked up the mail. "What did you do today?"

"I visited Ray and Meredith Stone this morning, went to Aqui Lobos this afternoon, and now I'm about ready to go pick up Briana."

"How is Ray?"

He noted that she didn't ask about Meredith, so he'd correct the oversight. "Funny thing, he was wandering along the road this morning. I took him home, and Meredith woke up soon after."

"How late does she sleep?"

"Mom, she and I didn't get home until two this morning. We were in Scorpion Ridge looking for Yoda, remember?"

"Yoda?"

"The wolf dog from BAA."

A tiny line formed right between his mother's eyes. Part of her wanted to jump in, ask questions, help even. But another part of her wasn't willing to accept Meredith as being back in the picture.

"I take it Yoda's fine."

"Yes, Meredith brought him home. Now she's got two wolf dogs. I haven't even told my editor yet."

His mother picked up *Nature Times*. "I'm not sure wolf dogs are the type of story your magazine runs."

He hated it when somebody told him what he already knew.

MEREDITH TOOK BOTH Yoda and Leia out for a run. Yoda stayed back, letting Leia take the lead. Leia clearly wanted off the leash and Meredith couldn't remember a time she'd been so winded after a run. Just two weeks after leaving BAA full-time and she was already out of shape.

It had to be all the pancakes she was eating.

It was close to four o'clock when she returned and perfect weather. She put Leia in the pen and left Yoda loose. He'd be fine as long as she was around. He contented himself with sniffing the premises, looking more than indignant when she scolded him for getting too close to the chickens.

Speckles, still not completely over his adventure with Leia just two days ago, scolded him, too.

Yoda cocked his head, enjoying all the attention.

Grandpa was back to watching television. Meredith headed outside. Well, one way to get into shape was to put up the outdoor Christmas decorations. She'd meant to start last week, but other things had come first: taking Grandpa to the doctor, getting Susan to the altar and discouraging Jimmy Murphy.

She was angry at herself for letting down her guard with Jimmy. She'd have to be extra vigilant when she was around him—which would be a lot in the next week as they got things ready for Susan's wedding.

"Grandpa, where's all the outdoor Christmas stuff, and what should I do first?"

"First, decide not to do it. You'll just have to take it all down in a few weeks."

"Ha-ha."

He pushed himself from the chair and came outside to look at his home of more than fifty years. "Last time I put up Christmas lights was Susan's senior year. She wanted them."

"I want them."

"I don't want to light the place up like some beacon. You never know who's out there."

"Have you had a problem with trespassers?"

He shook his head but pursed his lips. So, Meredith figured, the problem wasn't with a trespasser but with someone he knew.

"How did you get the hole in the screen door again?"

"Pepper did it. And don't ask me about it again."

Meredith was more concerned than ever, but she wouldn't get any more out of him now.

"Okay…if you say so."

She walked out the front door to stare at the small farmhouse. The weathered white paint had a few gray splotches, but the old place still looked nice. Nice and lived in. With Yoda running loose, coming to sniff at Grandpa's pants and then running off to chase butterflies—who weren't a bit afraid of him—it felt like the perfect place to be.

"All the Christmas decorations are in the shed," Grandpa said, "including the hooks that go on the gutter. Your grandmother always wanted bulbs on the flower boxes and under the side windows, too. Lord, she loved her perennials. Knew them by their fancy names too. Once, she planted some orange, yellow and red monstrosities that grew up to almost three feet before she'd let me help her repot and transplant them. Another time she planted something that must have yelled to the bees, 'Hey, come this way. All of you. Over here.'"

Meredith remembered.

To her amazement, Meredith thought Grand-ma's idea of stringing bulbs on the flower boxes might be fun. "The lights around the flowers will look nice when family starts coming," she said. "I mean, who knows how many people will be staying here when Susan gets married in two weeks."

Grandpa shook his head. "I don't want any-one staying here. I don't even want you here, remember. I wish…" His words tapered off, his expression vague.

Gone was his good mood, the shared memo-ries, the Grandpa she recognized and understood. Much too quickly his mood had changed.

She tried again. "Grandpa, what's bothering you? Why don't you want people here?"

"I'm tired. I just want to be left alone."

"Not gonna happen."

He walked away, his words coming back to her, ominous. "That's what I'm afraid of."

Meredith followed. "Grandpa, I've held down the head of a rhinoceros so he could get a shot. If there's something or someone bothering you, I can help. Really."

"You can't help."

She followed him inside, practically on his heels, waiting and hoping he'd tell her what was wrong. He settled in his favorite chair, turned on a judge show and said, "Nothing's bothering me except getting older."

Meredith decided that when he fell asleep, probably in about an hour, she'd go snooping. In the meantime, she searched for an outdoor power source. She found one on the porch, but only one. This was going to be fun and explained why Grandpa had a dozen extension cords. It took more than an hour, but Meredith checked to make sure all the bulbs still worked and the cords weren't frayed.

But Grandpa was still awake.

Next, Meredith fetched a ladder, hammer and bucket. Soon she was prying away rusty nails and whatever else got in the way. The new nails she drove in didn't quite form a straight line and she wound up with a more slipshod design: some nails high, some low, a few exactly where she meant them to be. Luckily, she didn't have any fingernails, so the only thing at risk was the rest of her body. The last thing she needed was a broken ankle or such.

Next, she started affixing the fasteners.

"Did your grandfather ask you to remove the gutters?"

Jimmy was back, and this time he had brought his daughter.

"Wow," Briana squealed. "Great dog! Is he the one who knocked down Aunt Holly?"

Looking down, Meredith had a grand view of Briana on her knees in front of Yoda. The wolf dog seemed to be smiling.

"His name is Yoda, and Leia is the one who knocked down your aunt Holly. Leia's in the barn."

As if knowing that someone wanted to meet her, Leia howled.

Shaking her hammer at Jimmy, Meredith said, "I can't believe you're back again. Have you forgotten where you live or—"

"Or maybe I just like being around you," he finished.

She made a face.

"The gutters on this house are actually fairly permanent." Jimmy was completely serious. "You could have just painted them. That's what you're doing, right? Getting ready to paint the house?"

"No, I'm putting up Grandpa's Christmas lights."

He had the good grace not to laugh. "Okay, but you do know that nails aren't what you want to use. They put holes in your house."

"Plenty of holes are already here. I just made a few more."

"They also rust and attract electricity."

"Who died and made you the Christmas-light expert?"

She'd expected a chuckle but instead got a full-blown laugh.

"How about I help you," he offered, coming to the bottom of the ladder and holding it steady. Behind him, Briana chased Yoda, who danced and howled and ran, always checking behind himself to make sure Briana was following.

Jimmy watched his daughter and Yoda for a few moments and then turned his attention back to Meredith. "Something interesting happened while I was picking Briana up from school."

"Something that involves me?" She climbed down the ladder, practically landing between his arms. She hesitated just a moment before she pushed him away.

"In a roundabout way."

She started gathering the shingles that had fallen to the ground and put them in a wheelbarrow. "Why didn't you text or call?"

"I wanted to see your face when I showed you this." He pulled his cell phone from his pocket, punched a few buttons and then showed her a picture. "This beauty was in the station wagon in front of me while I waited my turn to pick up Briana. I almost rear-ended them I was so surprised. Instead, I hurried out, explained who I was and got them to park so I could ask a few questions."

"It's a wolf dog," Meredith breathed.

"Two and a half years old. High-content. They were told the bitch was a malamute."

Briana ran by, screaming with joy, Yoda following right behind as they barreled into the tall grass behind Grandpa's house.

"Where did they get him?"

"Answered an ad in the paper. I showed them the phone number I'd been calling. They didn't recognize it. They said they'd driven up to the picnic area by Thompson Creek. They met a man, said he was probably in his late twenties to early thirties. He had three puppies and they chose this one."

"And they thought that process was okay?"

"While they were there, another family drove up and picked out a puppy. Kid told them that having a wolf dog was like having any other dog."

"They still believe that?"

"No, but they're ranchers, too, and they were able to close in an old horse pasture for Baby. That's what they named their puppy. He's the father's dog, mostly."

"What else did you ask them?"

"I asked them how much they paid."

"And?"

"Eight hundred dollars."

"Litters can run as high as seven pups. That's almost five thousand dollars a litter."

"I also," Jimmy said, "asked if they remembered the name of the breeder. They said no. I asked if they knew the other family who'd picked out a dog. All the mom could remember was that the other family had driven up from Adobe Hills."

"Maybe we need to go visit the vet you called earlier. They might be willing to give us a few names of people who have wolf dogs. We could pay them a visit, see how many look like Leia."

She realized that he'd managed to make her forget that she was angry with him. But she was interested in tracking down more wolf dogs, and there was something to the old adage "Keep your friends close, keep your enemies closer."

Leia howled again, and Yoda popped out from behind the shed and made his way over to Meredith. Briana was right behind.

"Look what I have!" she yelled. "It's a bone."

Yoda waited expectantly; surely all bones were meant for him.

"I found this one," Briana shared, "while we were digging."

"Where?" Jimmy asked slowly, moving closer to Yoda but not acting as if he was going to take the bone. Good, the man not only knew how to research but understood when to act—or in this case, not to act—based on what he'd learned.

"By the shed," Briana answered.

Jimmy took the bone from Briana, gave Yoda a respectful glance and then ran his fingers from the tip to the bottom.

"This is a femur."

Meredith felt the first stirring of dread, understanding dawning before Jimmy said his next word.

"Human."

"Like the other bone we found," she breathed. "Could there be a whole body buried under the shed?"

CHAPTER SEVENTEEN

MEREDITH STARED AT the old, yellowish bone. Jimmy half expected her to hand it to him. It was about twenty inches long, with a knob on one end and what could only be described as a ball joint on the other. It was speckled brown and white in places.

"It's probably from a horse," she said.

"No." He was sure it was human.

"Have you ever seen a human femur bone?"

"Yes, in Marrakech. I was doing a story on wild boar. We were on the outskirts of town, near a paupers' burial ground. A sandstorm uncovered some remains. One of my crew knew all about bones and identified them for us. I don't remember why he was so knowledgeable. I think his dad was a medical examiner."

Meredith made a face, then said, "I'll make a mental note not to die in Marrakech. Should we call the sheriff?"

It was her grandfather who answered, his voice strange and louder than usual. "No, just leave it be. There's bones all over this land. It means nothing."

Jimmy watched the expression on Meredith's face. It was guarded. She didn't like her grandpa's words or the tone of them.

"Yes, we need to call the sheriff," Jimmy advised. "It's a fifteen-minute drive from town, and human bones are not a typical find. The fact that this is the second one we've found is reason to be concerned."

Meredith went inside where her grandfather kept the important numbers on the refrigerator. Gesippi didn't have a police station, just an office. One officer worked six to two, the other worked two to ten. If anything happened in the middle of the night, one of the deputies from Adobe Hills took care of the call.

While Meredith called the police and then put Yoda in the barn with Leia, Jimmy went to his truck and got his camera before walking around the shed. He wanted to get down on his hands and knees and dig—do some fieldwork—but this was a possible crime scene, and he knew enough to leave it alone.

Still, he had a dozen questions circling his mind. One kept rising to the top: Was there a whole body buried here? And why was Ray taking such a hands-off stance?

Jimmy took pictures of all four sides of the

shed, paying special attention to the side still splayed open after Leia's misadventures. Besides the broken boards, the ground was torn up. What better place for a bone to appear? Leia's paws could have unearthed it and no one would have noticed.

How far down would Jimmy need to dig before finding something else? But, again, he reminded himself that law enforcement wouldn't take kindly to interference, and just because Jimmy happened to be stateside with his camera didn't mean he, wearing his reporter hat, would be welcomed.

He couldn't imagine a more unsettling place to find a human bone. And surely where there was a femur there was a foot. He wanted to find it, photograph it, solve the mystery.

His daughter, however, didn't feel the same way. Briana was in the house washing her hands for the third time. She was half thrilled that she'd get to tell her friends at school that she'd touched a human bone. The half that wasn't thrilled wanted to go home and cry.

Jimmy watched as Meredith left the barn. It didn't matter what kind of day she'd had, she managed to look in control and totally beautiful. Dusk was settling, and the giant moon seemed to throw a spotlight on her. Her blond hair shimmered in the night sky. It had long ago come out of the ponytail she insisted on wearing. Today she wore a black sweater and tight jeans. Her brown boots were designed for work. She opened the door to the porch and went in. He watched as she bent down to talk to her grandfather. Jimmy couldn't hear the words, but he could make out the tone. Meredith was trying to soothe Ray, but he was having none of it. He was agitated. Jimmy couldn't remember hearing the man act or sound so irrational.

Briana came onto the porch and sat on the arm of Grandpa's chair. She looked smaller, suddenly, and lost.

"We don't need to involve the police. This is nothing," Grandpa said for the fifth time.

Meredith met Jimmy's eyes before saying, "Grandpa, this is important. We have to find out how these human bones got onto your property."

"Human bones aren't on my property. The fool dog brought them in. Could come from as far away as that zoo of yours."

Just then, the sheriff's SUV turned into the driveway, its lights cutting across the Stone property. Meredith left the porch and waited at the bottom of the steps. Her grandpa and Jimmy's daughter stood at the top, Ray's hand on Briana's shoulder.

Ray had always had a way with children.

Stepping from the SUV, Sheriff Rafael Sala-

zar said, "Never a dull moment when you're involved, Meredith. Janie told me you were over
here taking care of your grandfather."

"I can take care of myself," Ray said.

"Grandpa, this is Sheriff Salazar from Scorpion Ridge. He's the best around. He's the one
who brought down that drug ring just last year."

"Don't need a police officer and certainly don't
need a sheriff," was Grandpa's response. "There's
no drug ring here."

Meredith paid no attention to her grandfather
and said, "I am surprised that you're taking the
call, Rafe. How did you get here so quickly?"

"We had a domestic dispute up near Mailbox
Mesa go…" His words trailed off as he noticed
Briana.

Jimmy stepped up and introduced himself,
adding, "And this is my six-year-old daughter.
She's the one who dug up the bone."

"I was digging for treasure," Briana ascer-
tained. "That's not it."

"I'll bet Yoda thought it was for him," Salazar
said. "I heard he was with you now, Meredith.
Where is he?"

"He's sequestered in the barn."

"Poor guy. Seems like lately he's been spending a lot of time alone in barns."

Now Jimmy was curious. How did the sheriff
know so much about Yoda and Meredith?

"He's not alone," Meredith said. "We've a female with him, Leia. She showed up two days ago. I think it was Leia's antics that uncovered the first bone."

"Antics?"

"She got a bit excited by all the people and chickens her first day here. Let's just say neither the chickens nor the shed will ever be the same."

Jimmy added, "Her nails tore into the ground and we think that might be where the first bone was—it was small, probably a finger. I took some pictures."

"Jimmy Murphy, huh?" Sheriff Salazar studied Jimmy much the same way Jimmy had just been studying him. "You're the guy who works for *Nature Times*."

"That piece of information gets around," Jimmy admitted.

"You were saying something about Mailbox Mesa," Meredith reminded Salazar, lowering her voice.

Salazar glanced at the porch. Briana had settled down on the front step. She leaned against the wall and looked as if she wasn't paying attention. Nevertheless, Salazar also lowered his voice. "I was helping with a domestic dispute. Husband and wife were fighting. She called us. We got there shortly after he set the house on fire with her in it."

"You get her out in time?" Meredith asked.

"Her and their two children, along with three cats and four dogs."

"Any wolf dogs?" Jimmy asked.

"Didn't know to ask, but none were as big as Yoda. Why do you ask?"

"There seems to be a lot of wolf dogs in that area," Jimmy said.

Sheriff Salazar raised one eyebrow, then went back to the issue at hand. "Let's see this bone."

Meredith retrieved it from the porch, walking around her grandfather, who didn't move out of her way.

The sheriff didn't hesitate to touch the bone, turning it this way and that. Then he wrapped it back in the towel Meredith had put it in.

"Could be human. This close to Mailbox Mesa, I wouldn't be surprised. But it could simply be from a horse, and truthfully, that's more likely. I know the forensic anthropologist in Tucson. I'll give her a call."

"You have to do that often? Send bones in for testing?" Jimmy asked.

"I haven't found any bones in my county, human or otherwise," Salazar said, "until now."

Salazar's cell phone rang. Soon, he was talking to his wife and it became clear that Meredith and Salazar's wife were acquainted.

"No, you don't need to come out here," Salazar

said into his phone. "Meredith's with family and friends. She's fine. I'll call you before I leave."

"He's married to a friend of mine," Meredith said, coming to stand beside Jimmy. "I helped with his wedding just a year ago."

Jimmy nodded. Seemed there were lots of weddings lately in his old stomping grounds.

"Janie, his wife, was kidnapped and taken to Mailbox Mesa."

That got Jimmy's attention. His mother had mailed him an article from the newspaper about the events. Now he wished he'd taken a few hours to research the story a bit more. He just remembered smiling at the line his mother had added about being glad Jimmy wasn't in Gesippi, as crime was getting out of hand.

He'd been in Ukraine, where a whole culture was contemplating civil war while Jimmy photographed and wrote about the brown bear.

"The last five years, we've had too many strange occurrences between Gesippi and Scorpion Ridge," Salazar said. "It's to the point I investigate everything that happens in the county."

"I've got something else for you to investigate," Meredith said. She quickly filled him in on Leia and the wolf dog saga. "I want to find the family who purchased the other wolf dog pup. That might lead me to the breeder. Could be a man named Paul Livingston. He's up to something, and it's hurting animals. And…" She hesitated, then, "I find it odd that Yoda dug up a bone so quickly after Leia showed up here. Add to that the families having to drive to Thompson Creek, right next door to Mailbox Mesa, to get the pups. Then, you happen to be in Mailbox Mesa right when we need you. You said the family had dogs? Maybe they're wolf dogs."

"You're grasping at straws. The sheriff already said that the animals didn't resemble Yoda," Jimmy responded.

"I wouldn't be so quick to dismiss it, though," Salazar responded. "There are connections everywhere, and we're just seeing them."

"You think there's a possibility these human bones are connected to the wolf dog pups?"

"Nothing is coincidence," Salazar said. "There's a reason all this is happening now. Kid found a wallet more than a week ago with two thousand dollars in it. No one's come forward to claim it. Your grandfather's phone number was on a piece of paper folded inside. We still don't know why. Things keep popping up, little markers in the desert leading to a crime."

SOON ENOUGH, RAFAEL finished walking the Stone land. "I'll be back tomorrow when it's daylight. Right now, I want to head to the station and run Paul Livingston's name through the system. Then

I'll spend some time talking to the guy from Mailbox Mesa. My deputy took him into Adobe Hills for lockup. The wife and kids went to stay with a friend."

Rafael turned to Meredith, "I'm glad you called me. I'll use the wolf dog angle. It gives me even more of an excuse to knock on some doors."

Jimmy had a wide-eyed look on his face that Meredith remembered from high school. It was an act. He was hoping feigning innocence would trick somebody into spelling out the whole story for him. This time, however, no one knew the whole story.

"I'm doubtful the wolf dogs had anything to do with the bones, other than finding them. The bones have probably been there for years."

"Not true," Salazar said. "If that bone had been on Stone property for any length of time, you or one of the dogs would have found it sooner. It's a recent addition."

"But not a recent death," Jimmy started. "The bone's too clean, and the color is—"

"The wolf dog brought the bone here," Ray said, even though Meredith had already said that wasn't possible. "This has nothing to do with us."

Meredith wasn't sure what to think except that she had enough responsibilities here in Gesippi without adding Grandpa's house as a crime scene to the list.

Meredith was baffled at Grandpa's stance. The Grandpa she knew and understood would be standing with Rafe and Jimmy, questioning and marveling.

There was no mystery to why Rafe wanted to connect the bones to other cases he was working on. He was hoping they'd trace back to Mailbox Mesa so he could use them as keys to unlock a few cases there. Understandable.

Jimmy alone thought the bone belonged on Stone land. But he wanted to find the rest of the body so he could write a story, document a case, never mind who got hurt.

"I'm tired," Grandpa said. "It's time for you all to go home."

"You go on inside, Mr. Stone, rest," the sheriff said. "Meredith and Jimmy can answer the rest of my questions."

Grandpa harrumped and just followed them anyway. Jimmy looked at Meredith and then back to Briana on the porch. After a moment, he went to the porch and sat by his daughter.

Rafael turned to Grandpa. "What's the strangest thing you've found on your property in the last ten years?"

"A two-headed rattlesnake." Ray didn't hesitate.

"What about wolves or wolf dogs? You know anything about them?"

"Just what my granddaughter tells me."

"How do you chase trespassers away?"

Meredith noticed that Rafe asked "how" not "if." Her grandpa, unfortunately, didn't catch on to the misdirection.

"Right now, I ignore them."

"Grandpa, you always go out and talk them to death," Meredith tried to lighten the mood. Being outside this late, looking for human bones was not in her comfort zone. The night was too quiet, too still. Rafe told them where to stand and made his way to the shed, the beam of his flashlight bobbing up and down.

"How many people have been this way?"

"Today?"

"That's the best place to start."

Jimmy answered from the porch, his voice echoing in the late-night wind. "My daughter, Briana, was playing with Yoda in this area for a good hour before she dug up the bone."

"Were any of you over here?"

"I took some pictures but didn't touch anything," Jimmy admitted.

"I've been over there off and on since Leia joined our family. I needed to fix the damage she caused," Meredith said.

"Wolf dogs can do a lot of damage," Salazar agreed.

"You don't seem surprised that we're finding so many wolf dogs, or that they might be connected to a crime," Jimmy noted.

Salazar looked at Meredith before saying, "Animals around these parts seem to have a way of getting into trouble."

"And not just wolf dogs," Meredith said. "A few years ago we had two young bears over at BAA. Crisco, a black bear, was found with his head stuck between the posts of a fence. Luke helped get him loose with the help of a jar of Crisco, thus his name. Before that, we had Scoot, who was dropped off out front..." Her words tapered off as she glanced at Jimmy. He already had way too many man-versus-nature stories where man was the bad guy.

"Out front of where?" Jimmy asked.

But, man was also the good guy in this example. "Of BAA. We get animals dropped off there all the time. Guess some people are smart enough to realize that not all wild animals belong in the wild."

Jimmy decided to ignore her dig. "Go on about Scoot."

"Someone had declawed him, but they'd done a hatchet job and had fed him improperly. He died."

"We've always thought he and Crisco were from the same mother," Salazar added.

"You want to connect them to the wolf dogs, too?" Jimmy asked.

Meredith had a quick response. "You can make a few thousand dollars on a good litter of wolf pups. A bear's gallbladder can earn you a lot more."

"So," Jimmy said, "this supports my earlier argument. Mankind surely knows how to make money off of caged wild animals."

"But," Meredith flipped back, "we don't rescue wild animals in order to cage them. We rescue abused animals in the hope that we can return them to the wild."

"Only it wasn't humane to release either Crisco or Scoot back into the wild."

"That's right…" Meredith said, surprised at his words.

He just smiled. "I'm learning."

Before anything else could be said, another car pulled into the circular driveway. Jimmy's mother got out and came over. He had called her earlier and she'd offered to pick up his daughter. Briana left the porch and hurried to her grandmother. "I touched a human bone, Grandma. When we get home, I'm taking a bath."

"Everything okay, Ray?" Debbie asked.

"Maybe." Grandpa stared at Meredith and

Jimmy. "It's sure heating up around here for the middle of December."

It was the sanest thing Ray had said since they'd found the bone.

CHAPTER EIGHTEEN

THE PHONE RANG at nine the next morning. Once again, Meredith raised her head, sleep deprived and grumpy, looked at the clock and frowned. If she kept this up, she'd soon be sleeping until noon.

The smell of pancakes convinced her to get out of bed. The sound of Grandpa on the phone got her moving a little faster. After pulling on a pair of jeans and shrugging into a button-down shirt, she headed for the kitchen, where Grandpa stood at the stove, the phone back in its cradle.

"You have a checkup in town today, right? Was that the doctor's office calling to confirm?"

"Why would they call to confirm? I've never missed an appointment. Of course, this visit is a complete waste of time. I feel fine. If an old man goes to the doctor every time he falls, soon he'll be spending all this days at the doctor's."

"Maybe the person belonging to that bone we found didn't go to the doctor enough," Meredith said, still grumpy herself.

Grandpa frowned at her.

"It wasn't just that you fell," Meredith continued. "You were a mile away from the house and—"

"And looking for your wolf dog. The one I fed this morning."

No wonder Yoda and Leia hadn't woken her up with their howling. Grandpa had saved the day. And, best of all, the dogs hadn't knocked him down.

"If the doctor says I'm fine," Grandpa said, "then I want you to go back to your job, full-time, and stop worrying about me."

"The fall is only one thing, Grandpa. There're a few other things, too. The house needs attention and—" What she really should have mentioned was the hole in the screen door and the human bones.

"I can hire someone for that." Grandpa took the frying pan from the burner and turned toward the sink. He paused for a minute, looking out the window past his property line and toward the area he'd gone missing that first day.

"What's out there, Grandpa? What has you so out of sorts? Are you worried because of the bones? Why do you keep trying to get me to leave?"

Grandpa shook his head. "I'm not out of sorts. I'm not worried. Nothing you need to concern yourself with. I'm just used to being alone, is all."

Now, *that* was a lie. Grandpa had been married sixty-plus years. He'd raised a son, and had taken in his grandchildren off and on over the last twenty years.

Meredith wasn't about to leave. Grandpa needed her. And when Zack got here tonight, she was going to press him to help her. It wasn't like Grandpa to try to shove people out the door. He'd always been a come-on-in kind of guy.

"Who was on the phone?" Meredith asked.

"Jimmy. He was heading to the train station in Adobe Hills. Guess they have some family coming in for the wedding. He wanted to know if we were all right."

For a moment, Meredith was annoyed that Jimmy had called Grandpa's landline instead of her cell phone. But that didn't make any sense. She didn't owe Jimmy anything and he shouldn't worry about her.

"I'll be working on the gutters again today," Meredith said. "Monday, I'll start painting. On Tuesday, all the girls in Susan's wedding party are getting together and heading into Phoenix. We'll be trying on bridesmaid dresses. She's getting married in just two weeks. You know that, right, Grandpa?"

"Seems awful quick."

Meredith agreed, especially since she was the one in charge of "awful quick." Good thing Holly was willing to share the decorations from her wedding.

An hour later, Meredith chauffeured Grandpa into town. Like last time, she escorted him into Doc Thomas's waiting room. And, like last time, once Grandpa was settled in, she headed for the old library.

Agatha was sitting at her desk searching the internet. At first, Meredith thought the aged librarian hadn't heard her enter, but soon Agatha said, "Find a seat, find a seat. I'm just trying to figure out what audiobooks to order. Used to be I kept ten bestsellers on hand for people to check out and listen to. They'd last a year. Lately, though, folks have been checking out about ten a month, and people keep asking for more."

"More people driving back and forth between Gesippi and a bigger town for work?" Meredith asked.

"I think so. Now, how can I help you?"

"Did you hear about the wolf dog I have out at Grandpa's?"

"Yes, and I heard that Yoda, the wolf dog you had at BAA, is out at your grandfather's place, too," Agatha said. "He got into some kind of trouble?"

"He escaped his enclosure, probably looking for me, and wound up on a neighbor's property. He went after one of their dogs."

"Jimmy says it's the second time Yoda's gotten into trouble."

"When did you talk to Jimmy?"

"He was here this morning. A lot of people in Gesippi are concerned about the wolf dogs. They worry a kid might get hurt."

"Yoda wouldn't hurt anyone. Jimmy knows that. Briana and Yoda played for hours last night."

"And that's when you found the second bone," Agatha said.

Jimmy must have been chatty this morning. The *Gesippi Gazette* wasn't due out for five more days, yet the story had already reached its audience.

"Jimmy says it's human. I hope it's from a horse. I mean, if there were human bones so easily accessible on Grandpa's property, we'd have found them years ago when we played in the dirt."

"Lots of bones in the desert. Many of them are human."

"What do you mean?"

"In the Arizona desert, death happens all too often. A few years ago the *Gazette* ran a story about immigrants from Mexico. It claimed that one dies each day trying to cross the border."

"If a wolf dog carried the bone to Grandpa's house, it wouldn't have been Yoda. He's not been off the property. It would have had to have been Leia."

"The one you found."

"The one Holly and I found, yes, but it's more like she found us. Or, rather, Grandpa's chickens."

"Then maybe she brought the bone in."

"So you're saying Leia might have found the bone of someone who died years ago trying to cross the border and carried it to Grandpa's shed?"

"I've been thinking about it all morning. He or she might not have been dead all that long. The desert's not kind to the dead. What the heat doesn't melt, the buzzards cart away."

"I just don't buy it," Meredith said, wondering when Agatha had become so fixated on death. "Leia could eat the bone whole. Plus, Grandpa's land is not close to the border or close to the interstate. It's not part of the well-trafficked corridor."

"You're probably right. But prepare to hear all kinds of speculation in town," Agatha warned. "Herb Taylor thinks this is proof that a drug ring still exists in our own backyard."

"All from two bones?"

"More from the fact that we had that major drug bust last year. He's still mad that he worked on a committee with that teacher and never suspected her of being a criminal."

It was all Meredith could do to keep her jaw from dropping. It was a small world, indeed. She'd had a connection to that drug bust, too. Janie, one of her best friends, had turned in the first evidence that had led to the arrests.

What had Rafael said last night?

No coincidences.

Now Meredith had a wolf dog and two human bones.

The best place to start was the wolf dog.

"I'm trying to trace Leia's lineage. It seems this area has a healthy wolf dog population. And one name keeps popping up—Paul Livingston. Jimmy searched online but can't seem to find anything on the man. I thought maybe you'd be able to help."

Agatha's fingers started trembling and she took them off the keyboard. For a moment, she looked uncertain.

"You know the name?" Meredith accused.

"I think so."

"Think?"

"You ever meet Victor Lucas, the man who owns the Crooked Feather Indian Trading Post across the street?"

"No, but his daughter Kristi was in my grade. She dropped out junior year."

"There's no reason for you to have met Victor. A trading post is not really a place teenagers hang out," Agatha said. "I remember feeling lucky that you still came to see me every three weeks when your library books were due."

"I came more than that!"

Agatha smiled. "You did. But, back to Victor Lucas. I used to wonder how he kept the place going at all. He sells mostly junk. He claimed it was Native American but no one believed him. A few years ago, he reorganized and had a grand reopening. Now, not only does he seem to have a lot of Native heirlooms, it seems the man's become an artist. He makes kachinas. They're quite good."

"I've seen them at the Drug and Dine," Meredith remembered. "They are good."

"He comes to all the town meetings and has quite a bit to say about things. He complains about taxes. And don't get him started on paying BOA dues."

Meredith decided not to ask what BOA stood for.

"Well," Agatha continued, "here's what's got me concerned. I've met his wife. She helps out at the store sometimes, and I try to go over there when I know he's not around. She barely says boo but she loves to read. So I used to take her some books, lend them to her without him knowing. I get the idea Victor keeps her on a short leash."

"So short she can't get to the library?" Meredith couldn't tolerate someone wielding that much control over her.

"Not everyone's as lucky as us," Agatha reminded. "Raised with love, surrounded by the type of family that steps in when needed."

As a teen, Meredith had occasionally confided in Agatha about what it was like for her at home, with her mother and father working constantly. Agatha had listened, not judging, and allowed the library to become another home for Meredith.

"Once, Maude gave me one of her personal books by accident when she was returning the ones I'd lent her."

So far, what Agatha had shared didn't seem too informative. "I'm not getting the connection. What does this have to do with Paul Livingston?"

"I'm getting there. Inside that book was a photo that she seemed to have been using as a bookmark. The picture was of three young men and one young lady. When I turned it over, I noticed that someone had written the names on the back. Two of the young men had the last name of Lucas. Her sons. The other two names were Kristi and Paul Livingston."

"Kristi married a man named Paul Livingston?

That's great. Well, not really, not for Kristi, but I can just go over and ask—"

"No, you can't. Since I returned the photo, she's not accepted any of the books I've offered. And real soon after, she had a black eye. I don't know if it's connected to her accidentally giving me the book, or me going over there and questioning her, or what. But it was real clear from the moment I gave her back the photo that she was afraid."

"All because of a family photo?"

Agatha stood, walked to the stairway and headed upstairs. Meredith followed. In the time they'd been talking, no one had ventured into the library. It was quiet. Agatha opened the door; the wind almost shut it before she could step outside.

A tumbleweed blew down the street, getting caught in the undercarriage of Herb Taylor's Cadillac parked at the barbershop. The Drug and Dine was doing a brisk business. The Crooked Feather Indian Trading Post had an orange open sign in the door, but the windows were dark. Funny, Meredith had never noticed how unwelcoming the store was.

"Has it always been that dark?"

"Yes. No one in the photo was smiling. They did not appear to be a happy family. But the guy named Paul Livingston, he looked downright mean, and I realized I'd seen him a few times."

"Where?"

"He's always unloading his old black truck, handing stuff off to Victor."

"That doesn't sound suspicious," Meredith remarked. "Maybe his job is going around and buying Native American art."

"Maybe," Agatha agreed, "but why do I only see them unloading his truck when it's late at night, usually midnight?"

"What are you doing up at midnight?"

"I've always had a hard time sleeping. Of course, I've not spotted the young man or his truck in a while."

"How long?"

"It's been at least six months." Age certainly wasn't slowing Agatha down.

"You've got a good memory."

Agatha smiled. "You want to know why I remember it? It's because your brother was in that day. I was helping him find textbooks. He was starting a new college class and worried about costs."

That would be like Zack. Her schooling had cost plenty, but she was slowly paying her grandfather back. But Zack, aiming for med school, would need triple what Meredith had spent.

"Maybe I'll go over there, to the store."

"And do what? If you ask questions, they'll clam up."

"For now, I'll just go in and buy something."

"I still think they'll suspect your motives."

"I do need to buy a wedding present for Danny. He's getting married tomorrow. It's the perfect excuse."

Agatha had the good grace not to mention that ten years ago Agatha had been the one buying a present for Danny Murphy's wedding.

For Meredith.

IN THE BACK of his truck, Jimmy had enough bottled water to fill a pool. He'd also found the tablecloths his soon-to-be sister-in-law wanted. He'd grabbed extra, too, because Joe and Susan wanted a Christmas wedding, and if Jimmy didn't buy them now, he'd just be hunting for them later.

Funny, Joe hadn't called since Monday night.

The wind concerned him. He hoped it didn't turn into a December storm, not with his brother's wedding tomorrow. As he stopped at the town's one traffic light, he noted Agatha Fitzsimmons standing on the front step of the courthouse. Her skirt blew with the same whipped determination as the American flag just to her left.

The library would still be open. He continued to drive by, crediting Agatha's standing in the doorway to a whimsical desire to admire Gesippi's Christmas decorations. But then he noticed Meredith's SUV parked nearby.

He knew Meredith used Agatha much the same way he did: for information. So where was she?

He should have called her the moment he woke up this morning, asked her about the dogs and the bones and her grandfather. He'd started to. But he couldn't think of what to say. Truthfully, all he'd wanted to ask was how was she doing? What was she doing? When would he get to see her again? Could she forgive him? Could they have a second chance?

Instead, he'd called Ray just to make sure everything was okay. And Ray said everything was fine.

It wasn't.

His timing couldn't be worse. His brother was about to marry the girl of his dreams. And Jimmy didn't need to cause a rift because he couldn't stop thinking about the girl that had one time dominated both their dreams.

Still, whatever was going on with the wolf dogs and the bones, Jimmy and Meredith were in it together.

He parked in front of the courthouse, and, skipping every other step in his hurry, he climbed the eight marble stairs until he joined Agatha.

"You trying to decide who on the street has been naughty or nice?" He stuck his hands in his pockets and pretended to be as interested in the street sights as she was.

He didn't notice anything out of the ordinary.

"You never were a comedian," Agatha deadpanned. "Always so concerned about what you could and could not do."

Well, she certainly knew how to put him in his place.

Immediately, she apologized. "I'm sorry. I'm just worried. Meredith's been in Lucas's store almost thirty minutes, and I'm concerned."

"Been in where?"

"The Crooked Feather Indian Trading Post. I told her that Paul Livingston was probably married to Victor Lucas's daughter, and she decided to check out the store. I should have gone with her."

Jimmy frowned. "I'll go in and see."

"Don't you be gone for more than thirty minutes," she advised. "I don't need to be worried about both of you."

Jimmy left his vehicle in the city hall parking lot and crossed the street. He'd never entered the Crooked Feather, mostly because he wasn't a shopper. Should a birthday or holiday come around, he was more a gift-card kind of guy.

When Jimmy got to the door, he held it open as a man and woman—clearly tourists—exited. Everything about the couple proclaimed they had money, from the turquoise belt loop the man wore to the squash-blossom necklace she wore.

Jimmy hadn't seen a squash-blossom necklace since his grandmother died.

Entering the trading post, Jimmy paused, letting his eyes adjust. The place was full of stock and not in a good way. One wall held all kinds of shoes, from beaded moccasins to leather boots. Giant orange sale stickers were on almost every pair. Judging by the dust, the sale had been going on a long time. Another wall displayed dolls of varying sizes, all with feathers and fringes and/ or headdresses. On a rack in the middle of the store was a collection of fake bows and arrows, cowboy guns complete with holsters and such. The last wall displayed baskets, rugs and etched pottery.

Some kind of flute music played on the CD player behind the cash register. Jimmy figured if he looked hard enough, he'd find the recordings on sale.

But nothing Jimmy saw should have appealed to the couple just leaving.

He paused long enough to let the music fade into background noise and heard Meredith's voice. Following the sound, he headed for the rear of the store and entered a partially opened door marked Private that took him into a second, much smaller room.

This room was very different from the main room. It was clean and bright, and featured expensive jewelry and antiques.

"I inherited a slave bracelet from my grandmother," Meredith was saying to an older man standing beside her. She was fingering something she held in her hand. Today she wore a black silky top and matching knit sweater. Her jeans were hip-huggers. The same work boots she'd worn yesterday adorned her feet, but on her, they were almost sexy.

The older man, Jimmy estimated he was around sixty, frowned at Jimmy. "I don't usually open this room to the public. This is by special invitation."

"He's with me, Mr. Lucas," Meredith said.

"And you received a special invitation?" Jimmy asked Meredith.

"No, I just followed another couple in here. They were looking at a Navajo cross necklace."

Lucas didn't seem happy about either Meredith's or Jimmy's misadventures.

Jimmy made a mental note to check out the man's prices. He figured the items in this room went for top dollar. Lucas confirmed Jimmy's speculation. "This room caters to true collectors. I put a lot of time into finding just the right pieces to display. Most people walking in off the street wouldn't be interested in either the articles I sell here or the prices."

"I'm looking at the slave bracelets," Meredith told Jimmy. "My grandma said slave bracelets weren't Native American at all, so I'm curious why they're here."

Lucas didn't roll his eyes, but Jimmy could tell he wanted to. Instead, he said, "They're here because they sell, and they sell well."

"Because they're made out of turquoise and silver," Meredith agreed. "But you shouldn't tout them as Native American. It's misleading."

"The slave bracelets in the main room are made out of silver and turquoise," Lucas said. "And I buy them on the reservation, so it's quite legitimate to say they are Native American. The one in here—I only have the one, and it's extremely rare—is made of diamonds and gold. You're right. It's not made by Native Americans. This particular gem came from South Africa. It would look quite nice on your hand."

Jimmy knew a bit about the diamond business in Africa. It often wasn't a pretty story.

"Mr. Lucas—"

"It's curious," the man said, "that both of you know my name and we've not been introduced."

"You're a business owner," Jimmy said. "Your name's not a secret."

"I told you," Meredith said, "I went to school with Kristi."

"Kristi's never mentioned you."

"It's been ten years," Meredith said. "I'm in town taking care of my grandfather. I've always meant to check your place out. Now seemed as good a time as any."

"And you're in the market for a diamond-and-gold slave bracelet?"

To Jimmy's surprise, Meredith was quite the actor, and the look she gave the jewelry actually indicated that she was indeed in the market.

She responded, "Not for the price you're asking, at least not for a Christmas present. Do you have something that's of better quality than what's in the main room but not quite so—"

"How much is it?" Jimmy asked.

"Five thousand, two hundred and fifty-three dollars," Victor said.

Jimmy nonchalantly glanced around the room. He didn't like what he saw. He'd actually spent a few months in a small South American village. He'd been filming the golden lion tamarin. One evening he'd dined with a local reporter who was doing a story on antique collectors who would do anything—including rob the graves of the dead—for certain goods that could fetch hefty prices. He'd advised Jimmy to be very wary of any antique dealers that were selling items such as ceramic pottery, baskets, fetishes, textiles and even clothing without being able to account for their origin. Dealers like Victor Lucas.

"Where did you get this?" Jimmy pointed to a mask in a locked case. "I've never seen anything like it." On top of the mask was what Jimmy suspected was the remnants of animal fur. The mask's face might have been made out of tree bark, with zigzag carvings on the cheeks and nose. Something red jutted down from where the tongue would be.

"It's a nightway mask, extremely rare."

Jimmy believed the man. The price was in the five digits. "Meredith, did you see anything in the main room that you'd like to purchase?"

"No." Meredith handed the slave bracelet to Mr. Lucas and said, "Tell Kristi I said hi and that I'm looking forward to meeting her husband and…how many kids does she have?"

"One, and she and Paul are no longer together."

As Jimmy hurried Meredith from the trading post, he heard Victor Lucas mutter, "Good riddance."

He could have been referring to Paul Livingston's departure from Victor's daughter's life.

Or he could have been referring to Jimmy and Meredith.

CHAPTER NINETEEN

"I'M GLAD YOU showed up. I was getting spooked," Meredith said mournfully once they'd returned to the library. "How on earth did you figure out I was in there?"

"I saw your car and then went to talk to Agatha. She was worried," Jimmy said. He took a seat next to Meredith at one of the library study tables. They'd done their homework here a time or two. Well, Meredith had done her homework; he'd copied her answers. His thank-yous had been in the form of kisses. He was bigger now, a man, could do his own work, and took up a lot more space. She liked having him next to her, so close she could touch him, smell him, dream of him.

What a morning. She'd marched into the trading post all curious and willing to conquer. Being alone in there, in a tiny back room full of items belonging to the long dead, had made her feel very vulnerable.

Until Jimmy showed up.

Yes, he hadn't been totally honest with her about the trip to the rescue, but over the past few days she'd gotten glimpses of the changes in Jimmy. He wasn't the narrow-focused teen or the close-minded journalist he'd once been. He'd made some concessions. But now the bigger question was, could she do the same?

He took a tiny notebook out of his pocket and wrote for a moment. "Here's what we've learned. Paul and Kristi are now separated, and Lucas has a private room that only a select few are invited into."

"People who have too much money to spend." Meredith scooted over so she could read what he'd written and watch him sketch the mask.

"Collectors," Agatha said, coming out from the back room where she'd been resting. "It makes sense now how Lucas has been able to stay in business all these years. He probably has a pretty good mail-order business under a different name. Interesting about Paul. And to think of all the times I saw that old black truck of his parked in the back and both those men unloading things."

Jimmy held up his drawing. "Agatha, you ever see anything that looks like this?"

"A sacred mask," Agatha said in wonder.

"It was ugly." Meredith had forgotten that Jimmy could draw. It was just one more thing he was good at.

Agatha swiveled her chair to the computer and started punching keys. In a moment, she said,

"I was right. It is sacred. It's called a nightway mask. It's not one you're likely to come across often. Most Native American tribes have tried to discourage nightway masks being displayed in museums due to Native American traditions."

"Traditions," Meredith encouraged.

"The only people who should see a nightway mask are Native Americans who've gone through a certain ceremony. How utterly amazing that Victor Lucas would have one in his shop. It must be a copy."

"It seemed old," Meredith said.

Jimmy stroked the drawing with one finger. "It's not a copy. It's the real thing. I'd stake my career on it."

"We should mention this to the sheriff," Meredith said.

A minute later, Jimmy put a piece of paper in front of her and instructed her to write down any item she remembered from the private room.

"The only item that didn't fit the Native American theme," he told Agatha, "was a slave bracelet that had a South African design."

Jimmy had given Agatha a job, too. First, he wanted all the information she could find on nightway masks. Then, he wanted a picture of Paul Livingston. Surely Agatha knew someone who knew someone who knew the whole Lucas clan.

"On Monday," Jimmy said, "I intend to drive out near Thompson Creek. It's time to track down Livingston's black truck. It seems to follow that he'd be selling the wolf dog pups around his home."

"Monday," Meredith reminded him, "you'll be working on the farm. Danny will be on his honeymoon by then. It's why you're here, right?"

"Right," he said slowly. "Chores first, story last."

He looked somewhat forlorn.

"It's not forever," she soothed. "Just two weeks."

His expression didn't change and she remembered that he'd said his job was on the line if his editor didn't go for the wolf dog story.

"I'll finish my list at home. I need to go see if Grandpa's finished his doctor's appointment."

"I'll have a stack of information for you tonight, Jimmy," Agatha said. "There're articles about the nightway mask, but they're few and far between. Getting a photo of Paul Livingston will take even longer. The name is as common as John Smith."

"I'm going to pick Briana up from school and then do a little research into that slave bracelet. It didn't belong in that back room. I wonder how Lucas came to have it?"

"Lucas is not a purist," Agatha said. "He might

have built his reputation on Native American artifacts, but he'll take anything that will bring him money."

"Not many trading posts deal with rare artifacts," Jimmy said. "I've never been in one that had a private room where items cost tens of thousands of dollars."

"Now I want to see this room," Agatha said.

"No!" Meredith and Jimmy said together. Jimmy finished with, "It's bad enough that both Meredith and I showed up today. If you go traipsing over, he'll really suspect something's up."

Before either of them could say more, a rumble sounded in the distance. Then wind hit the building. Meredith grabbed her purse and headed for the stairs. Grandpa had weathered many a storm, but she needed to get him home and take care of the animals. Plus, the sheriff had mentioned stopping by. Zack would be there soon so she could head to Scorpion Ridge and to work at BAA this weekend.

Behind her, Jimmy was talking to Agatha. "Call me if you need me when the library closes."

"I won't need you. It's a two-minute walk to my house. I've been praying for rain." She didn't stop there. "I think I like it when you two are on the same side," Agatha said. "It makes things a whole lot easier."

BRIANA WAS MORE than excited about the wedding when he picked her up from school. She chatted nonstop about wearing her flower-girl dress and carrying flowers and having all the bridesmaids and bride and grandmas wear the Rainbow Loom bracelets she'd made.

She wasn't as enthralled with the ring bearer. He was a boy in her class and apparently he picked his nose.

"I'm not going to touch him," Briana informed Jimmy.

That night, he put aside his thoughts on Paul Livingston and wolf dogs and nightway masks to focus on the last wedding practice.

The whole family, including some cousins Jimmy hadn't seen in decades, had gathered in the living room before heading to the church for the rehearsal. Jimmy's mother was busy making sure everyone had what they needed.

Danny looked ready to throw up.

Jimmy's wedding had happened so fast, he'd not had a chance to get nervous.

"Holly's called three times," Danny told his mother. "She and her family and friends are already at the church."

Debbie gave Jimmy a dirty look. He'd been the one to show up late. Then, there'd been introductions. And Briana had been desperate to show everyone the bracelets she'd made. Plus, she had to get enough rubber bands to make a few more for newfound relatives.

"There are no kids here," she whispered to Jimmy. "Am I the only one?"

"Until your uncle Danny decides to take his turn," Jimmy said.

Now Danny really looked as if he would throw up.

It was after six when they finally left the farm. Luckily, it was just a fifteen-minute drive into town. The lights were on in the Stone place as he drove by. Meredith's SUV was in the driveway. She should have left for Scorpion Ridge a good hour ago. The dust storm had faded to nothing. He'd call her later, see if something was wrong.

The moment they walked into the church, Danny stopped looking nervous. Just the sight of Holly did the trick. His only comment as he walked to his almost-bride was, "We should have eloped."

"I suggested that, remember?" Holly said.

"I'd have disowned you," Jimmy's mother quickly interjected.

Jimmy's dad, usually quiet, agreed. "You only get married once."

"We hope," one of his aunts muttered.

The rehearsal went perfectly.

Afterward, the entire party moved to the Hospitable. A few people gave toasts, a few people got tipsy, one of them being Danny, who really didn't drink.

Jimmy sent Briana home with his mother and helped Danny into his truck.

"Boy, I hope you don't have a killer headache tomorrow."

"I werwon't," Danny made up a word.

The night was velvet, little trace of the dust storm left.

Danny threw his arm around Jimmy in a way he'd not done since they'd been on the high school football team together. "You should have married Meredith."

Jimmy stopped. "What!"

"She only ever loved you. I wouldn't have made her happy."

"But you—"

"I know. After you left, I wanted things to stay the same. We always had so much fun. I just didn't realize that without you, there was no 'we'."

"I'm sorry. She did love you—"

"Shh," Danny said. "I never held a grudge. Truth is, I was kinda relieved when she took off. I just wish she'd have done it before the actual day. I sure hated facing a crowd, especially a crowd that felt sorry for me. That was what took me a while to get over."

"Things happen for a reason," Jimmy countered. Jimmy wasn't sure if his younger self would have made Meredith happy, either. It had taken him this long—and the example of his brother and Holly—to understand what true love really meant.

CHAPTER TWENTY

THE DUST STORM barely graced the town of Ge-sippi with its presence—not so Grandpa's house, just outside the town's limits. The Christmas lights that Meredith had hung were no longer attached to the house. They looked as if reindeer had tangled them in their hooves attempting to play jump rope.

Yoda had gotten scared and now lay in the middle of the living room watching Meredith's every move. She marveled at how right he looked—alert, happy. She paused from her work to rough up the gray fur at the nap of his neck.

"Nothing's going right," Grandpa muttered, as Meredith swept dust out the front door. "Still wish you'd go to work."

"When I called, Katie said they were just fine without me. I decided to take off until the new year. With Susan getting married and all, I need the time. What's worse is I probably should go to Danny and Holly's wedding tomorrow just so I can see what Susan and Joe's wedding should look like."

"I got married that fast."

"You what?"

"Got married in just three weeks."

"That's right," Meredith remembered. "You were shipping out to Korea."

"Lots of couples got married in haste then. Difference was, we did it in front of a justice of the peace. We didn't try to have a full-blown event, expecting family to do the preparations."

"Grandma was an only child, right?"

"What's that got to do with it?"

"She didn't have a sister like me to help her."

"Not too many sisters are like you. You try to do too much, always have."

Meredith pushed the last of the dirt over the doorstop and came back into the kitchen. She'd made hot dogs earlier, and Grandpa had eaten one without complaint.

"Where's your tree?"

"In the shed your dog destroyed. Probably covered with dust now because there's a big hole in the shed letting the elements in."

Meredith paid him no mind and headed for the shed. She found the box for the Christmas tree and carried it inside, happy it was awkward more than heavy. When they were kids, they'd go out near Bandit Hideaway and chop down a tree. A moment after they'd gotten it up in the living room, Grandpa would be sitting in his chair offering ornament-hanging advice and memories, Rowdy curled at his feet.

Turned out, some things never changed. "You made that Leggs egg nativity when you were but three" was his first offering after she'd put the tree together, followed by "Your dad painted Santa Claus pictures on all those papier-mâché ornaments."

Meredith couldn't imagine her father doing anything artistic. He'd never so much as colored with her.

"Susan preferred doing things with egg cartons. Annoyed your grandmother because Susan would snatch the cartons Sandy had saved for gathering eggs."

Meredith remembered.

"Zack painted that clothespin reindeer pink because it was your mom's favorite color."

Now, *that* was something Meredith didn't remember. But then, Zack had always been the nurturer. Then the memory came. Meredith combing Susan's hair while Zack sat at the kitchen table. He'd been drawing a picture for their mother using every shade of pink crayon he could find. Meredith had thought it silly. Susan wanted Zack to color her one, too.

Zack had fallen asleep before their mother had gotten home. Meredith had put the picture in a kitchen drawer.

Maybe it was still there.

And, if Meredith really thought about it, maybe some of the jewelry Dad had purchased for her mother was still there, too. Like the slave bracelet! Meredith would love to compare it to what she'd seen in the Crooked Feather.

Outside, the wind whistled. In the distance something fell. Then the wolf dogs howled. Grandpa sat up. "You hear that?"

"It was a trash can, I'm sure."

He settled back, still ill at ease.

"You ever going to tell me why you don't want me here and why you're always looking over your shoulder?"

"I'm expecting death to come creeping up, and I know I need to run."

"Not funny."

"You're right. It wasn't, I'm sorry. Guess I've just been worried more lately about how I'm feeling. I still need to get Zack and Susan through college."

"I'm helping."

"And I appreciate it. Every penny you pay me goes right to Zack's account. I don't want him to even think about getting a second job. College, and particularly his major, is hard. I wish your parents had planned more."

"Do you ever wish you'd gone to college?"

"No, this land's the only thing I've ever wanted."

Meredith hung the last angel. It used to be Susan's job. Back then, there'd be the smell of Grandma's cookies wafting through the house, and noise from whomever had gathered nearby: family, friends, Jimmy.

It always came back to Jimmy.

She always came back to Jimmy

THE MURPHY FAMILY hit the ground running Saturday morning. Danny, Jimmy and the other two groomsmen had already picked up their tuxes. Then Danny had headed into town for a haircut and some errands.

Jimmy was at the church making sure all the last-minute stuff got done. The flowers were in place. Since they weren't real, none were drooping. Susan wanted poinsettias for her wedding, which was a good choice. After Christmas, she could get them on sale. The candles were already up front. He set up his equipment and readied the slide show. Before the wedding march started, the guests would watch Holly and Danny grow— first as children with their families and then together as a couple.

Jimmy went through every slide. Danny and Holly had gathered their pictures several days ago. Just two days ago, Danny had added a new slide, one with Meredith in it.

The last picture was of Danny and Holly. Jimmy knew a happily-ever-after when he saw it. He wanted Danny's children to see it, too, and so he made sure his cameras were at the ready to record Danny and Holly's next chapter. With an energy he'd not felt since Regina died, he checked the angles, lighting and equipment one last time before leaving the church.

Tonight, after doing groom duty, he'd be a roving photographer. He loved being behind the camera, the ideas one could capture on film forever. He'd snagged some great candid shots this morning at the house. Danny hopping on one foot: one sock on, one not. He'd managed one of his mother with some green gook on her face, an old robe tied around her waist and tears shimmering with both joy and sorrow. Her baby was getting married. Then his father had moved in and nestled her from behind, his chin on the top of her dark hair. Jimmy'd blow that one up to frame it. She'd have a love-hate relationship with it for the rest of her life.

Briana was with Grandma now, getting her hair and nails done. She'd not been able to sit still this morning, not at all, and Jimmy half expected her to return with slashed hair and nail polish up to her elbows.

His little brother was getting married. This time, the thought of it allowed Jimmy to breathe. The last time, it had paralyzed him.

It was a hazy day. The dust storm had left tiny remnants of itself floating in the air. Getting into his car, Jimmy headed for the Hospitable, where Danny and Holly's reception would be. But as he drove down Main Street, he noticed a black truck up ahead. It turned.

Black trucks weren't unusual. Every teenage boy wanted one. But Agatha had last seen Paul Livingston driving a black truck.

Now was not the time to investigate. Jimmy's brother was getting married in six hours. He still needed to do some chores around both his dad's and his uncle's places, help Briana with her duties and call Meredith and insist she be his date.

No, now was not the time for that, either, especially not to be his date to his brother's wedding.

He turned down the street and watched the black truck disappear down an alley behind the Crooked Feather. Jimmy kept going, parked the truck and then leisurely walked back toward Main Street.

He couldn't see the truck down the alley. It must have pulled into the tiny rear lot. Except for trash cans, there were no hiding places in the alley. It was either risk detection or do nothing.

Jimmy had never been a do-nothing kind of guy. He made it to the tiny back parking lot and spotted the truck. Taking out his cell phone, he took a photo of the license plate. It was a start. The back door to the trading post was open. The same flute music from before was playing. Peeking in, he saw a tall, slender man with long brown hair in a ponytail offering two brown shopping bags to Victor Lucas.

Lucas just looked mad. He set the bags down without opening them and held out his hand, palm up, wanting something. Car keys? No. The man—it had to be Paul Livingston—was backing up and shaking his head. Jimmy didn't need to hear the next words; he could read lips.

You owe me.

Livingston held up his hands in surrender. More than anything, Jimmy wished he had the guts to try taking a photo of this.

Trash cans did come in handy. Jimmy ducked behind the ones belonging to the Crooked Feather just as Paul Livingston came out the door muttering, "I can't give him what I don't got."

Once Livingston had driven out of the alley and completely turned the corner, Jimmy peeked back into the trading post. From the first bag, Victor Lucas pulled out a brownish-red clay pot, about sixteen inches wide. It was intact. The second bag held something smaller. At first, Jimmy thought it was some kind of fetish. It took a moment, but finally Jimmy figured out what it was: a mummified human hand with gnarled fingers.

CHAPTER TWENTY-ONE

THE CHURCH'S PARKING lot was full. Not even her grandpa's handicap-parking decal could get them close to the front door where carolers, dressed in period clothes, sang Christmas songs. Meredith drove up, parked and ran around to help Grandpa out. She turned him over to her dad.

"Your mother's inside. We've saved you a space," he said to her.

She wound up parking on the street and hurrying back to the church. Dust storms did something beautiful to the Arizona horizon. The December sun was setting, a bright orange orb in the distance. A gentle breeze pulled at Meredith's dress, which was really Susan's dress, as she scurried to the church's entrance and waved to her friend Jasmine who'd just finished singing about figgy pudding.

It was a good thing that Susan discarded clothes the way snakes shed skin. The dress that Meredith had borrowed, though not her usual taste, was gorgeous. It was a light blue silky one-piece that hugged the hips but flared at the knees.

Susan's white sandals—with a strap that kept coming loose—weren't the most comfortable, but they rounded out the ensemble nicely.

Blue definitely stood out at a Christmas wedding. Meredith apparently had missed the part of the invitation that asked attendees to wear Christmas colors.

Wait! She'd not received an invitation. She was either a wedding crasher or tagging along as the unmarried daughter of Burt and Karen Stone. She wasn't fond of either choice. She entered the church and spotted her family. Zack looked uncomfortable and tired sitting next to their father. They'd spent the day cleaning up the house and yard so Susan could hold her reception there next Saturday. He'd be more uncomfortable later when Meredith told him about the human bones and the fact that Grandpa still insisted that he didn't need any help.

The lights dimmed and a slide show appeared on the church's white side wall. The first image was of Danny Murphy as a baby. Then Danny a little older, tucked in his brother's arms. Danny tossed in the air by his father, baking cookies with his mother, riding a horse.

Danny, Jimmy and Meredith looking down from the tree house.

"They chose the right picture," Zack whispered.

In the photo, Danny was off to the side. Meredith and Jimmy were nestled so close to each other they appeared as one. More than a few people glanced her way: some had questions in their eyes and others just smiled as if knowing a secret.

What had she told Jimmy when he'd asked her why she'd not married Danny...

I didn't love him, not the way you're supposed to love the man you marry.

She felt like crying, like she'd missed something huge and wouldn't be able to swallow, breathe, unless she got it back. But the lights came on again and no way did she want the people of Gesippi to wonder what had made her cry.

The music started. The church was full, so much so that folding chairs were necessary to make up three extra rows.

The ceremony was simple. Just what Danny needed.

It was homespun. Just what Holly wanted.

There were only two bridesmaids—a Murphy cousin and a girl who must have been Holly's best friend—and no maid of honor. The two groomsmen were Danny's best friend and Jimmy.

Whoa, Jimmy looked amazing in a tux. Not like a small-town boy or a farmer but like a Hollywood superstar, rugged and cocky.

Briana came down the aisle all seriousness and

smiles. The ring bearer handed her his pillow and, finger in his nose, ran to sit with his mother.

Then, Danny's father walked Holly down the aisle while his wife wiped away tears in the front row. When the preacher said, "Who gives away this woman," the entire Murphy clan said, "We do!"

Holly was exactly what Danny needed.

While the preacher performed the service, Meredith studied the church's auditorium for Susan's wedding. All the candles could stay, and so could the fake flowers. Susan wanted to add poinsettias, the touch of red that would separate her wedding from Holly's, which Meredith thought a good idea. Susan had always loved bells, so maybe they could add a few of those. Instead of carolers, maybe there was time for Meredith to arrange a horse and buggy. Decked out for Christmas, it would be an awesome way to exit a wedding.

It was too late for Susan to book the Hospitable, not that there was money on the bride's side to pay for that, so Susan and Joe were getting married a bit earlier in the day and then everyone would be invited to Grandpa's for a potluck.

Grandpa wasn't crazy about the idea, but when someone mentioned having a barbecue, suddenly potluck was okay.

Too soon the wedding ended, the pictures

began and the guests headed for the Hospitable, first mingling in the foyer and then stopping to admire photograph albums spread out on a front table. It paid to have Jimmy in the family. There were enough pictures to plaster a wall. Once she'd done enough oohing and aahing to satisfy the crowd that she was really over Danny, Meredith let Zack take over Grandpa duties.

Grandpa was slower at his oohs and aahs.

At a round table set for nine just inside the doors, she sat next to her mother and leaned in to whisper, "You look good, Mom."

"Thank you. The wedding wasn't as hard to attend as I thought it would be."

Funny, in all these years, not once had her mother mentioned Meredith's interrupted nuptials. Meredith reached out and took her mother's hand, noting how smooth it felt, how small.

"I felt the same way."

Amidst the centerpiece's spray of green leaves and red berries were three disposable cameras. Jimmy must be cringing. Meredith retrieved one and took a picture of her grandpa, Dad and Mom.

"What a great idea," Agatha said, joining them. She reached for a camera and took a picture of Meredith. "I might never see you in a dress again."

"About time our kids start to get married," Meredith's mom said.

Agatha only smiled, looked at the centerpiece and said, "Holly for Holly. I think that's why she so wanted a Christmas wedding."

"And Danny would have given her the moon" came a voice over Meredith's shoulder. Jimmy Murphy had arrived.

"Great wedding," Meredith's father said. "They look amazing together."

Meredith's mother nodded to her and Jimmy. "Like you two do."

Jimmy didn't seem to mind. "I love the wedding present you gave her."

Meredith smiled. "Didn't cost a cent. Only elbow grease."

"Only Meredith would give someone an old used Maytag washer," her mother said.

"You know this is a buffet," Jimmy nudged. The food is set up in the back."

"I'll get your mother a plate. Why don't you get Grandpa's," her father suggested to Meredith. The restaurant was filling up. Half the town had been invited. Tables took up one side, a dance floor the other. Already a DJ messed with his equipment.

"Don't trip," Jimmy warned. He bent down and adjusted the sandal strap that had been giving her grief. On one knee, he looked up at her and something caught in her throat. Something about the expression in his eyes, the way his hair was already mussed.

Reaching down, she grasped his hand to help him up. Before she could, Agatha took a picture and said, "I love these cameras."

Someone called Jimmy's name, and he was gone, but not before whispering in her ear, "After I dance with my cousin, I'm dancing with you."

NEVER HAD JIMMY so wanted to be in three places at once. He wanted to be at the Crooked Feather, just in case Sheriff Salazar did something. He'd called the sheriff with what he'd found and sent him the photos before heading to the church. Not knowing what was going on was killing him, which made Jimmy think that maybe his future could involve something besides wild animals. Even if his call with his editor didn't go the way he wanted it to on Monday, it wouldn't be the end of him. Jimmy was starting to realize, after being with his family and with Meredith these last few weeks, that he had nothing to prove and no one to best. He would be okay.

Unfortunately, the sheriff hadn't been nearly as impressed with his information as Jimmy thought he should be. He'd merely taken the information, repeated it and promised to look into it.

"If the appendage is mummified this is probably more of a criminal-trespass offense than a murder," the sheriff said.

"What?"

"This is probably a case of grave robbing. You say one bag held a clay pot and the other a mummified hand. Chances are your guy is a looter, and Victor Lucas might deal on the black market. That side room you told me about is something I'll definitely look into."

Salazar hadn't said when, though.

The second place Jimmy wanted to be was exactly where he was—at his brother's wedding. It had gone off perfectly. It made Jimmy rethink how he wanted his future to look. And not just job wise.

The third place he wanted to be was on the dance floor with Meredith in his arms. What better place to announce to Gesippi that the Murphy clan no longer cared about the past but instead looked toward the future?

After signing witness papers, dancing with his cousin and Mom, taking Briana to sit on Santa's lap—because Holly had thought of everything—he then turned his daughter over to the parents of her best friend so the two little girls could make Rainbow Loom bracelets for anyone who wanted one. Should they need advertisement, he wore one on his wrist, as did both Danny and Holly.

Briana intended to sell them for ten dollars

apiece. Her little friend was more practical and hoped for fifty cents.

It felt like an hour from the time he'd promised to dance with Meredith until he finally got the chance. She was sitting with Agatha, both of them critiquing the wedding for ideas to use next week at Susan's wedding.

Maybe he should run; weddings could be contagious.

Meredith had a piece of paper out and she was drawing. Agatha tapped her bright red nails on the paper and said, "Are you sure this is what Susan would want and not what you want?"

Jimmy had to clear his throat before Meredith looked up.

Funny, a moment ago there'd been three places he'd wanted to be.

Now there was only one. With Meredith.

"Oh, my," Agatha said.

"May I have this dance?" he asked.

She stood, put her hand in his and followed him to the dance floor. Around them, old, young, married, single, friends all danced. But once he put his arms around her, drew her close, inhaled her scent, they were alone.

"You didn't use to like dancing," Meredith reminded him.

"I've had a change of heart."

"I'm glad."

"I've had a change of heart about a lot of things. You've opened my eyes, Merry, and I promise to try and keep them open."

She tucked her head against his shoulder and for a while they just danced, no need for words, just the need to touch.

"What are we going to do?" he finally asked.

"You're only here for two more weeks," she said. Her words were muffled.

He was glad she wasn't looking in his eyes. He didn't want to remind her that he had no idea what his plans were. If his editor didn't go for the wolf dog piece, sure he could propose another one, but where would that take him? And was it in his daughter's best interest to pull her out of school? He could take his career in another direction, but which one. He didn't want Meredith to see his indecision and think it had something to do with her.

Them.

"A lot can happen in two weeks. You're here for how long?"

"I've taken off work until New Year's."

"Ha," he said. "That's two weeks and two days!"

She turned so she was now looking at him. "I don't work that far away. I can be back home in a little over an hour."

The song changed, a few people left the floor

and Meredith pulled away a bit more to confess, "I'm still worried about Grandpa." Just like that, the mood switched from romantic to tense. He wanted romantic back, but this wasn't the time.

"In the week you've been here, he seems to be better. Did Zack take him home or your parents?"

"Zack."

"Did you tell Zack about Ray's phone number being in that wallet?"

"I forgot."

"What about finding what we think are two human bones?"

"That I told him about. I also said we don't believe it's recent, so he's not worried."

"Maybe he should worry." As much as he liked her head tucked under his shoulder, he also wanted her informed. He gave her a rundown of his morning, explaining about the black truck and Victor Lucas and the clay pot and mummified hand. He ended with, "And Sheriff Salazar thinks we might have grave robbers working in the area."

"Around my grandpa's land?"

"It makes sense. That property's been in your father's family for a century or more. It would explain the bones, and it might also explain why Leia was abandoned there and why Ray hears things in the night and tries to explore."

"It doesn't explain the hole in the screen door

or his phone number in a mysterious wallet, though. No one but family ever calls him." She paused. "That's not true. We also get calls for changing our cable company, installing solar panels and investing in time shares."

"I'll come over early next week and we can walk your grandfather's property, see if anything looks out of place."

"If there are Native American ruins, they're not in plain sight. We'd have found them when we were kids."

"If a grave robber found something, he'd leave the area disturbed. I just want to look."

"Speaking of looking," Meredith said. "We need to start gathering photos of Susan and Joe so we can have a slide show like you had for Danny and Holly. Joe talked to you about doing that, right?"

"I'm having his mom bring photos to church tomorrow. Why don't you come over Monday with photos of Susan and we'll start putting the slide show together."

There it was again. Them working together. He wondered if she noticed, like he was, just how good they were together. Again.

The song changed again and Jimmy decided they'd done enough talking. All he wanted to do was hold her, breathe her, love her. The music swayed and so did they, moving together almost as one.

To the tune of "Could I Have This Dance," he decided that if he couldn't dance with her for the rest of his life, then it wouldn't be much of a life.

HE DIDN'T GET to see Meredith at church on Sunday as he'd planned. Briana, who'd been looking forward to exploring the Stone place with Yoda by her side, woke up with a fever. Jimmy spent the day helping his mother prepare a last-minute Christmas because "Briana has to have a tree" and sitting with Briana while she watched TV and made bracelets. Whenever Briana napped, he planned his Skype meeting with Thom. His pitch was unlike any proposal Jimmy had made. He threw in everything: the story of Bridget's Animal Adventure, giant snakes dropped off at its door, the declawed bear and now the wolf dogs.

Man was necessary.

Hopefully, Briana would be in school tomorrow so he'd not be interrupted when Thom shot the whole thing down and Jimmy terminated his employment as lead feature writer.

He'd mentioned this meeting to Meredith, but he didn't want to mention it again, and in fact he hoped she'd forgotten about it. He wanted to figure out his next move. His thoughts on what was best for the wolf dog had changed. His thoughts on zoos had changed, too, somewhat. He just hoped she could trust him when he proposed they work together on a documentary on Bridget's Animal Adventure.

Maybe this time he could make a difference.

If she'd let him.

At one, Joe's mother brought two manila envelopes full of Joe's photos. She'd pulled out her favorites and had them paper clipped.

Jimmy carefully removed the paper clip so there'd be no crease.

Just after three, the phone rang. Sheriff Salazar had a few questions, mostly about what Jimmy had seen in the private room at the Crooked Feather. This time the sheriff was a little more forthcoming. It seemed the good sheriff already had Victor Lucas under investigation and because of Jimmy and Meredith, would be moving up his sting operation. Now Jimmy understood why he hadn't been able to be definite the day before.

"We want the supplier more than the dealer," was Salazar's point. Another piece of news, albeit small, was that Salazar had talked to the butcher in town, the name Meredith had recognized from the wolf dog-owner list.

"He said his brother had a wolf dog, one that the county sometimes used for rescue."

"Another give-and-take between man and beast," Jimmy said.

"What?" Salazar had no idea what Jimmy was talking about.

At five, Meredith called, both excited and irritated. "Someone dropped off a wolf dog in my front yard this morning while we slept!"

Not her grandpa's front yard but hers.

"The new wolf dog okay?" he asked.

"Scared and a little underfed, like Leia was."

"You'd just talked Luke into trying a wolf dog pair. How do you think he'll respond to three?"

It took her a while to answer. "I don't know."

For a few minutes they talked about Susan and Joe's wedding, moved on to Briana and the family, and finally settled on what the upcoming week looked like, what they'd be doing together.

Briana went to sleep at seven. Jimmy ate with his parents and then worked at the kitchen table, laying out his ideas for Thom and finally emailing the document to his editor.

Tomorrow, he'd either get a do-over or he'd have to start over.

CHAPTER TWENTY-TWO

MONDAY'S WARM, SUNNY WEATHER was the reason people moved to Arizona. Jimmy did the first of Danny's chores, amazed at how good it felt to be outside, doing physical labor, getting his hands dirty. Next, he took Briana—fully recovered— to school. When he got back home, he picked up the to-do list Danny had left him. Great, today at Uncle Mitch's Jimmy would have to play with compost for an hour or two...until his appointment with Thom.

His dad was outside working, and his mother was in the apartment over the barn, cleaning it and adding all kinds of special touches so Danny and Holly would have someplace special to return to after their honeymoon.

Danny had already picked out a parcel of their dad's property for himself, and knew exactly what he wanted his future house to look like.

Except for the dogs and a radio playing in someone's empty room, there was nothing to distract Jimmy from his conversation with Thom. It only took a minute to connect, both visual and audio worked. To Jimmy's surprise, Thom actually looked excited.

"This is great!" Thom said, not even waiting for Jimmy to pitch. "You sent me so much stuff, at first I thought you'd sent me your notes instead of the final proposal. I had no idea you had an inside source at a zoo."

"Huh."

"We can get three issues out of this!"

Jimmy almost fell off his chair. Three issues? That meant he could remain in Gesippi for a couple of months, Briana could stay in her school and he'd be close to Meredith. In the distance, he heard a door slam. His mother, probably, finishing up the apartment. She'd be thrilled to keep her granddaughter close.

"First, we do the bears' story. I've been doing some research. There are actually people who sic their dogs on bears. It's called bear baiting. Next, you can do the wolf dogs. I know you really want to dig into that one. I saw the YouTube video of this Meredith you keep talking about. She sure looks like a bossy little thing. Then, let's do the whole Bridget's Animal Adventure. Did you know that Katie Vincent is the daughter of a man who exploited animals—"

"Her name's Katie Rittenhouse. She—"

"Her married name is Rittenhouse. Her maiden name is Vincent. Her father was a famous animal trainer in the nineties. One of his cats attacked his four-year-old daughter, leaving a permanent scar."

That would be Janie, who was married to Sheriff Rafael Salazar. Jimmy didn't like the way this was going.

Thom went on. "You didn't tell me you could get into a zoo where an orangutan actually sits in a chair and acts like he's reading the paper."

Jimmy hadn't caught that show.

"His trainer is a guy named Jasper Dunbar, he's gotta be near ninety. I love what I find on the internet. He'd worked with animals for almost seventy years. Do you have any idea of the atrocities that happened to animals in the 1960s? He should have plenty of stories to tell."

All Jimmy remembered of Jasper Dunbar was an old man standing out in the dark night helping them search for a runaway wolf dog.

No, Jimmy didn't want this job.

Thom finished with, "We'll make this a full multimedia package. Heck, maybe we can even go IMAX. I really hope this Dunbar fellow has some old black-and-white photos, 'never seen before' type thing."

IMAX? His boss was talking 3-D?

It was the next level in the journalistic world. Their magazine sold for just over six dollars, fifteen if it was a double issue. And since the e-revolution, revenue had been down. As for the documentaries, much of their funding came from investors who expected to get paid back first.

"We won't even need to put a disclaimer at the end," Thom said gleefully. "It won't matter that every minute's not in the wild because we won't be in the wild."

"I—"

"So," Thom interrupted, "flesh me out a schedule of what and who you need. This Bridget's Animal Adventure is just perfect. I consider this a done deal."

Jimmy opened his mouth. *No!* his brain shouted. On the computer screen, Thom disconnected.

Behind him, something crashed to the ground. He turned just in time to see Meredith flying out the kitchen door clutching two photograph albums.

The slamming of the door hadn't been his mother.

"Meredith! Wait."

He almost knocked his laptop to the floor as he hurried after her, stumbling to the porch. He caught a glimpse of her face as her SUV skidded out of the driveway. Surprise, surprise, she didn't look angry.

Instead, the combination of acceptance and

disappointment in her eyes almost brought him to his knees.

His cell phone rang. He grabbed it, slid it to answer and said, "Meredith?"

It was Gesippi Elementary School wanting him to come collect his sick daughter.

MEREDITH STOMPED FROM her SUV and all the way into the house, flinging open the door. Jimmy Murphy'd used her again! The first time, gaining entrance to Aqui Lobos, she'd expected. Her heart had been cold. Today, though, her heart had been his, and he'd once again tossed it back to her, essentially telling her to keep it.

If he were a wolf dog, she'd neuter him!

"Grandpa! Where are you?"

Only silence echoed. A quick search took her through all the rooms and to the back door. A large black truck was parked by the barn. Looking around, she half expected to see somebody from church delivering folding chairs. They'd need them for Saturday's wedding reception. Meredith doubted the black truck was the visiting nurse her father still promised.

Fear pooled in her stomach.

She had been talking to Jimmy about someone who owned a black truck.

She heard the howls, three animals now. Instead of their usual yelping, "Me first. Come see me," she detected something a bit more frantic in their forlorn call.

"I've already fed you," she muttered.

Before she got halfway to the barn, they'd stopped. Yoda was at the entrance, waiting for her, tail wagging and wanting attention. Leia and the new wolf dog were pacing back and forth, agitated.

"What is it?" Meredith felt the edge of her anger ebb. She had something new to worry about: Grandpa.

Off in the distance, Pepper barked, at least Meredith thought it was Pepper. Meredith shivered, and not from the December breeze. Last time Pepper'd been that far out, Grandpa had fallen.

But what about the black truck? She patted her back pocket, checking to make sure she had her cell phone.

"Grandpa!" She hurried back into the house. Instead of cookies and a *TV Guide*, Grandpa's chair had a word search. In the corner, they'd set up a puzzle table. There were presents under the tree. The house no longer looked lonely.

Except without Grandpa answering, it felt lonely.

She pulled her cell phone out and went to stand before the list of emergency contacts on the refrigerator. Darn that Jimmy Murphy. Her first inclination would have been to call him. He was back on the speed dial. She'd trusted too quickly, too deeply.

Pepper had stopped barking.

She bent forward to read Jimmy's uncle's phone number, but before she could punch the first number, someone grabbed her from behind, viselike, cutting off her breathing and relieving her of the cell phone.

"You must be Meredith," a male voice whispered in her ear. It wasn't a question.

She squirmed, at first unable to move, unable to get away from the smell of potato chips and sweat, but finally the man relaxed his grip enough that she could turn and see him.

He was tall with brown hair that was pulled into a low ponytail, accentuating his thin face and watery eyes. She didn't recognize him.

"Where's my grandfather?"

As if cued, Pepper barked again, followed by wolf dog howls.

"He's a tough old man," the intruder sneered. "And, yes, he's out there, hidden and hurt. You might not find him in time."

White-hot anger erupted within her. She took a quick step, fists raised, but she was jarred to a stop when once again his arms went around her like a restraining jacket. Thumbs digging into soft flesh.

She'd have bruises.

"You're going to do something for me, little Merry. That's what your grandpa calls you. Guess you were born around Christmas."

It was such an illogical syllogism that she had no reply.

He held up her phone. "I'm punching in the number to Gesippi's patrol officer. I want you to tell him that since you've been here, staying with Ray, your grandpa's feeling a lot better. So much better that he's remembered that the wallet, with two thousand dollars, was indeed his. You can identify it as rustic red, and one of the card sleeves is slightly torn. Tell the officer the name and phone number were put there by your dad because your grandpa kept losing the wallet. Say you'll be by to pick it up in about thirty minutes."

"What does my grandpa have to do with your two thousand dollars?"

"Nothing except his phone number happened to be inside when I lost it."

"Go get it yourself."

"Can't. I have this little problem called a warrant in the system. I come in contact with Officer Sykes and I'm going for a three-to-five year vacation, courtesy of the state of Arizona. No thanks."

"You hurt my grandfather or me, you'll have a forever vacation."

"Call. And, if you do anything except say exactly what I just instructed you to say, I'm leaving. I'll be long gone by the time you get someone out here and you'll never find your grandfather. I've left lots of false trails in case you use the dogs. Why do you think both Pepper and the wolf dogs are so upset?"

His eyes narrowed and she saw in their depths that Paul Livingston was the kind of guy who would hurt a woman and not think anything of it.

"Call."

The only weapon she could get her hands on was the cell phone. It wouldn't do any damage, it would only piss him off.

She didn't know Officer Sykes. He'd joined the force a few years ago, after she left. No way would he realize that her voice was shaky. She prayed, though, that he'd question her, give her some time to slip in a clue. Good cop that he was, he answered on the second ring. She gave him the information, all the while trying to figure out what to do, how to overpower this guy.

Sykes didn't question her at all, merely accepted her claim with, "Elderly people often forget where they've stashed money."

Not what she wanted to hear.

After she ended the call, she said to the man,

"I've done what you wanted. Tell me where my grandfather is."

"No, and right now he doesn't want to be found. See, this is why I picked you to help me get the wallet. Your grandfather's not innocent in all of this. If I get in trouble, he gets in trouble."

"What are you talking about?"

He made a face, shook himself a little, and then snarled again. "He and I are partners, of sort. Best you do what I say and not go squealing to the police. A vacation courtesy of the state would be Ray's last vacation. I just want to get this done. Two thousand dollars will take me a long way."

Working in an animal habitat had strengthened her. She could hoist fifty-pound poly bags of feed. Once she'd lifted the neck of a sleeping rhino.

But the man had ushered her into her SUV before she could come up with an escape plan.

"Don't you want your truck?" she asked weakly.

"No, too easy to trace."

"My SUV's pretty noticeable. I've got vanity plates."

He rolled his eyes and started the ignition. "I don't want your car."

"How do you know I won't tell the cops what you're doing?"

He leaned close, his neck as long as a snake, his eyes suddenly beady instead of watery. "Because your grandfather's a grave robber. How do you think he's been putting you through school? The fines for such crimes are in the six digits, and the jail time longer than three to five. If they put your grandpa away, he'll die in jail."

That shut her up.

He'd managed to get them a half mile down Pioneer Road before Jimmy Murphy drove by, going a little fast and clearly on a mission. Meredith knew Jimmy's destination. He was coming for her. Any other day, he'd be the answer to her prayers, but not today.

Because in Jimmy Murphy's backseat, curled up against the window and asleep, was Briana.

FUNNY, MEREDITH USUALLY didn't drive fast. She always had an animal or two or three with her in the car and had learned to drive safely. He started to honk, but his fingers paused on the horn.

Meredith wasn't driving.

And he recognized the driver. It was Paul Livingston, the one who'd given Victor Lucas the clay pot and mummified hand.

If it weren't for Briana sleeping in the backseat, Jimmy'd have said all kinds of bad words. As it was, he could only bite his tongue and turn the car around. He fumbled for his cell phone, and in his nervousness it slid out of his hand and onto the floorboard. No way could he give chase and bend down to get it. He tried anyway and his truck hit a bump that almost knocked the steering wheel from his grip. Luckily, it also skidded the cell phone a bit closer to him.

"Daddy, you're going too fast."

Great, he'd wakened Briana, and she didn't need to see all this.

"I know, honey, but Meredith might be in trouble. Go back to sleep."

Oh, man, he had to figure out what was happening with Meredith and keep Briana safe. He had to get the stupid cell phone.

Briana sat up. "Why is she driving away from us?"

"She's not driving."

It went against every parental gene in his body, but this was a desperate moment. "Briana, take off your seat belt and climb up here. I need you to get my cell phone from the floor. When you have it, punch the number two so I can talk to my dad."

Briana didn't hesitate. She was out of the seat belt, crawling into the front, fumbling for the cell phone and handing it over to him in under a minute.

Jimmy didn't think he'd ever barked orders at his father, but he did now. "Dad, run out to your car and head toward Ray Stone's house. If you see Meredith's brown SUV, make sure it doesn't get by you. You have maybe one minute. Do whatever you have to do. Block it. Also, have Mom call both the Gesippi police and Sheriff Rafael Salazar over in Scorpion Ridge. Tell them—"

"What's going on, son, I—"

Jimmy didn't have time to finish or answer. Meredith's car suddenly skidded to a stop, backed up, and, in a funnel of dirt, did a U-turn, heading straight for Jimmy.

"Get your seat belt on, Briana!"

Briana started crying and obeyed.

The brown SUV came right for them. At the last moment, he saw Meredith grab the steering wheel. Her SUV went into the ditch and slid on its side with a loud crash.

The driver's door opened and Paul Livingston climbed out, jumped down and ran into open farmland, not stopping to check if his passenger was okay.

No way was Jimmy leaving Briana or Meredith to go after him. He quickly unbuckled his seat belt and then his daughter's. Carrying her, he ran to the overturned SUV.

Briana could stand by herself, so he set her down in the grass near the SUV. As if sensing the seriousness of it all, she stood quietly, glancing around, anxious. If Paul Livingston came back, Jimmy could jump in front of Briana, shield her, do whatever he had to do to keep her safe.

Inside the SUV, Meredith was slumped over, looking young, vulnerable and pale.

She wouldn't have been vulnerable if he'd not been such an idiot. She'd have still been at his house, going through photos with him. Using one wheel as a stepping stool, he climbed up to the door Paul had left open. Before crawling inside, he gazed around. He wouldn't leave his daughter exposed if Paul were anywhere near.

In December, the crops weren't tall, so Jimmy could see Paul zigzagging through open fields.

"Meredith, wake up. Talk to me."

She didn't respond.

He lowered himself into the front seat, careful not to disturb her. He felt helpless. Every time a woman he loved was in trouble, he was too late.

That was going to change.

He wasn't about to lose someone he loved twice.

"Meredith, I need you to wake up. I can't move you because something might be broken. You have to wake up."

"Daddy, your phone's ringing in the car. Should I go get it?"

He glanced out the window. Paul was still running, now quite a distance away. "Yes, go get it."

Meredith's lashes fluttered, then her eyes opened. He'd never been so glad to see her determined green stare.

"How do you feel?" His hands went to her face, neck, shoulders, anywhere he could reach, tracing the strong bones and making sure nothing was broken.

She swallowed, and he wished he had some water.

"He did something to Grandpa," she whispered.

"Paul Livingston? What do you mean he did something?"

Her voice got stronger. "Grandpa's somewhere on the property. Pepper was barking out by the foothills. Livingston said Grandpa was hidden and would be impossible to find."

Jimmy could hear Briana talking, telling someone that Meredith was hurt and that they were on the road where it was dirt and bumps.

Good girl.

"Tell me everything."

She did, without hesitation. She'd just finished when both Jimmy's parents and Officer Sykes drove up.

She reached down and undid her seat belt. For a moment, he thought the movement had taken the last of her strength, but then she reached for him and said, "Help me out of here."

"You sure?"

"We need to look for Grandpa."

Jimmy helped her out; his father helped her down. Already, Jimmy's mother was with Briana, telling her what a brave little girl she was.

Quickly, Jimmy relayed to his dad and Officer Sykes what Meredith had shared.

"Grave robber? Ray Stone? I don't believe it," Jimmy's dad said.

Sykes didn't answer, which told Jimmy it wasn't so far-fetched. Maybe Paul Livingston had given them a germ of the truth. It wasn't cheap putting three people through college, especially when one was heading for med school. He wouldn't have implicated Ray except that he was in such a dire situation.

His mother took Briana home and everyone else moved to Meredith's farm. Soon, others gathered, and once again—just two weeks after the first time he'd gone missing—a crowd was setting out to find Ray Stone. Meredith wouldn't lie down, wouldn't go to the doctor. She intended to search, too.

"Quite a story, huh?"

Jimmy agreed. "I've never heard anything so fascinating."

"You'll include it in your 'Done Deal'?" she asked.

He wanted to reach out, pull her to him and

explain everything to her, but now was the not the place or time. When it came, he'd be ready. He already had the ring.

"You're the only 'Done Deal' I'm considering" was his best response, but either she didn't hear or she didn't believe him, because she didn't respond.

DINNERTIME CAME AND WENT, and there was still no sign of Grandpa. Meredith's mom had put together sandwiches; Jimmy's mother and Briana had brought watermelon and iced tea. A search-and-rescue team from Adobe Hills had showed up. The helicopter was on its way.

"If he's hidden," Meredith told her brother, "the helicopter's no good."

"Sure wish Pepper would start barking again," Zack said.

No one had seen Paul Livingston. The police had talked to his ex-wife, Victor Lucas and all the neighboring farms. Nothing.

"Victor confessed," Rafael said. "He'd been buying from looters for the last ten years."

Meredith had enrolled in college ten years ago.

"And you think my grandfather...?"

His lack of a response gave her the answer.

The grid was drawn, labeled A–G, and groups assigned. Meredith, a knot on her forehead and a left ankle that protested every time she took a step, went a lot slower than she wanted to. She was assigned section A, the closest area to the farm, and where the Murphy boys and she had played as children. With her foot, it made sense not to send her farther. The sheriff thought Jimmy would do more good with him.

"I'll walk with you," her father said.

He kept his gait equal to hers. His expression was terse, his body tense. She looked east and he looked west. They stopped, called Ray's name, checked under bushes, behind trees and called his name some more.

Meredith received a text from Jimmy. He'd been assigned area B and so far had found nothing except a baseball cap he'd lost in tenth grade.

"I can't remember the last time I walked back here," Burt Stone said after the first hour. "Probably when I was a kid."

Meredith didn't respond. Her father had never walked back here with her when she was a kid.

When they got to the tree house, her dad climbed up. "I don't think Dad would be up here, but maybe I can see something from up there."

A moment later, he climbed down having found nothing. "I'm surprised the tree house has held up so well. Dad and I built it. A few things have changed, though."

"I didn't know Grandpa built it with you," Meredith said.

"It was my ninth birthday present. I wanted a minibike, not splinters in my hands from something I had to build myself."

"Grandpa and I added on to it. So it's a little bigger. What else changed?"

"The engravings on the wall. I remember carving I Hate Girls. Now, instead, there's a *MS* loves *JM*."

Meredith blushed. "That was a long time ago."

To her surprise, her father came toward her and put his arm around her. "We'll find Dad. He's a tough old guy."

"It'll be cold tonight," Meredith sniffed.

Past the tree house, civilization dropped away. Meredith's tennis shoes crunched in the dirt as she called Ray's name. Arizona sycamore and walnut trees were scattered among the purple cacti. Dirt turned to stone and then rock. Meredith kept a steady pace, her father right behind her.

"We played for hours in these rock formations," she said.

"I hated them," her father admitted. "I was an only child. I always found it both scary and lonely out here by myself. I always thought I'd get lost."

She wasn't sure how to respond. How could he hate the granite that made Grandpa's place special?

"Zack, me and the Murphy boys all played pirates hiding treasure out here. Then, we were pioneers seeking shelter from a storm. Our favorite spot was right down there."

It was only a bit of a decline. Meredith gingerly stepped down, not wanting a loose stone to send her stumbling. Her father took her elbow and helped.

They ended up in a tiny cave that was really no more than an indentation in the earth. A granite shelf was above them.

"One time Jimmy and I stayed in here for an hour while it poured outside. He tried to build a fire but couldn't."

"He was pretty important to you," her dad said.

"Yes."

"I almost asked you not to marry Danny."

"What! Really?"

"Really," he admitted. "But you always seemed to know what you were doing. You had the maturity of a thirty-year-old when you turned three. Your mom and weren't sure what to do with you."

"All us kids ever wanted was your time."

"Yeah, and you found that with your grandparents instead of us."

"Grandpa and I love the same things—the open spaces, animals, pancakes."

"I'm glad he was there for you when I couldn't

be." There was silence, except for the wind and insects. Finally, her dad offered, "It can be different now, Meredith."

It was a beginning. "Thanks, Dad."

"If we find Grandpa, we'll make him a big plate of pancakes," her father suggested.

"Not if, *when*," Meredith said.

Overhead, the wind shivered through the trees. The temperature dropped, and a lonely cicada droned. Off in the distance came the sound of someone calling, "Ray! Ray!"

Then Meredith heard it, a muted whine. It wasn't in the tiny cave, but somehow next to it.

"Grandpa!"

Another whine was her only response. Meredith, unmindful of her ankle, scurried outside. The whine had come from the left. She got on her hands and knees and crawled toward a tiny opening in the ridge. Just big enough for her to squeeze through.

"Dad, hand me the flashlight."

"I can crawl in."

"Flashlight."

It was another cave, bigger than the one where Meredith used to play but with a tiny opening that had been hidden for centuries, at least from the kids.

Grandpa was in the dirt, his eyes open and full of pain. Pepper was curled against his side.

"He's here!" she screamed. "Call Mom, call Jimmy."

"He shot Pepper," Grandpa whispered.

"Can you move, Grandpa."

"No, but I'll be all right. I'm just thirsty. We need to get Pepper help. He wouldn't leave me."

Already the helicopter whirred above. The distant sound of an engine and the whinny of a horse fought each other in the wind. Help was on its way.

Meredith sent her flashlight beam around the room and almost screamed.

No wonder Grandpa hadn't been afraid of the bones discovered near his shed. Here was a room of bones. That wasn't all. There was also pottery, spears, tools and a mask just like the one for sale at the Crooked Feather.

Meredith and Jimmy, for all their exploring, hadn't realized what was next to the cave they so loved as youngsters. It had been left by the Hohokam. Grandpa had known, though, and had left it alone because it was sacred. Until he'd gotten desperate.

Then, nothing had been more sacred than the love he had for his family.

CHAPTER TWENTY-THREE

"PAUL THOUGHT I was taking him to the artifacts," Grandpa said from a hospital bed. "Really, I was leading him in circles, trying to figure out a way to lose him without getting shot."

"Grandpa," Meredith said. "You should have told me all this when I moved in. We could have—"

"I made my bed. I had to lie in it. I'm just sorry it was Pepper who got shot."

"How did that happen?" Jimmy asked.

"I think Pepper got tired of going in circles. He took off running. I said, 'He's going to the cave.' Paul took off after Pepper. I ducked into the real cave, heard a shot, and soon Pepper came in after me. Not even whimpering. That dog's smart. I heard Paul fumbling around. Then, I heard nothing. Problem was, neither Pepper nor I could get up. Sure was glad when you showed up."

Meredith got herself checked out, as well, and went home, exhausted. The next day, Zack went back to Tucson; he had to pack up his things. He'd be staying with their parents during Christmas break. Meredith's dad went back to work. He'd be helping with medical bills for the next year. Meredith's mom took over with Grandpa.

Grandpa stayed in the Adobe Hills hospital. He'd be out on Friday, attending Susan's wedding on Saturday and then moving in with Meredith's parents for a short while. Her mother had agreed to care for him. "I can do it," Meredith's mom said. "It's my turn."

Ray made a face but didn't refuse. Meredith whispered to him, "It's a beginning."

Tuesday morning, just five days until Susan's wedding, Meredith had already spent a few hours at the hospital and was now busy scrubbing down the cabinets in the kitchen. Last night had erased all trace of the thorough cleaning she'd given Grandpa's house. She was back to square one, alone, well, a slow moving and bandaged Pepper was at her side, and needed to have it spick-and-span for the reception.

"At least scrubbing cabinets is easier than cleaning the panther pen," Meredith told herself.

Cleaning also gave her plenty of time to reflect. According to Rafael, the Tohono O'odham Nation didn't seem inclined to press charges against Grandpa. They just wanted their artifacts back, and Grandpa had kept a list of everything he'd taken. The local law authorities appreciated

Grandpa's willingness to help. The state looked forward to the hefty fine he'd be paying.

Both bones found by the shed were from the same burial site. Grandpa confessed that he'd gone out roaming because Livingston had threatened to hurt his family if Grandpa didn't turn over enough artifacts to equal two thousand dollars.

Exactly the amount that Paul had in the wallet he'd lost—the amount Victor Lucas wanted him to pay back. Problem was, Grandpa didn't have the strength to get to the cave on his own.

Meredith stopped cleaning when she heard someone drive into the grooved area of the front yard. Meredith's breath caught. Living here, alone for now, with Paul Livingston on the loose, made for some sleepless nights. Luckily, she had three wolf dogs keeping watch.

"Hey, you in there," Jimmy called.

"In the kitchen."

He came in carrying his camera, his laptop, a stack of papers and a bag of donuts.

Jimmy'd been the first one to climb in the cave and help her with Grandpa. She'd never been so glad to let someone else take care of her. It had been a lesson for her.

"I've got something to show you," Jimmy said.

"About yesterday, Grandpa and Paul Livingston?"

He shook his head, brown hair standing straight up, making Meredith want to pat it down. He was dressed in a dark blue T-shirt and jeans. On his left wrist, he wore a new red bracelet, courtesy of his daughter. Meredith had its twin.

He'd already put in a good morning's work, Meredith figured, doing chores and getting Briana to school.

She swallowed.

"You don't need to show me what you're doing for *Nature Times*. I understand. It's business."

"I don't work for *Nature Times* any longer. I meant what I said to you. That's what I want to show you."

She set the dust rag down. "You quit? But you love your job!"

"I did," he agreed. "I loved it for many years, but what I did didn't really change things. I didn't take in stray animals. I didn't nurse a baby bear that had been declawed or turn a wolf dog into an ambassador for his breed. I want to work with you."

Meredith had never been very good at partnerships because she'd always wanted to be the one in control. But she'd lost that control over the last few weeks, and it had been the best thing that had ever happened to her.

Yes, she'd be happy to be this man's partner.

He set his laptop on the kitchen table. "This,"

he said, holding up a small white box with a cord, "is an external display box. I can show you a slide show right here in the kitchen."

"I can't believe you found time to put Joe's pictures in order."

He frowned. "I still need to do that."

It took him all of ten minutes to get the laptop set up and the projector working. The only wall without decoration was above the kitchen table, so Jimmy had to man the laptop from the stove across the room.

The album he'd put together wasn't of Susan and Joe. It was of Meredith and Jimmy.

Meredith leaned against the counter and watched. She hadn't remembered that their first date was at ages one and two, swimming in a little blue pool.

There were pictures of church picnics and school events. There were family outings and dates.

"There's a ten-year void," he said sadly, "where I have no pictures of you, of us."

A final slide went on the kitchen wall. It was from last Saturday, at Danny and Holly's reception. It was of Jimmy down on one knee, staring up at Meredith, an expectant look on his face.

"You fixed my shoe," Meredith remembered.

"Yes, but doesn't it seem like I'm doing something else in this photo?"

It did. It looked for all the world like he was proposing.

"Tomorrow's Christmas. I bought you a present."

Eek. She hadn't bought him one!

"I bought it ten years ago," Jimmy said, getting down on one knee—just like in the picture—and reaching into his pocket.

He pulled out a ring.

Part of Meredith wanted to say, "You've got to be kidding." Another part wanted to say, "What took you so long?"

"Ten years ago, I didn't listen or understand when you asked me to wait. I promise to listen and to try to understand, but I don't want to wait anymore. I don't want to have any more gaps in my—er, our—photo album."

Meredith couldn't answer. Her throat was closing, and she thought she might faint. She couldn't even blame it on the goose egg.

Jimmy continued, "I'm a single father, unemployed and I live with my parents. What more could you want?"

In the living room, something, probably an ornament, slipped off the Christmas tree. Outside, first one wolf dog and then another started howling.

What more could she want?

She knew the answer. "I want a Christmas

wedding. I have just the place and the decorations are already up. Briana is already an expert on how to be a flower girl. I'll keep my job at BAA and you could write and make documentaries about the animals here. There's Yoda, and Crisco the bear and—"

He didn't let her finish.

And she agreed with his reasoning.

Kissing was so much better than talking.

* * * * *

LARGER-PRINT BOOKS!
GET 2 FREE LARGER-PRINT NOVELS PLUS
2 FREE GIFTS!

❦HARLEQUIN®

Romance

From the Heart, For the Heart

YES! Please send me 2 FREE LARGER-PRINT Harlequin® Romance novels and my 2 FREE gifts (gifts are worth about $10). After receiving them, if I don't wish to receive any more books, I can return the shipping statement marked "cancel." If I don't cancel, I will receive 4 brand-new novels every month and be billed just $4.84 per book in the U.S. or $5.24 per book in Canada. That's a savings of at least 19% off the cover price! It's quite a bargain! Shipping and handling is just 50¢ per book in the U.S. and 75¢ per book in Canada.* I understand that accepting the 2 free books and gifts places me under no obligation to buy anything. I can always return a shipment and cancel at any time. Even if I never buy another book, the two free books and gifts are mine to keep forever.

119/319 HDN F43Y

Name	(PLEASE PRINT)

Address		Apt. #

City	State/Prov.	Zip/Postal Code

Signature (if under 18, a parent or guardian must sign)

Mail to the **Harlequin® Reader Service:**
IN U.S.A.: P.O. Box 1867, Buffalo, NY 14240-1867
IN CANADA: P.O. Box 609, Fort Erie, Ontario L2A 5X3

Want to try two free books from another line?
Call 1-800-873-8635 or visit www.ReaderService.com.

* Terms and prices subject to change without notice. Prices do not include applicable taxes. Sales tax applicable in N.Y. Canadian residents will be charged applicable taxes. Offer not valid in Quebec. This offer is limited to one order per household. Not valid for current subscribers to Harlequin Romance Larger-Print books. All orders subject to credit approval. Credit or debit balances in a customer's account(s) may be offset by any other outstanding balance owed by or to the customer. Please allow 4 to 6 weeks for delivery. Offer available while quantities last.

Your Privacy—The Harlequin® Reader Service is committed to protecting your privacy. Our Privacy Policy is available online at www.ReaderService.com or upon request from the Harlequin Reader Service.

We make a portion of our mailing list available to reputable third parties that offer products we believe may interest you. If you prefer that we not exchange your name with third parties, or if you wish to clarify or modify your communication preferences, please visit us at www.ReaderService.com/consumerschoice or write to us at Harlequin Reader Service Preference Service, P.O. Box 9062, Buffalo, NY 14269. Include your complete name and address.

HRLP13R

LARGER-PRINT BOOKS!
GET 2 FREE LARGER-PRINT NOVELS PLUS
2 FREE GIFTS!

HARLEQUIN *super romance*

More Story...More Romance

YES! Please send me 2 FREE LARGER-PRINT Harlequin® Superromance® novels and my 2 FREE gifts (gifts are worth about $10). After receiving them, if I don't wish to receive any more books, I can return the shipping statement marked "cancel." If I don't cancel, I will receive 6 brand-new novels every month and be billed just $5.69 per book in the U.S. or $5.99 per book in Canada. That's a savings of at least 16% off the cover price! It's quite a bargain! Shipping and handling is just 50¢ per book in the U.S. or 75¢ per book in Canada.* I understand that accepting the 2 free books and gifts places me under no obligation to buy anything. I can always return a shipment and cancel at any time. Even if I never buy another book, the two free books and gifts are mine to keep forever.

139/339 HDN F46Y

Name _____ (PLEASE PRINT) _____

Address _____ Apt. # _____

City _____ State/Prov. _____ Zip/Postal Code _____

Signature (if under 18, a parent or guardian must sign)

Mail to the **Harlequin® Reader Service:**
IN U.S.A.: P.O. Box 1867, Buffalo, NY 14240-1867
IN CANADA: P.O. Box 609, Fort Erie, Ontario L2A 5X3

**Are you a current subscriber to Harlequin Superromance books
and want to receive the larger-print edition?
Call 1-800-873-8635 today or visit www.ReaderService.com.**

* Terms and prices subject to change without notice. Prices do not include applicable taxes. Sales tax applicable in N.Y. Canadian residents will be charged applicable taxes. Offer not valid in Quebec. This offer is limited to one order per household. Not valid for current subscribers to Harlequin Superromance Larger-Print books. All orders subject to credit approval. Credit or debit balances in a customer's account(s) may be offset by any other outstanding balance owed by or to the customer. Please allow 4 to 6 weeks for delivery. Offer available while quantities last.

Your Privacy—The Harlequin® Reader Service is committed to protecting your privacy. Our Privacy Policy is available online at www.ReaderService.com or upon request from the Harlequin Reader Service.

We make a portion of our mailing list available to reputable third parties that offer products we believe may interest you. If you prefer that we not exchange your name with third parties, or if you wish to clarify or modify your communication preferences, please visit us at www.ReaderService.com/consumerchoice or write to us at Harlequin Reader Service Preference Service, P.O. Box 9062, Buffalo, NY 14269. Include your complete name and address.

HSRLP13R